The Therapist

The Therapist

Latoya Chandler

www.urbanbooks.net

Urban Books, LLC
300 Farmingdale Road, N.Y.-Route 109
Farmingdale, NY 11735

The Therapist Copyright © 2019 Latoya Chandler

ISBN 13: 978-1-62286-252-8
ISBN 10: 1-62286-252-X

First Trade Paperback Printing December 2019
Printed in the United States of America

10 9 8 7 6 5 4 3 2 1

Distributed by Kensington Publishing Corp.
Submit Orders to:
Customer Service
400 Hahn Road
Westminster, MD 21157-4627
Phone: 1-800-733-3000
Fax: 1-800-659-2436

The Therapist

by

Latoya Chandler

CHAPTER ONE

Closure . . . Keep on Moving Candice . . .

As I sit in my master bath, half of me feels overwhelmed with happiness because I know I am blessed. However, the other half of me feels a sense of guilt and unworthiness with it all. I've learned everything happens for a reason, but did we have to endure so much pain and abuse in our lives in order to get to where we are right now? I'd never question God. I sometimes don't understand how and why we had to be abused physically, mentally, and emotionally to see what the other side of poverty and unhappiness looks like.

I flick on the bathroom television; my pastor just so happens to be on the screen. The more I listen to him, the more everything that I've been feeling fades away.

"We were all born in sin, and because we were born in sin, sin will run rampant and will have its way," my pastor says on the TV. "God gave us a choice between good and evil. Unfortunately, some choose evil. That evil is and can be fully packed and loaded with hate, mistreatment, abuse, lying, stealing, cheating, you name it . . ."

As tears of clarity and understanding drench my olive-brown skin, I turn the television off. I have heard all that I need to hear. It confirmed what my new therapist said to me earlier today. I've been struggling with adjusting to her, as I am so accustomed to Dr. Binet and the way she says and does things. However, some good things have to come to an end, so others can flourish, but that bitter-sweet moment still stings a little. I think back on it now.

"Good evening, Candice. I want to have a word with you, if you don't mind?"

"Of course, Dr. Binet. Have a seat. Is it serious? You're being extremely formal right now."

"I apologize. It's not serious. Well, maybe it is . . . but nothing for you to be alarmed about."

"Okay. I am listening."

"First, I want to say how proud I am of you. You've come such a long way, and I am honored to have been a part of your journey."

"Thank you, Dr. Binet." I started to tear up.

"Now you're making me tear up," she said as she wiped an eye. Then she took a deep breath. "Okay, let me take a different approach." She exhaled. "You know that I've grown to love all of you, as if we are family, right?"

"Yes, some or one more than the rest of us." I giggled.

"Yes, which is the reason this is so hard for me. In order for me to work here at New Beginnings, as well as further my blossoming relationship with Jenna, I must discontinue counseling you. It would be a conflict of interest for me to continue counseling you and the other girls. I will eventually speak with each of them. I just wanted to come to you first, because there is so much more at stake. I hope you understand, Candice, but I cannot be what you need me to be here at New Beginnings, and I cannot be what I need to be to Jenna if I continue being your therapist. It's just too much. I've played different scenarios in my head, but ethically, I cannot do both, in all honesty."

"Dr. Binet, you owe me no explanation. I had a feeling it would come to this. I just didn't expect or want it to happen so soon."

"You did?"

"Um, since when did you start canceling and rescheduling sessions? We haven't met in about two weeks, even though I have seen you and have spent countless hours with you during those two weeks."

"Now, you know I was here getting things situated for the grand opening, Candice."

"I'm just kidding. But I had a feeling we'd have to part ways at some point because it'd become too much on your plate eventually."

"Mommy, can you tell Dylan and Darren to *get out* of my room?" Amiya shouts from the other side of the door, pulling me from my thoughts.

"I'll be in there as soon as I get out of the bathroom, Amiya." I shake my head.

These kids. I grin.

After getting the kids settled in bed for the night, I make my way back to my bedroom to take off my robe and put some pajamas on. As I shuffle through my delicates drawer, my hand swipes over the latest assignment that my new therapist gave me. Dr. Raysor said it'll bring closure for me. However, I'm afraid it might end up leading me into opening up a new can of wounds and reinjuring myself. I know one thing: the assignments in school are so much easier than those dealing with my issues. I'm great at being an ear and offering a word of advice for everyone else, but I don't seem to have much to offer myself.

When I move a pair of socks in the drawer, I see the letter. My problem is that I shut down every time I see this letter. From the onset, being moved from New York to Connecticut's Hope House, it was a place that was supposed to live up its name and give hope. Instead, it stripped us of that very thing. Having the place demolished was the best thing that I could have done for myself and for my house sisters in terms of our ability to move on. During the demo work, the demolitions expert in charge of leveling Hope House found a locked safe, and inside it were additional monies that Ms. Nancy had left behind and a letter she had written to me. I've never read that letter. When I received it, I tucked it in this drawer, and it has been here ever since. I've tried so hard to ignore it, and once I even decided to throw it away, but I couldn't. Something in me won't allow me to rest until I read it.

When I mentioned this to Dr. Raysor, she informed me that an abuse survivor needs to find closure with his or her abuser. Although Ms. Nancy didn't physically harm me—Paul and Anthony did that—she's considered an abuser because she allowed it to happen. Dr. Raysor said my refusal to open the letter is an indication of my hurt and pain. In order for me to completely let go, it is crucial for me to face the contents of that letter. No matter how big or small that letter is, I need to face it. She also said that reading this letter would bring the closure that I need. And I also need to take it a step further by writing my own letters to my abusers and then burning all the letters together.

"I guess there's no time like the present," I say aloud to myself. I take a look around me, and then I slowly remove the letter from the drawer and fumble to get the envelope open. I slip the letter out of the envelope, unfold it, and then I read it silently to myself.

Dear Candice ,
First and foremost, I want to extend my sincerest apology to you first and then to Nakita, Samantha, Simone, and Judith. I have realized that I am and was my own problem. I blamed all black women for my failed marriage. I am a white woman who was married to the most amazing man. He just so

happened to have been African American. That man is your father, Dale. Before I met him, I didn't think love or falling in love was in the cards for me. But when I heard his voice the day that we met, there was something in him that made my heart stop. Especially the moment we made eye contact. Right away I felt a connection. One that I've never encountered or experienced with another human being until this day.

After two months of getting to know one another, we married. I thought my life was complete. I know you don't want to hear about this. I just wanted you to see your dad through my eyes. Also, to try to understand how hurt I was to learn that he'd been taking monies from me the whole time we were together. The day I came to this realization was also the same day he served me with divorce papers, saying he had to do right by his unborn child. I then automatically assumed it was with an African American woman.

I thought I could move on with my life following our divorce. However, I developed a deep-rooted hatred toward women of color. Because of my hurt, I allowed Paul and Anthony to have their way with all the girls of color who were sent to Hope House. My heart dropped when your mother called to have you sent to me. After talking to her, I learned she was a woman like me, and my hatred for black women redirected itself to you. Hence Anthony's obsession with you.

I blamed you for my unhappiness due to your father leaving me. I wasn't able to take on responsibility for myself, and in turn, I took it out on you. It was unfair to you and the other girls. The more of a bond that you built with them, the more I resented you. Especially your relationship with Nakita, as she no longer needed me because she had you. I allowed your connection to fuel my already lit fire and my anger toward you. For this, I sincerely apologize.

Neither you nor the other girls deserved any of this. I hope and pray that you can find it in your hearts to forgive me. I pray I am long gone by the time you read this. If I am not, please come up to the hospital, so I can apologize to you face-to-face.

Please allow yourself to grow and move on from all this. You are a great mom to your children and epitomize the perfect daughter that I longed for.

Again, I am so sorry for all this, so much so that I want to leave everything to you.

Apologetically,
Ms. Nancy

"Ugh," I cry out, drop the letter on the floor, and swipe everything off my dresser with one hand.

"Mommy, *what's wrong?* Are you *okay?*" Amiya asks me through the bedroom door.

"Y-Yes." I clear my throat. "Yes, baby. I am fine. I will be out in a minute."

I tie the sash on my robe, and then I gather myself as much as I can and open the door.

"Mommy, why are you crying?" Amiya looks concerned.

"Mommy's okay, Amiya. Why aren't you in bed? I just tucked you in."

"I couldn't sleep. Can I sleep in your bed?"

"How about I go in your room with you and stay until you fall asleep? I want you to get used to sleeping in your own pretty bedroom. You're a big girl now," I tell her and sniffle.

"Can Adrianna come and sleep over here with us?"

"I will see if they're awake. After tonight, Amiya, you have to sleep in your room. Okay, baby?" I say as I lead Amiya back to her bedroom.

"Yes, Mommy." She jumps up on her bed, grinning from ear to ear.

"Candice, what happened in here?" Nakita gives me a worried glance as we stand in my bedroom, staring at the mess on the floor in front of the dresser.

"Are the girls in bed?" I say, avoiding her question, as I pick Ms. Nancy's letter up off the floor.

"Yes. They're asleep. Now tell me what the hell happened in here."

"That evil woman Ms. Nancy happened. That's what happened. I don't want *any* of this anymore, Nakita. I want nothing from her." I begin knocking everything within reach off the nightstand.

"No, Candice. Please stop! Don't let her take you there. What happened?" Nakita drops to the floor and wraps herself around my waist.

"I can't do this, Nakita. I don't want her guilt money. I don't want any of this."

"This is yours. I don't care how you got it, but it's yours. You're the first one to say that God is a mystery that neither of us can comprehend. He doesn't cause evil acts, but they happen. I know the only reason you're this upset is that you read that stupid letter." Nakita pauses and looks up at me. "I tried to steal it on many occasions," she confesses as tears stream down her face.

"W-Why did you want to take it?"

"I knew no good could come from that letter. I am no therapist, but I know my heart couldn't take all of that. Sometimes things are better left unknown."

"I don't want to live in denial, Nakita. I want to face what needs to be addressed."

"Candice, you already knew what that woman did and why she did it. What more could she have to say in a letter?"

"You're right. I just feel horrible, as if I am being paid off to forget what happened."

"No matter how hard we try, we will never forget. We will move forward, but pieces of our past will always live with us. That doesn't mean we have to pick up those pieces and put them back together again."

"Listen to you," I say, my voice cracking with emotion.

"I guess all that therapy is paying off."

"Or we traded places. Look what I've done to my bedroom." I shake my head.

"Girl, it's about time. Getting mad is good for the soul. Now that that's out of the way, you mentioned that Dr. Raysor said to burn the letter and let it go."

"She said to write letters to all my abusers and burn them all. However, I don't have anything to say. I feel like I've said all that needed to be said during my sessions. I am glad I read the letter, because knowing it was here bothered me. I sort of feel a sense of relief, if that makes sense."

"It makes a lot of sense. I do think burning that letter will do us both some good."

"I think you're right," I tell her, holding up the letter.

We head to the kitchen, where I retrieve a box of matches, and then we step out onto the back patio. I strike a match and light a corner of the letter, and as a flame races toward my fingers, I release the burning paper. It lands on the flagstones, and we watch as fire devours the words and red and yellow sparks fly.

"I am done. It is finished," I declare when ashes are all that remain of the letter.

CHAPTER TWO

To Forgive Others, You Must Forgive Yourself Nakita . . .

Although my life has done a complete 180, I am not completely happy. It's crazy, because I want for nothing at this point. The little black girl that once used safety pins to hold her bra together now has bras and panties in every color and with every design you can think of. My daughter will never see a day of lack. I can provide for her and then some. However, there's a part of me that is uneasy. Material things don't make you a parent or a person, and I think those are the areas in which I am failing or will fail.

I am anxious all the time, and I feel like it is almost impossible for me not to be anxious at this point. I'm scared that I'll regret having my Adrianna. Sometimes I wonder if she is a blessing or a mistake, as horrible as that sounds. I don't ever want to look at her as a mistake. Adrianna has brought an enormous amount of happiness and love to my life, as well as a boatload of fear. I thought having her would make me complete, but instead, I've been a complete mess ever since she was born.

Sometimes I wonder if we would all still be at Ms. Jasmine's place if Candice didn't get all that money and share it with me, Judith, Samantha, and Simone. Things were so much easier before the settlement. I always had Candice, the other girls, and Ms. Jasmine there around the clock. It's not like that any longer, and I don't trust myself alone with Adrianna for long periods of time. I'm afraid I'll do something wrong and hurt her by mistake.

I was beginning to have a meltdown when Candice phoned last night. But she was able to talk me down off the ledge. She's talked me down one too many times, and yet I still find myself climbing my way back up to the top. Since Dr. Binet concluded treating us, I haven't seen or talked to anyone besides Candice. I don't do well with change, and all this is too much for me. I believe my therapy sessions have run their course, so it doesn't really matter to me that they came to an end. Candice believes that I am making a mistake, that more therapy would be a good thing, but I disagree.

Adrianna and I are together in my bed now, and Adrianna is finally asleep. She went to bed a little upset and disappointed. The kids wanted to have a sleepover tonight, but I ended up having to bring her back to the house because she was not feeling well. She has a mild fever. Candice said it could be just a head cold. I have been giving her Tylenol Cold, and it appears to be working.

Adrianna's coughing pulls me from my sleep about three hours after she settled down.

"M-Mommy," she says in a small voice.

Exhausted, in a bleary-eyed state, I grab the Tylenol Cold from my nightstand, pour some in the dosage cup, and give it to her. Sometime later, she coughs again, and I repeat the process and give her more cold medicine. As I lie back down, the realization dawns on me that I mistakenly gave her the medicine too frequently, and so she has taken too much.

"Oh my God. Adrianna, wake up," I yell and grab her.

Seeing that she's still asleep, I reach for my phone and dial Candice.

When she picks up, I stutter, "C-Candice, I th-think s-something is wrong with Adriana—"

"Hang up and call nine-one-one," she orders, interrupting me. "I'm on my way over there."

This had to be one of the scariest nights of my life. It never fails; I am bad luck to anyone within arm's reach. Adrianna wound up with a bad stomachache and the runs, but overall, the mild overdose didn't do anything to her. Since I really don't trust myself with her now, I wanted Candice to take Adrianna home with her, but she refused. I wasn't in the mood to argue with Candice, but I didn't see why she just couldn't keep her over there for now.

I have been nursing Adrianna for three days now, and I'm so tired. I just want to sleep. I am going to ignore the knocking at the front door. But then Candice barges into my bedroom.

"Nakita, what is wrong with you? Open these curtains. Get up."

Almost jumping out of my skin, I stare at her, wide-eyed, before turning my back to her.

"You forgot I have a key. I need you to get up. It has been three days. You cannot sit in this room in the dark. It smells in here too." She pulls the curtains back.

"I have a headache. Just leave me alone right now."

"From what? This?" She storms over to me and waves an empty bottle of wine in my face.

"No, Candice! Now let me be."

"Your daughter needs you, Nakita. It was an honest mistake! You cannot continue to beat yourself up."

"A mistake that could have *killed* my daughter, Candice." I break down.

"But you didn't. Adrianna is fine. I just checked on her. You've been taking great care of her. You're fine, Nakita."

"I am not fine, Candice. I can't do this anymore."

"Do what? What are you talking about? Every day won't be perfect. We are not perfect. And guess what?"

"What?"

"We all make mistakes. You cannot give up on yourself and life because you made a mistake. You have to fight. Yes, we went through hell and back, but you can go through hell and still be happy."

"It's hard to fight for a life that you've given up on for so long."

"Well, you have to keep fighting, Nakita, no matter what. You also need to go back to therapy. It *was* helping."

"I'm not starting over with someone else. I don't need to talk about anything anymore. All talking does is dig everything up that I buried. I am sick of resurrecting my dead issues and demons. I am done talking about all of that, and I'm done talking to *you* right now. Now, *please* leave me alone for a little while."

"I will leave you alone for now, but I will be back bright and early tomorrow morning. You know what tomorrow is, and you know that I need you there."

"Fine. Now shut the curtains and close the door behind you. Thanks."

CHAPTER THREE

When in Doubt, Follow Your Heart
Jenna . . .

For as long as I can remember, I have always admired and had a thing for older women. Women that I've seen on television, in malls, teachers, you name it. I thought I was weird at first, but I then realized boys my age—and boys, period—didn't interest me. Initially, I told myself I was looking for a mother figure. I had say to myself, *I don't want to hold hands, kiss, or take long walks on the beach with my mother. Or do I? Minus the kissing?*

In actuality, I've never had a relationship with a woman, or with a man, in all honesty. I have never had a boyfriend, a girlfriend, or been on a *real* date. I remain a virgin. I have never been able to interact with women on anything more than the level of friendship. I've had a few casual "dates," which consisted of a one-on-one girls' night out, but nothing serious. Until Brianne. So of course, with Brianne, I was intimidated at first. Without question, she saw right through me. She is an amazing woman. When we met, I had no idea of her relationship status, and with my insecurities, I could never have imagined that she would be interested in someone like me.

During the family counseling sessions I attended with Candice and my dad, Dr. Binet—I mean Brianne . . . I'm gushing just mentioning her name—would always have her hair tied in a ponytail that she'd slicked back and wrapped into a tight bun. Glasses and little to no makeup to accompany her everyday ensemble. Not even lipstick. She was always professionally dressed in dark colors, such as gray, black, and navy, and she wore blazers paired with skirts or pantsuits. Pretty much a plain Jane, so I never really paid her that much attention to her physical appearance. I admired her intelligence, but not in a romantic way, so to speak.

That was until Candice's graduation day. A few months back, Candice received her associate's degree in mental health. She swore then that Brianne and I were already an item and in love, because of the way I watched her and stared at her. I disagreed for the simple fact that I wasn't attracted to Brianne romantically. And for the fact that she was a therapist and knew all my dark secrets. Maybe I was in denial. I had never really looked at a woman of a different race in that manner. Primarily because I had thought all of them looked, smelled, and acted like my evil stepmother. Either way, Candice's revelation was on point and smacked me dead in the face. Brianne walked into the auditorium for the graduation, she took my breath away. I remember that moment now.

"She's absolutely stunning," I mumbled.

"Excuse me? What did you just say?" Alonzo joked.

"N-Nothing."

"And you're st-stuttering? Yeah, you're in love," he said, ribbing me.

The person who was once plain Jane was no more. Dr. Binet had transformed into sexy Susie, as radical a change as Clark Kent into Superman. Dr. Binet was absolutely breathtaking. For starters, the tight bun that she wore had been freed from the top of head, and now her kohl-black, curly tresses plunged over her shoulders.

Her eyeglasses, which usually covered her brown eyes, were gone, and I found her glance hypnotizing. I didn't think I could stare in her eyes any longer. Dr. Binet wore a black wraparound dress that flowed just right and hugged her curves in all the right places.

In an instant, her beauty matched her brains, and I fell completely in love. The perfect woman. *At least that was what my mind told me as she closed in on my personal space.*

"Hey, Jenna!"

"H-Hello, Dr. Binet."

"It's all right for you to call me Brianne."

"No problem, Brianne," I whispered, though I wanted to shout.

"Are you okay? You're sweating." She brushed the perspiration from my brow.

"I think you took her by surprise, coming in here looking like America's next top auntie or model," said a male voice behind me.

"Alonzo," I said. My eyes pierced him.

"My bad. No disrespect, Dr. Binet, I mean Brianne. Jenna is a little shy, and I think she's blown away by your beauty. The same way I am blown away by the graduate's beauty." He beamed as the color vanished from his face.

Sheepishly, Brianne suddenly became interested in the stitching of her pointy hazel pumps.

"I love your shoes," I told her in order to change the topic.

"Thank you. I search for reasons to dress outside of my professional garb."

"You look like a totally different person," I noted.

"Everyone says that when they see me outside 'the office.'"

"They aren't lying."

"Well, thank you, Jenna."

"You're welcome. I'm not sure if this is out of place or wrong, but would you mind joining me for coffee sometime?" My heart dropped.

"Of course. Why wouldn't I?"

"I understand if it's a conflict of interest. I don't even know if you're married or—"

"Jenna, she said yes. Save that conversation for Starbucks," Alonzo remarked. He shook his head. "Rookies," he added.

Ever since that moment, Brianne and I have been inseparable. I love being around her. Candice feels I've become too attached, too soon, and that the relationship could take a turn for the worse. She thinks I should make sure of what I really want, because sometimes I sound like I am confused and unsure of myself. One thing for sure is, I know that I have almost always become very attached to older women whom I admire. This has been happening without fail since I was young. It's like I meet or have an encounter with an older woman and instantly fall in love.

It began with a few of my teachers while I was in high school. I'd do whatever I could to get their attention. Even if it meant purposely failing a test so that I'd have to stay after school for extra help. No other students would be in attendance at these sessions the majority of the time. The end result was undivided attention, and I devoured it. With Brianne, all I have to do is be myself, because she loves being around me just as much as I crave her presence.

Lately, things have become a little uncomfortable for the two of us. It's so easy to get carried away when you first meet someone you're attracted to, before you really get to know the person. The endorphins are flowing; the possibilities seem endless. Well, not all possibilities.

Although I savor every moment as if it is the last time we'll occupy one another's personal space, each time Brianna attempts to take things to another level, I withdraw. The truth of the matter is, I am a young woman who has always been attracted to woman romantically, but the idea of sex or any kind of intimate contact *terrifies* me.

I finally have someone who simply doesn't care about image, race, or my imperfections. She accepts me for me. However, when it comes to sexual contact, I choke up and find myself almost on the verge of tears. Don't get me wrong. I cherish taking long walks with Brianne, holding hands, cuddling in our pajamas on a Saturday night with a good movie, popcorn, and wine. Unfortunately, my fear of and struggle with intimacy appears to be driving a wedge between us. I don't know if I should feel guilty or upset and disappointed with Brianne. Without question, each time things don't go her way, she immediately turns into Dr. Binet and dispenses a handful of diagnoses, as opposed to allowing me time to get comfortable, considering all this is new to me.

I hope and pray this evening with Brianne at her place goes smoothly. She's been in the bathroom for a while, now that I think about it.

"Bri, what are you *doing* in there? The movie is about to start. The popcorn isn't good when it's cold, and it will be at the pace you're moving," I shout from the sofa.

"How about we skip the movie tonight?" she says as she creeps up behind me.

"Wow! What's the occasion? You're so beautiful, Bri." I admire her as she stands in front of me on her ladders to heaven, wearing a sexy black fishnet bustier featuring open cups, a matching thong that reveals her womanhood, and fishnet stockings.

"I thought I'd throw something simple on to spice things up for us."

"If that's simple, I'm clearly in a league of my own," I tell her.

As the corners of her mouth slide upward, Bri uses her magic wand of a remote to distract me with the sounds of Goldfrapp's "Ooh La La." As the words "Coils up and round me, teasing your poetry. Switch me on. Turn me up" serenade me, she activates her hips and dances and models her body in between running her hand all over it. After gliding closer to me, Bri brings her face down the side of my head until she finds what she's searching for. My ear. As she tugs and sucks on my ear with her mouth for a few seconds, Bri causes me to laugh. Then I try to suppress my laughter, and it turns against me and I sputter out like an old faucet.

"Jenna, how is any of this amusing to you?" She steps back, using her hands to conceal her exposed flesh.

"I—I apologize. You were tickling my ear. You know I am ticklish."

"I really don't get you, Jenna. You profess this undying attraction to me, and then you clam up when you have my undivided attention. All you yearn for are fragments of the perks of being in a relationship. You're not ready for any of this, or for me, for that matter. Sometimes I wonder if you're attracted to me."

"Bri, you know that is not true. I just need time. I am a virgin to all this. That includes sexually and emotionally."

"I can understand you being hesitant with exploring my secret places. That's a given. However, you refuse to allow me to explore and make my own intimate memories with you."

"I'm just not there yet, Bri. Why can't you understand that? You said we could go as slow as I needed to go as long as we didn't stop. Yet when I don't fold, you take it personally."

"Personally, Jenna? You laughed in my face."

"You're not playing fair at all. I never laughed *at* you. It tickled me. I cannot help that I am ticklish."

"Immature is more like it."

"That was a low blow, Bri." I shake my head.

"I didn't want to go this route with you. Unfortunately, in order to get this long-standing white elephant out of our relationship, I have to be honest with you."

"White elephant?"

"Yes, those troublesome things that have been lying dormant inside you—"

"I'm confused," I say, interrupting her.

"Please allow me to finish." She grabs her robe off the floor, where she dropped it earlier. Taking a moment to cover up and to pull her hair into a tight ponytail, she continues, "Unfortunately, some hold on to the negative images that we see and have created within ourselves, which causes us to become resistant to being seen any other way. Fear from what you've been through is making it difficult for you to grasp or accept the possibility and the reality of being loved. So much so that you've built up a wall to resist love. Because of your unresolved issues, you are forced to reject love and intimacy, and instead, you create tension to push away anything close to what you're in fear of."

"Well, if you did your job right, those issues that you've convinced yourself I suffer from would have come to the light a long time ago, and not as a result of me not being ready or comfortable with being intimate with you, Bri," I retort. "And how am I resistant to love? When did we start loving each other? Besides, the last time I checked, sex or intimacy isn't love."

"I know how I feel about you even if you're in denial about your feelings toward me. You really need to challenge your negative attitudes toward yourself and not push what you long for away. I can help you overcome your fears of intimacy, so you can enjoy all that being loved and becoming intimate have to offer. Love isn't hard to find. I am right here. Whether you accept it or not, you found it. It is just difficult for you to take and tolerate right now."

"How about you show this love that you profess to have, instead of diagnosing me all the time? I'm no therapist, but I do know that would go further than your 'therapeutic love' for me. Listening to you right now, I realized you cannot get past what you've learned in those textbooks. I am no more than another client to you. I wonder if I am one of your case studies for your book. There's no way in the world you have real feelings for me. It's all work for you."

"You just proved what I just said to you. Your ill feelings about yourself force you to create things that simply are not there. You've become defensive to dampen the mood. I can promise you this isn't in a book," she asserts, her tone angry. She knocks the wine and the popcorn off the table before she adds, "I need time to myself. Please leave my home now."

CHAPTER FOUR

It Still Hurts. . . . I'm Still Bleeding Brianne, aka Dr. Binet . . .

Jenna reminds me of myself when I was her age. Being nine years her senior, I've seen, experienced, and dealt with some of the same demons that are tormenting her. So much so that after dealing with those dark moments and places in my life, I fell in love with the process designed solely to decrease misery and improve one's life. As a result of my newfound love, I became a therapist. It was a long journey down the road to recovery, but I made it safely.

It took a very long time for me to get to where I am as a therapist. When I reflect on the early days of my "training," I realize that a seed was planted in those moments when my family and friends confided in me when they were dealing with a crisis. Hearing their pain hurt me, but I took it as an honor to be the person they turned to in their vulnerable moments. In the early days of my internship as a rape crisis counselor for survivors of domestic violence, I found myself drawn to complex trauma and developed a more profound love for my role as a therapist. Although the work was deeply challenging, I found it incredibly rewarding.

There's an old saying that resonates with me because it encapsulates my life story. "No matter what side you're on, you will never be able to explain how it feels to be in that position." Point being, the dark places inside me push me to pour understanding and care into these girl's lives, I know what being alone is like.

In their eyes, I am a godsend. In return, when it's all said and done, I yearn for that same comfort and solace I provide them. I assumed me not being intimate or having someone in my life was stirring up these feelings. However, even being with and connecting with Jenna, I still feel lonely and alone, like something is missing or wrong. Like I am desperately seeking something that provides comfort, that fills a void. Don't get me wrong. I enjoy us, but on the inside, something is missing for me, and because of it, she and I have been clashing lately.

From the onset of my practice, I have felt energized just from working with clients. Nothing, whether it is good, bad, or indifferent, can alter those feelings. The reward of witnessing a person accomplish goals and make progress in life alone is what I think of as the ultimate satisfaction. It has been especially satisfying to see how far Candice and the girls have come. Especially Candice. One can barely imagine the things she has endured and overcome. And to think that I took part in helping her get to this point of self-sufficiency . . . That alone gives me a level of fulfillment that is tremendous.

But working at New Beginnings and remaining the girls' therapist poses a conflict of interest. The crux of the matter is that I believe my attachment to them has begun to muddle things for me. On the one hand, I have operated as a professional in assisting the girls with overcoming the traumatic events that took place in their lives. On the other hand, in the back of my mind, I have been envisioned myself assisting them in brutally punishing their abusers. This has come out of nowhere. I have never before found myself second-guessing myself or contemplating anything of the sort. As a result, I have recently sought out therapy for myself, and so I have found myself sitting on the proverbial couch from time to time.

Because I don't want any of this to show up in my paperwork, and I certainly do not want my colleagues or, God forbid, my clients to catch wind of this, I first connected with a family friend of a friend who practices as a therapist in New York. Well, I didn't feel comfortable with her, so I moved on to a second therapist. She accepts only cash payments. In any event, right now, I need a clear mind: I cannot allow anything to cloud my judgment and disrupt any of my clients' progress. Especially since the New Beginnings grand opening is in a few days. I will be taking on new vulnerable clients, and they will need me at my best and on my A game.

Speaking of my new therapist, Dr. Felita Ness, I am in the reception area of her office, waiting to meet with her now.

"Ms. Binet, Dr. Ness will see you now," Claudia, the receptionist, informs me, extracting me from my thoughts.

"Thank you, Claudia."

"No problem. Right this way," she says, directing me to Dr. Ness's office.

Every time I enter Dr. Ness's elegant yet soulful office, which features a full wall of windows, I am reminded of the upgrade that my home office is in desperate need of.

With a warm, comforting smile, Dr. Ness says, "Good to see you again, Brianne. Please have a seat. How are you doing today?"

"All is well. And you?" I reply as I take a seat on a comfortable armchair.

"I am great. I think we should pick up where we left off on Monday. How do you feel about that?"

"That sounds great. Thank you again for doing this for me."

"No problem at all—" she says and cuts herself off, looking at her notes. "Speaking of our last session, from your viewpoint, what went wrong with your meeting with Dr. Kruk, the first therapist you saw?"

"Honestly, I am not here to talk about that. Right now, I am struggling to separate my personal feelings from my professional feelings, and that's what I really need to discuss. It pains me to hear the abuse that my clients have endured."

"We will discuss that in depth. But right now we need to get to the root of the problem. That's why I have brought up Dr. Kruk."

I shrug. "You and I both know Dr. Kruk could never take me serious," I respond automatically.

"Please elaborate as to why you feel this way, Brianne."

"For one, I am a woman, and a therapist at that. I know from my own experiences in life that men won't hear or listen to me in a profound way. You and I both know that men don't listen deeply, especially ones with authority. And that goes for male therapists. A male therapist would use his platform only to minimize and trivialize my concerns and pain. All based on the simple notion that I am a woman. He'd generally be dismissive with me because I am a woman *and* because he is threatened that I wear the same hat as he does. So that alone means two strikes against me."

"At what point during your session with Dr. Kruk did you feel he was minimizing and trivializing your concerns?"

"He didn't get a chance to. Due to my own negligence, I learned Dr. Kruk was a male while I was seated in his reception area. I failed to do my homework on him prior to going to his office. At this point in my life, I refuse to allow a man to mistreat me. Especially in the vulnerable state that I am finding myself in these days. So I canceled the appointment while there, in his office. Now I am here with you."

"Do you feel all men act this way, or do you expect this from just Dr. Kruk and other male therapists?"

"No offense, Dr. Ness, but let's cut to the chase. You and I both know how this works, so how about we omit the probing questions and we get straight to the point?"

The brooding expression in her dark eyes spoke for her, and she said nothing. She didn't have to. I continued to speak and clarify things.

"I was married for three years. Shortly after two years of being married, the man I vowed to spend the rest of my life with left for work and never returned. A perfect stranger came into our home that evening. To make matters worse, he wasn't alone." I pause as I begin reliving the most horrific time of my life. Tears threaten to fall.

"Take your time," Dr. Ness suggests, handing me a tissue.

Nodding my head, I continue. "The day my marriage ended was the first time in my life that I've ever felt so dirty. It was as if I were a piece of nothing and had transformed into my husband's mistress. Going into the marriage, I dealt with the chronic criticism and even overlooked his controlling tendencies. Never in a million years could I have unraveled the fact that my growing business, which caused me to have less time or energy for him, would turn him into a monster and a pimp."

"Would you like—"

"Dr. Ness, please allow me to get this off my chest. I haven't talked about this in so long, I didn't know it was still a soft spot for me. Usually, with my clients, when I see they are having a breakthrough, I allow them to unload without interrupting them."

After turning her hand, folding her fingers in toward her palm, Dr. Ness pointed her thumb skyward.

Shaking my head, I say, "Did you really just give me a thumbs-up? How professional is that?"

"It is clear you refuse to allow me or anyone else to do their job. It doesn't matter if the therapist is male or female. The fact is that Dr. Binet has to remain in control. Let me let you in on a secret. For this to work, you have to allow me to do things the way I do things. I am fully aware you have your practice. However, you are human, and you cannot continuously hold on to your skeletons from the past. It will spill over into your work. You need these sessions more than you think, and I perceived that within fifteen minutes of listening to you. So, my question for you is, Is this therapy session really what you want to do, because the last thing I want to do is waste your time or mine?"

"You're right. I haven't been on the other side of the room in so long, I got caught up. Please forgive my arrogance."

"As you stated, you were having a breakthrough. Do you mind discussing the things that transpired the day you feel your relationship with your ex-husband dissolved?"

"It has been a nightmare that has replayed in the back of my mind for twelve years. I married at the wrong time in my life, but I was needy back then. My only saving grace has been my practice. Without it, I would have probably lost myself in a deep depression." I exhale before continuing. "Mason came home extremely late that evening. Which just so happened to be my thirtieth birthday." I close my eyes, allowing myself to revert to that exact moment in time.

"Happy Birthday, Bri-Bri," he exclaimed, toting a dozen birthday balloons, a dozen red roses, as well as an adult-size gift box.

"Oh, my goodness, Mason. What have you done? What is it?" I said, glowing.

"It's my surprise. Why don't you go upstairs and put something sexy on for me?"

Taking two steps at I time, I dashed upstairs and into our bedroom and pulled out a red negligee and paired it with matching red heels. With my heart racing a mile a minute from excitement, I anxiously disrobed, took a quick shower, and slid into my sexy ensemble.

I'd been home all day, having my own pity party, thinking he'd forgotten about my birthday, and look what he had done. It had been so long since I had been this happy, since he'd called me sexy. Better yet, it had been a long time since he wanted to see me in something sexy. A little over a year, to be exact. For so long we'd gone about our everyday lives as if we were roommates instead of husband and wife.

"Bri, what are you doing up there?" he called up the stairs.

"I'm here, my love," I said, and then I sashayed down the stairs. I stopped in my tracks when I reached the last step.

"This is my surprise, hon. You remember Chuck? I decided to unwrap him for you myself since you were taking so long."

I open my eyes and snap out of my flashback. "I hate him so much." .

"Would you like a moment, Brianne?"

"No. I am so *upset* with myself." I take in the room around me. "I apologize, Dr. Ness. I will try to calm down. I am just so upset with myself. I cannot believe I am still harboring this anger. I probably will never get over this. How can I? The man that vowed to love me up until I was on my deathbed and then beyond that took turns with his best friend in insulting and raping me for hours. Happy thirtieth birthday to me, right? That was also the last day that I laid eyes on Mason. And to add insult to injury, I was impregnated by one or both of them that evening."

"A baby? You never mentioned you have a child."

"Ha-had a child." I sniffle. "Sienna was three months when she . . . when I . . ." I burst into tears. "My therapist at the time said it was postpartum depression combined with depression brought on possibly from giving birth to my rapist's child. I-It was one of the hottest and most humid days of the season. I couldn't get any of it out of my mind. I didn't think having a drink with my medication would alter my thinking. I never meant to leave Sienna in the car. I went to bed to sleep it off. I thought I had put her to bed, Dr. Ness. I didn't intentionally leave her out there to die. You have to believe me. I would never hurt my baby. You have to believe me." I sob uncontrollably.

"I will allow you time to gather yourself before we go on."

"I-It's fine. I've been here before. My heart is just still broken."

"In my professional opinion, Brianne, this is more than just a broken heart. You may require extensive therapy, and you are not in any condition to counsel anyone right now. I am not saying you should stop indefinitely. Right now, I believe you first need time to deal with these things that are still dealing with you. You cannot help anyone until you help yourself."

"You're *wrong*. My practice has been my saving grace. I *knew* this was a mistake. No wonder you're taking cash under the table from clients. You don't have a clue as to what you're doing." I quickly rise from the armchair and storm out of the office.

CHAPTER FIVE

Everything Affects Everything Nakita . . .

Another sleepless night and my thoughts are consuming me once again. I am a ticking time bomb. All I want to do is escape. No matter how hard I try, the voices won't shut up. They won't leave me alone. They're getting louder and louder.

You're no good.

Everyone will be better off if you were gone.

You should have been in the car, not Shakita.

You should just kill yourself.

"Shut up. *Leave* me alone," I whimper. I need to silence these voices. I look down at my phone and scroll through my contact list as I use my free hand to take another swig from my bottle of cabernet sauvignon.

"There she is." I press the telephone icon and dial the number.

This constant conflict between my unhappiness and my will to live is taking a toll on me. I need energy; I'm defenseless to fight this battle—the battle for my life—which is impossible to win. Ever since I was born, darkness has been my way of life. I was born like this. I don't want to pass any of this to my Adrianna. I've given her all that I can at this point. I can't fight off these dark thoughts. At this point, my only solitude or glimmer of hope is death. It will finally bring me the peace I so desperately seek.

Suicide feels like the best solution for relief, I think to myself as Dr. Binet's voice mail picks up.

"H-Hello? Dr. Binet? I didn't know who else to call—" I begin, but then I cut myself off. "Forget it." I disconnect the call, then take another swig from the bottle.

I need to do *something.* I have to try to get these thoughts under control. But I am a burden to everyone. I am to the point where I have no feelings of happiness or sadness. The only thing I believe is real is the emptiness that I feel on the inside. This on-again, off-again battle is making me weary. I am tired of acting like everything is all right when it's the complete opposite. This wine provides a temporary respite and briefly numbs the pain. But when it wears off, I find myself back here.

I make my way into the bathroom to do some cleaning. But I've scrubbed this place from top to bottom. How much more cleaning can I do? It's not working.

Why don't you just do it, Nakita?

I reach for the .357 revolver that Candice had in her safe for her protection. I snuck into her place while she was having her sleepover with Alonzo and took the gun. She deserves to be happy. I will get in the way of their happiness, with all my issues. This is my problem, not hers. Candice deserves to be happy. I know she will make sure Adrianna is happy and will give her what I cannot deliver to her—love and protection.

Yeah, this is for the best. Everyone will be happy. I smile for the first time in months.

I feel so calm and excited right now. I won't feel any more pain. It will be over.

After climbing into the bathtub, I pull the curtain closed and place the gun under my chin and pray. "God, please forgive me for what I am about to do. Please protect Candice, Adrianna, and everyone else."

As tears storm my face, visions of Adrianna dance inside my mind, causing my hands to quiver violently. The motion forces the revolver out of my hand, and it falls onto the porcelain at my feet.

"I am such a failure. I cannot even bring peace and happiness to myself the right way," I mumble. Then I drag my spineless existence from the bathroom.

You're such a failure. You can't do anything right, the voices mock.

"Leave me alone," I shout as I throw myself across the bed, knocking my phone to the floor.

After retrieving it, I locate my last call and dial the number again. The call goes straight to voice mail. I leave a message and hang up.

Everyone is sick of you. No one wants you around. You're a disappointment, the voices tell me.

"I'll prove you all *wrong*." I dart back into the bathroom, rip open the medicine cabinet, and search until I locate my original prescription.

I don't know why I bothered calling again. It's evident what needs to be done. I tried to seek help or a voice of reason, but I know I need no reasoning. God is calling me home. Yes, He is. It's time for me to be reunited with my twin sister.

As a sense of peace swallows me whole, I enter my walk-in closet and pull out the dress I purchased for the grand opening.

"This is so pretty," I say as I disrobe and change into the olive-green, formfitting dress. Giving myself a once-over, I notice my hair is in shambles. "Oh my. I need to do something with this head and maybe put on a little makeup. Yeah, that'll bring it all together."

Excitedly, I comb my hair into a tight bun ponytail and make my face up as I indulge in my wine and pills.

Turning to find my pumps, I am suddenly startled by the image standing before me. I immediately begin to weep. "Oh my God, Shakita, my deceased twin sister. When did you get here? How? I'm so sorry you went in the car without me, and I promise to make it up to you. I was in the process of getting myself together to come and get you."

I love you so much, Nakita. It's all right. I am here now. I just want to hold you and never let you go.

"Can you hold me until I fall asleep, Shakita? I am so tired. I just need to sleep."

Yes, I promise to hold you tight, she assures as we nestle together on the bed.

CHAPTER SIX

A Deadly Combination
Candice . . .

Pretty much every waking moment has been spent with the kids for the past seven years, twenty-four hours a day and seven days a week. Minus me attending therapy and school for the past two years, Nakita and I have dedicated our all to our little ones. We even homeschool them in the mornings, from 7:00 a.m. until noon. However, lately, with New Beginnings taking up the majority of my time, my schedule has changed. So much so that we've found ourselves trying to work with the kids in the late afternoon or evenings, and that's beginning to pose problems. Alonzo feels it's time the kids transitioned to private school, which would allot me the time that I need to get things done without distractions. Especially while they're in school.

Thoughts of Alonzo make me sigh, and I cross my arms as this unfamiliar, yet familiar smile creeps across my face. Things have been unbelievably great. Alonzo has shown himself to be a fabulous father and provider and is one of my best friends. Lately, my other best friend, Nakita, has been down and somewhat depressed. She spends the majority of her time alone at her place. I have been so busy that I haven't been able to be there for her like I'd like to. However, when I do go by, she pushes me away. The only time she wants to talk or has anything to say is when it's about Adrianna. It breaks my heart to see her like this, so I have been giving her time to clear her head.

On the flip side, I haven't had anyone to talk to or turn to other than Alonzo. He has been so much more than what I need him to be with the kids when time gets the best of me. It's as if he and Nakita have traded places. Those late-night talks about life, deep wounds, regrets, or whatever topics Nakita and I used to cover, Alonzo and I now have together. It has gotten to the point where we curl up in the bed together and watch movies, talk, and laugh the same way I have done with Nakita. He sleeps at my place more than he does at his own home. The crazy thing about it is, I feel comfortable with him. However, the feelings that are present are not the same ones that I experience with Nakita.

Now, every time my phone rings, I get a text, or I know that I am going to see Alonzo, I suddenly feel as if the inside my stomach is being tickled. I smile for no reason at the thought of him. I don't even know how to stop smiling anymore. I walk around nowadays with this slaphappy grin tattooed across my face. He gives me this warm, fuzzy feeling that makes me all tingly inside. All this scares the daylights out me, but I cannot shake it, and deep down inside, I don't want to.

Alonzo is actually on his way here now to help me with the kids so that I can put the final touches on things for the New Beginnings grand opening tomorrow.

"It's open. Come in," I call when I hear a knock on the door to my office, which is situated upstairs.

Alonzo walks in and finds me seated at my desk. "Hey there, beautiful. The kids are all set. They're downstairs, playing with your dad. Did you need anything before I head out?" he says as he closes the office door behind him.

Turning my head sideways to avoid eye contact, I stutter, "I—I d-didn't hear you come in the house. When did you get here?"

"Your dad let me in about a half hour ago. He said you were working up here, so I left you alone. But now I came by to make sure you're good."

"I . . . I'm all right, Alonzo. Thanks for everything."

"What's going on, Candice? Why can't you look at me? Did I do something wrong?"

As my eyes well up with tears, I manage to form a smile. "No, you've done everything right. Sometimes I'm so happy, I can't bring myself to believe it's real," I confess. "I have to pinch myself just to make sure I'm not dreaming. I am so afraid of how I feel about you, Alonzo, that it's driving me crazy."

Alonzo tries to talk and swallow at the same time, but he chokes on his words. As he gathers himself, he stares at me blankly. His eyes don't blink for at least thirty seconds. Maybe I jumped the gun. He probably really sees me as his friend. We just happen to have the same daughter. But why does he want to adopt the boys? Maybe he feels sorry for me.

"Oh my God, what have I done? I am so sorry, Alonzo, if I overstepped my boundaries."

"No, no, please, Candice." He takes a deep breath. "I have loved you since the moment I laid eyes on you at Burger King. You aren't and weren't like any person or woman that I have ever met. Your innocence was breathtaking to me. Do you know how long I've waited to hear something remotely close to the words that just floated from your lips?" He closes in on my personal space.

My head drops in embarrassment.

"Candice." He kneels before me and lifts my head so that I look at him.

"Ye-yes?"

"Can I kiss you?"

"I . . . I don't think I even know . . ."

"If you're not ready, I will wait until you are. We can take our time and go as slow as you'd like to, just as long as we don't stop or pause. My life will never be complete until I have all of you completely. I know it won't happen overnight. I just need to know that there's hope or a possibility for it to happen."

Without uttering a word, I allow my lips to join his in a French connection.

After breaking our embrace, with my chest heaving up and down, I confess, "I think I want this. I just don't think I am ready to be sexually intimate. I need more time for that."

"I don't want your body right now. I need your heart. The rest will come naturally."

"Candice, Alonzo, *please* come quick," my dad calls up the stairs.

Abandoning our moment in my office, Alonzo and I race down the stairs, unsure of what will greet us when we hit final step. My pulse pounds in my ears.

"Dad, what's . . . wrong . . . ? Are the . . . kids okay?" I ask frantically when I find my dad in the foyer.

"Yes. They're in the playroom. We went over to Nakita's earlier. Adrianna wanted to see her mom. She doesn't look good, Candice. She's unresponsive or is ignoring me. You know how Nakita is. She's probably in one of her moods and don't want to be bothered. Either way, I told Adrianna she was asleep. Please go check on her, Candice. I'm a little nervous about her."

Jenna charges into the foyer just then. "What's going on? I heard Dad shouting your name from out front."

"He said something might be wrong with Nakita," I tell her.

Jenn frowns. "What are we doing here? Let's go over there and check on her."

"You're right, Jenna. Alonzo, please stay here with Dad and the kids. We will go whup Nakita back into shape."

Nakita and I race over to Nakita's. I open the front door with the key Nakita gave me, and we both call her name, but she doesn't answer. The stillness in the air seems to muffle even the sound of our footsteps as we walk warily toward Nakita's bedroom. I knock on her bedroom door, but again, there is no answer. The silence Jenna and I share at this moment is the kind of silence that descends right before you get knifed in the back. This thought causes a sudden shiver to race down my spine. I can feel my blood chill in my veins as we enter Nakita's bedroom and dash over to the bed. I see Nakita lying there, unnaturally still.

"Nakita, why are you sleeping in that dress? You look so pretty. You're so—" I say, but then I cut myself short and panic. "Oh my God! Nakita, what have you done?" I put my hand over my mouth to stifle my scream. I can hear my heart hammering in my chest, and the sound echoes in my head.

"Candice, call nine-one-one. *Now*!" Jenna yells as she shoves me out of the way and hovers over Nakita. After picking up the empty prescription bottles on the nightstand and tossing them in anger, Jenna taps Nakita on the shoulder and shouts, "Are you okay? Can you hear me?"

I stand there watching, motionless.

"Candice, snap out of it! Please call nine-one-one." Jenna yells. Then she proceeds to turn Nakita on her back, intent on opening her airway. After tilting Nakita's head slightly, Jenna lifts Nakita's chin and begins to administer CPR.

While she does this, I dial 911 and cry into the phone, "My friend Nakita, isn't breathing. Please come to thirty-two twenty-six Terry Road. Hurry! Please hurry!"

After getting out of the ambulance and sitting in the hospital waiting room for hours, I am dying on the inside. Positioned on the edge of the chair, I place my hands on my knees, intending to stop them from bouncing every other second. I just want to know what is going on with my Nakita. This would not have happened if I hadn't been so caught up with everything else. I had seen her sinking deeper and deeper into a depression, and instead of dragging her out of it, I had given her time to herself.

"This is all my fault," I sob.

"You cannot blame yourself, Candice. Let's just pray she's all right. We can and will work through this," Ms. Jasmine says, consoling me.

"She's right, Candice. We are in this together and will work through it," Jenna chimes in.

As I stare at the faded green wall in front of me, I can feel the tension and anxiety consuming me. "I need air." I jump out of my seat.

"I'll walk with her outside," Alonzo says and grabs my hand.

Before we can make it the door, Ms. Jasmine summons me back. As I ran back to our seats, I see the doctor standing with everyone. The fear and sadness painted across their faces stops me in my tracks and drops me to my knees.

"Please, God, no. This cannot happen. How? Why?" I cry.

"They did everything that they could, Candice. I am so sorry. I love you girls so much," Ms. Jasmine says as she wraps her arms around me.

"I want a do-over. Please, God, let her wake up. C-Can I see her, Ms. Jasmine? I need to see her. She has to hear my voice. She's just sleeping. She's been sad and tired. She'll get up. You'll see." I use the back of my hand to wipe my nose.

"Candice, do you mind if I come in?" Dr. Binet calls from the other side of Nakita's bedroom door, then peeks her head in.

"Sure," I say and sniffle.

"Ms. Jasmine said you were over here. By the time I got to the hospital, you were gone. I am so sorry this has happened. I should have known and kept counseling her," she says, tearing up.

"I feel like it is my fault, Dr. Binet . . . I mean Brianne. I saw the signs. Hell, I know the signs. I just thought she needed time to herself. She was so upset when she gave Adrianna that medicine. It was like she turned into another person right after that. I had Adrianna with me more than she did. Never in a million years could I have seen this coming. Depressed and angry, yes, but not suicidal. Honestly, I don't think it was suicide. I believe she didn't realize the effects the wine would have in combination with the medication she was taking."

"I believe she knew what she was doing, Candice. She loved you and the kids more than she did herself. Nakita would rather endure hurt, harm, danger, or possible death than to see you and the kids suffer. I think she believed she was a burden to everybody, and so she sought to end it all."

"She has been drinking wine and taking her meds for a while, even before she went away. I mean, she may have been drinking a little more lately, but that doesn't signal a suicide attempt or a plan to me."

Placing her hand on mine, Dr. Binet explains, "No matter how often she was or was not drinking, it was dangerous to drink with her medication. I just don't understand how she managed to have Prozac and Seroquel in her system."

"She went to one visit with Dr. Raysor after our sessions with you concluded. Dr. Raysor changed her medication and advised her to discontinue taking the Prozac. Oh no, Brianne! She did kill herself. She took both medications together and finished this bottle of wine." I pick up the bottle and throw it across the room.

"Candice, you know as well as I do that sexual abuse and violence can have psychological, emotional, and physical effects on a survivor. Everyone deals with those effects differently. Some of us recover, and some of us don't. Unfortunately, sometimes even therapy doesn't help at some point. Some people just don't take to it. Nakita blamed herself for her sister's death and expected no good to come to her. She felt if she wasn't in the picture, you and the kids would be better off."

"Why would you say something like that? She never once said we'd be better off without her. She loved Adrianna. She loved me and the boys. She wouldn't leave us like that."

"Candice, this is hard for all of us, but you need to know the truth. She called me yesterday, but I . . . I missed her call. I had my ringer off, and my phone calls went to voice mail. If only I had answered my phone, she'd be here. I am to blame." She bursts into tears.

"Wait, Brianne. Wait. If you missed her call, how do you know this?" I blubber.

"Sh-she left me a message."

"I need to hear it."

"Are you sure you want to hear it? Maybe we should leave her bedroom and go to your place before you hear it."

"No, I want to feel her. I need to hear her voice again now. Please, Dr. Brianne. Please let me hear my sister one last time."

Dr. Binet pulls out her phone and retrieves Nakita's voice-mail message. Then she pushes a button to replay the message and hands me the phone.

"H-Hello? Dr. Binet? I didn't know who else to call." Nakita's words tumble together, a rush of barely distinguishable syllables, and then the message ends abruptly.

"Brianne! How does that message justify anything you just said?" I exhale forcefully through my mouth before continuing. "The only thing that's clear in that message is that Nakita was drunk and possibly high off the meds."

"Hand me back the phone and give me a moment. She left more than one message. I need to bypass the message that was left after hers to retrieve the next one that she left." She fumbles with her phone. When the message is about to play, she hands me the phone.

"Dr. Binet, I have to take a nap, but I wanted to try you again first, and still no answer. By the time you hear this message, I will probably have gone down for my final nap. I am so sorry. I could not be helped. I am poisonous. Everyone that I love either dies or gets hurt. It's best that I leave silently. Please do me a favor and tell Candice to continue loving Adrianna the way that she loves me. Tell her I love her, and that I made it this far because of her. But my time is up. Thank you for everything, Dr. Binet. I will always be with you guys in your hearts—" The message is cut short.

"Why, Nakita? Why? We could have worked through it. Why did you leave me, us, like this?" I wail in agony and sink to floor. Pounding my hand on the cold floor, I sob, "Nakita, you can't be gone. We made a vow to fight, no matter what. They're wrong. She's just sleeping. She said it in the message." I jump up, throw myself on top of the bed, and allow the pillow to hug my face. My tears dampen the pillowcase.

"I am so sorry, Candice. This is a tough pill to swallow for me. I want to console you and tell you everything is going to be all right, but right now, I am not sure how much of that I believe."

"No, Brianne. This is all your fault. She called you twice, and you waited an entire day to call her back. How could you be so selfish?" I screech. My eyes burn with rage, and my chest feels heavy, as if it is filled with lead.

"Candice—"

I hiss through clenched teeth, "There's nothing you can say to change this. She's gone. Forever. My sister is gone. How can I go on?" I jump from the bed and dropped to my knees. "Please, God, let this be a terrible dream. I am ready to wake up now. This is not how it is supposed to end. We need her here a little longer. God, please send her back. I won't mess up this time. I won't let her be alone this time. Please, God, let my sister wake up. We need her," I plead as memories flood my mind and the tears continue to flow.

CHAPTER SEVEN

A Child's Pain
Candice . . .

As I head toward my front door, the sounds of the kids' laughter spins me around in the opposite direction. Sobs rack my body as I stand there.

"Dear God, I can't do this. These babies . . . Adrianna, they don't deserve any of this," I utter as my body turns against me.

Without warning, the pounding of my heart gets faster and faster, and my lungs struggle to keep up with my heart. Not enough oxygen enters my body, and I instantly become light-headed and dizzy.

"Oh, God. I think I am going to pass out," I murmur, and then two strong arms grab me around my waist.

Looking behind me, I see Alonzo holding on to me as if our lives depend on it, and a shiver runs through me as we gaze at each other for a moment.

"A-Are you all right, Candice? I saw you from the window. You look flushed."

"I cannot look into those babies' eyes and break their hearts. I cannot break their hearts. We vowed never to break their hearts. How could Nakita do this? It wasn't supposed to happen like this. She promised we would do whatever we could so the kids didn't have to endure any heartache like we did. What am I supposed to do now, Alonzo?" I blubber.

"They will never endure that much pain, Candice. You are a brave woman. All of you women are. Please know you are not in this alone, Candice. We will make sure this is as easy as it can be for you and those babies. I promise never to leave your side. I know I cannot take away the pain or bring her back, but I will do everything in my power to try to alleviate some of the anguish and the burden for you, if you'll allow me to."

"I'd like that—"

"What's wrong? Is she okay?" Jenna shouts as she approaches us.

"She's having a hard time, Jenna," Alonzo says.

"I can't do this, Jenna. But I know I need to see and hug my babies. I need to see their smiles. How am I supposed to break those sweet babies' hearts, Jenna?" I wail.

"We will get through this. Ms. Jasmine and Dad are in there. We can all do this together if you want. Don't ever think you're alone. We will always be here," Jenna tells me, and then she bursts into tears.

"Mommy . . . Aunty," the kids sing in unison when Jenna, Alonzo, and I enter the playroom.

"Hello, babies. I love you so much," I tell them.

"Why are you sad, Mommy?" Amiya asks me. She can read me so well.

"What's wrong, Auntie? Where's my mommy? Is she still sleeping? I want to see my mommy, Aunt Candy," Adrianna says.

"Come here, babies, all of you." I kneel to their level and embrace them one by one. Then I take a deep breath, exhale, and say, "Adrianna, you know your mommy loves you, don't you?"

"Yes, Aunt Candy."

"Amiya, Darren, and Dylan, you know your aunt Nakita loves you, don't you?"

"Yes, Mom," the three of them chorus.

"Adrianna, your mommy wasn't feeling well. Her medicine didn't work like it should. She had to go to heaven, where the really sick people go," I say. Then I break down.

"Mommy can't go to heaven. She has to come back here, Aunt Candy. I need her here. Can we go and get her? Please, Aunt Candy? She has to come back now," Adrianna cries, her little body convulsing.

"Only dead people go to heaven, Mom. Where is Aunt Kita, Mom?" Dylan says as he brushes tears from his eyes.

I'm sorry, babies, but she's gone. We cannot go and get her. She's in heaven. She will always be in our hearts and watching over us. She loves all of you. Especially you, Adrianna."

"No, Aunt Candy. I don't want her in my heart. I need her here. Please go and get my mommy. Please." Adrianna jumps into my arms.

"I wish I could, baby." I weep, cradling her.

"Mommy, we *have* to go and get Aunt Kita. She *can't* go to heaven. She's not dead," Dylan insists as tears roll down his face.

"I'm so sorry, guys." Alonzo pulls Dylan, Darren, and Amiya into his warm embrace. "Your aunt loved you and will always be with you, like Mommy said. We love you, and we will get through this together."

"Yes, we will, babies," Ms. Jasmine says as she clings to me as I sit on the floor and envelope Adrianna.

Upon breaking from Alonzo's embrace, Darren races over and pulls Adrianna from my arms. "You can have our mommy with us, Adrianna. Don't cry. She's yours now too. Okay?" he whimpers.

"I can't," Jenna cries, and then she bolts to the bathroom, locks the door behind her, and throws up in the toilet.

CHAPTER EIGHT

The Truth Hurts
Jenna . . .

After assisting with getting the kids fed and settled in bed for the night, I make my way through the house to try to find Brianne. Her car is parked out front. She texted me earlier, saying she would be coming by, but I haven't seen her since I got here. I know things haven't been great between the two of us, but I know she has to be hurting like the rest of us. She was the first person that Nakita really opened up to and shared her truth with. Brianne blames herself for Nakita's depression. I kind of feel uncomfortable about all this. Had I not pursued Brianne, Nakita might still be alive. Brianne discontinued her counseling only because of what we were trying to build together. Now I am unsure if that's even happening, and to top it off, Nakita is gone.

When I can't find Brianne anywhere in the house, it dawns on me that she may be over at Nakita's house. So I walk over to Nakita's and search for the house key under the flowerpot by the front door and come up empty handed. That means someone is in there. The rule for Candice and Nakita is that if the key is missing under the flowerpot by the front door, they are home, and if they are not at home, then the key must be under the flowerpot. After allowing myself inside the house, I make my way to Nakita's bedroom, guided by the line of light that illuminates the bottom of the closed bedroom door in a house that is otherwise dark.

"Brianne, are you there?" I call when I reach the door.

"Y-Yes, I am here."

"Are you okay? I know this is a tough one for you, as it is for the rest of us."

"This is all my fault. I was selfish. I should have continued my sessions with her. How could I have abandoned her when I knew she was fragile?"

I slowly open the door, then step inside the bedroom. Brianne is standing in the middle of the floor. "Please don't put that on yourself. You did right by her and the other girls and found them another therapist. You didn't abandon anyone. You did what you thought was best."

"Best for who? No one. She's gone, and I am to blame."

"No you're not, Brianne. You just said she was fragile. So, this could have happened with or without you as her therapist. I believe the person or persons that are at fault here are the men and women that took advantage of her and abused her. Had none of those horrific things taken place, Nakita would still be here."

"I was responsible for helping her get through and past all of that. Look at Candice. She is stronger than ever. I knew she would have no trouble transitioning to a new therapist. Nakita wasn't there yet. I should have waited until she was able to handle that type of change. It was a mistake . . . All this was a huge mistake, and because of my carelessness, someone is dead. Again," she howls.

"Please, Brianne, don't do this to yourself . . ." I pause. "I'm sorry, but what do you mean, someone is dead again?"

"Never mind. Forget I said that."

"I don't think I want to do that. How can we move any further with secrets? How will you be able to even move past this and not take the blame for this when you're harboring secrets?"

"I am a horrible person, Jenna. I am surprised you even want to deal with me. That is probably why you're so turned off and cannot be intimate with me. You can see past my facade. I am not as perfect as everyone thinks I am . . . or thought I was, Jenna."

"I think Nakita's death is hitting you hard, as it is all of us, and it should. She was family to all of us. Blood didn't make us family, even though we are. Our bond and our loyalty to one another did that. However, no one thinks or thought you were or are perfect. None of us are or will ever be perfect. Leave that to God. I am not sure what facade you're talking about either. What I do know is, you were the strength that my sister and the other girls needed when they didn't know where to turn. God in heaven knows that we all blame ourselves in some way, shape, or form because we love her." I take a deep breath.

I go on. "Deep down inside, we know it wasn't our fault. I may not be a therapist, but I do know that some people cannot be saved, no matter how hard you try. Nakita felt this was needed in order for Adrianna to be happy. No, it doesn't make sense to us, but it made sense to her. I hate all of it. I wish I could have been here to stop her or something. It hurts like hell, but I know neither you nor I did this to her. My heart is bleeding like everyone else's is, but we cannot blame ourselves and end up in the same place that she was in, Brianne."

"I've been where she was, and sometimes, I find myself still there. No one deserves to be treated the way that those girls were mistreated. Someone deserves to pay, and it should not have been Nakita. My baby had to pay for what happened to me." Unable to hold in her heartbreak any longer, Brianne collapses on the floor, inconsolable in her misery, as tears flood her eyes.

"Baby? Your *baby*, Brianne? What are you talking about?" I move closer to her.

"I don't want to talk about it right now, Jenna."

"Well, I think it's good to talk. I feel like you need to talk. You would tell us that in counseling. Or should I say, 'You're at a breaking point, so please continue'?" Tears race down my cheeks.

"I am already broke, Jenna, so run now. I can help fix everyone except myself. What I will do is make sure none of my other patients get to this point. I will make sure their abusers pay."

"You're not making sense. You have no control over that, Brianne. Please talk to me. What baby?" I say, digging.

"Just let it go, Jenna. Please."

"I cannot and I will not let it go, Brianne. Please talk to me."

"I killed my daughter. I am a horrible person. Are you happy now?"

"No, I am not happy. What do you mean, you killed your daughter? What daughter, Brianne? You're not making sense."

"I am making perfect sense. Like I said, I am not as perfect as I appear to be. I have flaws. I too was raped and was possibly impregnated by my rapist. The downfall is I went into a severe depression, and my Sienna is no longer here because of those bastards."

"No longer here? How? What happened? I am so sorry, Brianne. I had no idea." I drop to the floor next to her as gut-wrenching sobs tear through my chest.

"I—I left her in the car. She died from vehicular heatstroke. I was so caught up in my own mess and so severely depressed that I left my child in a car by herself to die. I am a horrible human being. Like I said, because of my own selfishness, because I put my shit first, once again someone lost their life."

"I am so sorry, Brianne. It was a mistake. You didn't leave her in the car intentionally. You cannot blame yourself."

"I am to blame for Sienna, just like I am to blame for Nakita."

"No you're not. Don't do this to yourself."

"Do what? It is already done. Instead of handling the cowards that hurt me, I went into a depression, and now my daughter is gone. Now, once again, instead of putting Nakita's needs first, I selfishly discontinued her services to pursue something with you, and now she's gone. No more. This will never happen again."

"You can't take the blame for all this, Brianne. None of this is your fault. You were hurt, just like Nakita was. Your abusers are at fault. I had no idea. I am so sorry. I will do whatever is necessary to work through all this with you." I grab her hands to try to comfort her.

"I don't want your help. This is partially your fault. If you hadn't thrown yourself at me, Nakita would probably still be here. Please get your hands off me." She snatches her hands out of my grasp. "To add insult to injury, you're nothing more than a tease. So she's gone, and for what?" She shakes her head.

"I *threw* myself at you, Brianne? That's what I did?"

"Of course, out of everything I just said to you, that's all you heard."

"You're upset, Brianne. You don't mean that. Would you like me to go downstairs and give you a little time by yourself?"

"No, you can leave. I will be fine," she tells me, her tone cold.

"I don't feel comfortable leaving you alone right now. You're upset. We're all upset. We need one another to get through all this, Brianne."

"What? You think I am suicidal now? I am fine. I'd kill someone else before I'd hurt myself."

I frown. "You're really scaring me, Brianne. I know you're upset, and this is hard for us, but you can't blame yourself or push me away."

"How can I push someone away that I never had? That's impossible, Jenna. You're a beautiful, insightful, and intelligent woman. I think you need to reevaluate things and make sure that you really want to be with a woman and that you're not looking for a mother."

"That was cruel, Brianne." My chin trembles.

Distance is all that matters to me right now. The only sure way to escape this verbal lashing is to remove myself from her presence. I get up of the floor and walk toward the door. As I am about to leave the room, I stop in my tracks and turn around. Through my tears, I say, "I—I know you're hurting. You might even be dealing with a different level of pain, because you had a somewhat unique relationship with Nakita as her counselor and her friend. However, that does not give you the right to be rude, hurtful, or disrespectful."

"I am being honest. Life is too short, as you can see, to be walking on eggshells and trying to spare feelings. You and I both know the truth, so let's get through this rough moment in our lives with Nakita's passing and leave everything else where it's at."

"What does that mean, Brianne? What are you trying to say?"

"I believe I have been totally clear. You and I both know that I am not looking to be your mom. I want more, but you're unable to give me what I want other than a friendship."

"No problem." I dart from the room.

Allowing my tears to become one with my face, I pick up speed, head out Nakita's front door, and sprint back to Candice's place. As I reach for the doorknob, the door swings open, and I collapse into my dad's arms.

"Baby girl, are you all right? I don't think it was a good idea for you girls to keep going over there. It's too soon." He swallows me with his arms.

"I—I need to get away from here. Everything is falling apart around me. Nakita is gone, and now Brianne."

"Brianne? What's wrong with Brianne? Baby, what are you saying?"

"Can we leave, Dad? I don't want to upset anyone any more than they already are."

"Sure, baby. Let me go and make sure Alonzo and Ms. Jasmine are good with the kids. Oh, never mind. Here comes Tracy and Simone. They can be there with Ms. Jasmine and Alonzo. "

"Hey there, ladies," Dad calls. He and I greet the girls with hugs simultaneously.

"We feel awful, Jenna. How's Candice? How's Adrianna taking it?" Tracy says, sympathizing.

"Not good. This is a rough one," I say.

"Yes, it is for all of us," Simone interjects.

"We have to hold each other up through this. That's what family does," Dad declares.

"Yes, we do. Listen, my dad and I are on our way out. We will be right back. If my sister or the babies need anything, please text me," I say.

"Will do," Tracy throws over her shoulder as she and Simone walk by us and into the house.

"Dad, I don't have an appetite," I tell my dad as we sit in a booth at TGI Fridays.

"You have to eat something, baby girl. You're going to make yourself sick. Try a sandwich, even if you eat only half of it."

"You know I don't like processed food. I don't even eat meat, Dad."

"They have a black-bean burger. See there, princess? Right up your alley."

I smirk. "I'll give it a try, Dad. My stomach is in knots. I feel like I can't breathe, Dad. My whole world caved in right before me."

"Well, you wouldn't be able to talk if you couldn't breathe, so please take a deep breath and talk to me, baby. What's going on with Brianne?"

"She was so mean to me, Dad. I cannot believe she talked to me the way that she just did. She blames Nakita's death on me. I felt bad originally, because I know that had she kept going to counseling with Brianne, she might still be here."

"Don't do that to yourself. There's no telling what would or would not have happened. As for Brianne, she knows better. She's supposed to be a professional with this, so I am confused as to where all this is coming from."

"She has her own bag of skeletons, Dad. I think Nakita's death gave them a life."

"I am sure she does, baby girl. We all do. Right now, you need to focus on Jenna. Let me ask you a question, How do you know you prefer women?"

"Dad!"

He shrugs. "It's a simple question."

"I just find myself attracted to them. I don't see men like that at all."

"Is it because of me?"

I shake my head. "No, Dad. Why are we talking about this right now, anyway?"

"Because I really think you're looking for motherly love. I think you're confused. I want you to be able to mourn and be there with and for your sister. Nakita was family to all of us. I don't want this mess with Brianne upsetting you when this thing you have for her isn't real."

"Why does everyone keep saying that? I know what I feel." I dissolve into tears.

After moving to my side of the booth, Dad put his arms around me and holds me tightly, whispering, "I love you so much. I am sorry for not being what I needed to be to you. I am even more sorry that your mom wasn't here for you. I blame myself for all the ups, downs, and unbearable things that you and your sister experienced. I promise to make it up to both of you."

Snuggling closer, I reply, "I love you more, Dad."

I am not sure what my future holds when it comes to my sexuality. Dad and even Brianne have a point. Maybe I have been looking for a mother all along. No matter what I decide, I know Brianne isn't for me. She has turned into my evil stepmother. Just like Camilla when she's mad, Brianne verbally assaults. I refuse to allow myself to open that door to mistreatment ever again. My heart is aching, but it has more to do with wishing Nakita had given life another chance. She was the other half of Candice and, when I met them, of me as well. A cousin I didn't know I'd had and someone whom I'd grown to love from our first encounter is gone. How do we go on from here? I feel like I now have a bigger hole in my heart. One adjoined to the hole Mama left.

Dear Heavenly Father, if you're listening, please help me. I know I am probably the last person you expected to hear from. My sister said talking to you would help me, so I am talking. I need help, God. I am confused, hurt, and scared. Please help me, so I can help myself, I pray silently.

"Jenna, are you all right over there? Did I say something wrong?"

"Yes, Dad, I am fine. And no, you said everything right."

"I am happy to hear that. Let's get this to go. We can stop and pick up a couple pies and bring them back to the house for everyone."

"That's a great idea."

CHAPTER NINE

Breaking Point
Brianne . . .

Dr. Ness had no business telling me what I can and cannot do with my practice. She's the one taking clients under the table. That's more questionable than me being burnt out or still mourning the loss of my daughter. I should not have gone to see her. Had I not gone, I would have been available for Nakita when she phoned me. I'd been so upset with myself for wasting my time going to see Dr. Ness that I'd turned my phone off when I left her office. Now another life is gone because of my negligence and selfishness.

"I am so sorry, Nakita. I wasn't there for you, just like I wasn't there for Sienna. I promise to make it up to both of you by not allowing another person dear to me or a client suffer due to my negligence and selfishness. Everyone will have to pay for their sins one way or the other," I vow aloud through angry tears as I sit on Nakita's bedroom floor. "I can do this." I pick myself up off the floor.

As I pace back and forth, I refuse to let regret, heart-break, and sadness consume me any longer and promise myself that I will commit myself anew to my practice. "Yes, I can. I can do this," I affirm. "I am Dr. Binet, American Psychiatric Association Award recipient in two categories. I will not allow a minor setback to take my accomplishments away or diminish my practice."

At times, I used to see four or more clients a day, five days a week, and each of my clients came armed with heavy problems. I managed to help them through it all. Yes, some of it reopened my barely healed wounds. But that doesn't mean I am unfit to practice. Helping the girls helped me. It just eats away at me when their abusers get off easy. I know if their abusers paid for their sins, they'd heal faster and be able to move on with their lives without too many hang-ups. I honestly believe Nakita couldn't fully recover because evildoers who preyed upon her, Mr. Frankie and Paul, got off easy.

Simone, Tracy, and Judith, the other girls who fell victim to abusers and were at Hope House along with Candice and Nakita, still live together, because they're still afraid, despite all the extensive counseling they've undergone. They're scared to be alone. Samantha hasn't been the same since she parted ways with all the girls, as well as with her son Micah. Unfortunately, she married that clown of a lawyer who represented her in the proceedings against Ms. Nancy's estate and is now dependent on drugs. Money couldn't and didn't buy her or her children happiness. Ms. Jasmine now has full custody of Micah, and the state has Samantha's twin girls. Ms. Jasmine is fighting to get the twins as well. Therapy is so important for those girls, and they need closure. Because they have not had closure, they're still afraid and lost. They don't feel safe. How can they?

As for Simone, her abuser is a free man because no one believed her. I believe her story is what led me to believe wholeheartedly that more needs to be done for victims of abuse. And Nakita's sudden death has underscored my conviction. For two years, it was very difficult to extract information from Simone. It was like pulling teeth just to get a straight answer from her or to get her to open up. She was my most difficult case since I opened my own practice. No matter what direction I went, she wouldn't budge. The day I broke through to her, something broke in me. I did something I never had never done before in my practice or profession. I became personally and emotionally attached. I remember exactly what happened that day.

"Good afternoon, Simone. How are you doing today?" I said when she entered my office and took a seat.

"I am good, Dr. Binet. How are you doing?"

"I can't complain. How about you tell me what you'd like me to help you with?"

"We have been doing this for a few years. You're supposed to be the doctor, aren't you? Shouldn't you know the answer to that question by now?" Her eyes widened.

"You're absolutely right. Well . . . do you think you should be here? I know when you first arrived at Hope House, the girls suggested therapy, as it was their saving grace, as they mentioned to you. But do you think you should be here? Do you even want to be here, or is it just something for you to do? You can be honest with me," I replied, digging.

"Are you going to let me answer, or are you going to keep asking open-ended questions and answering them yourself?" she snapped.

"I suppose you still struggle with trust, considering it has been a few years since you started therapy, as you just stated."

"You're absolutely right. I do not trust you. You don't know me. You're just here to collect a check. This is your job. You couldn't care less about us. I don't need your pity either."

"This is more than a check for me, Simone. I was once you. I was hurt and taken advantage of by someone I thought loved me, and because of that, it's hard for me to trust anyone. What I do trust is my clients hurt and

pain, and what I can give of myself to help them tackle their pain."

Scanning her face for a reaction, I saw she didn't have one. Simone stared blankly as silence hovered over us.

"Would you like to end here—" I stopped short when I noticed tears illuminating her eyes like jewels.

Tearfully, she revealed, "I—I was only three years old. I don't' remember everything. I just keep having the same nightmare over and over of police officers removing me from our home. That was the last time I saw my parents. And in this nightmare, I am being placed in the system." She paused.

"Do you need a moment?"

"No. I think I need to get all this off my chest. It's time. I heard everything you've ever said to me. The only way that I've talked about any of this until now is in my journal, as you instructed me to."

"I am happy to hear this, Simone. That is huge. If you don't mind, I'd like you to continue talking about this now. Are you all right with that?"

Nodding her head yes, she admits, "When I was seven, I learned my mom and dad were arrested, and I, along with four other kids, were removed from the home during the raid. My foster brother at the time said it was all over the news. He was four years older than me and helped my foster mom out. Todd was Mimas's only son. She wanted to have more children and couldn't, so she took in foster kids."

"So, the other four children weren't siblings? And Mimas? Is that your foster mother?"

"Yes, Mimas was really the only mom that I've known. I vaguely remember my mom and dad. I was an only child. When I was old enough, I researched and found out my parents, along with my aunt, were arrested for having guns and cocaine in the house. Myself along with my four cousins were placed in foster care. The only family that I've known are Mimas, Todd, Kathy, Sabrina, and Terianne. Things were great until I turned ten." She used the back of her hand to wipe tears from her eyes.

"Please feel free to use the tissues to the right of you." I pointed.

"Thank you." She blew her nose before closing her eyes and taking me back to the exact day and time. . . .

"Kathy, Sabrina, Terianne, and you too, Simone, bring your smelly tails in here."

"Yes, Mimas?" we sang.

"Girls are supposed to be pretty and smell like flowers all the time. I want each of you to get yourself together, so I can give you a bath the right way. I have some pretty undergarments and deodorant for you girls that I want you to try."

"Yes, ma'am," we chorused, moping..

"What are the long faces for?"

"We wanted to finish jumping rope before the street-lights come on," Kathy explained.

"The lights are on in here. Now bring your smelly tails upstairs."

"You girls heard what she said," Todd said, chiming in. "Mimas, I'll give you a hand and help Simone and Terianne."

As Terianne and I entered the bathroom, Todd in-structed, "You two undress while I run your bath."

"No. Just run the water. You can't see our privates," I replied.

"No one is paying attention to your mosquito bites, Simone," he mocked. "But I will turn around."

Rolling my eyes but filled with shame, I removed my clothes, and so did Terianne.

"You two get in the tub. I'll show you how to clean yourselves real fast, and then I'll leave," Todd told us.

"Good," we said in unison, and then we jumped into the tub, splashing water over the rim.

"Stop splashing the water, before I call Mimas," Todd warned us.

"Tattletale," Terianne teased.

"Okay, stop playing." He pulled me closer and placed the washrag in my hand. With his hand over mine, he guided the washrag under my arms, across my training bra–sized breasts, and then down to my privacy. There he slipped his hand under the washrag and placed his middle finger inside me .

Simone sighed and gazed out the window of my office for a moment. "Dr. Binet, he helped us, all right. Todd had always been so sweet and protective of us. However, on that day he turned into one of the guys he professed to protect us from."

"Is that the only time Todd touched you?"

"I wish. Todd raped me up until the day Mimas made me leave. She didn't even believe me when I told her that Todd might be the father of my baby and that he'd been raping me. Mimas said I wasn't being truthful. She said she couldn't keep a fast, lying pregnant girl in her home or help raise a bastard baby." Simone began to sob.

"Do you need a moment, Simone?"

"No. Would you please stop asking me that question? If I needed a moment, I would take it. You have no compassion whatsoever. You said you were hurt and taken advantage of by someone you thought loved you. I shared this, thinking you could relate and that it'd be safe, and yet you sit there in front of me, stone faced."

With tears threating my eyes, I confessed, "Ethically, I cannot become emotionally attached, so it's best I allow you to finish before I say anything. It will give me time to process things, so I can say what you need to hear. This isn't about me."

"Ethically? I am no case study, Dr. Binet. I am a human being, looking for more than a 'Do you need a moment?'"

"This is about you, Simone, not me. Yes, I was hurt, and every day I am haunted by the memories of it. However, I shared too much when I said that. I apologize for getting personal."

"You're just like Todd. When he abused my trust over and over, all he did was apologize, right before he did it again. You're probably sitting there, speechless, judging me like Mimas did, because I am unsure who fathered Sage. Mimas didn't give me time to clear that up. So, before you go judging me, the reason I don't know is that Todd wanted to give his best friend, Robert, a birthday present, and 'the pretty, Chinky-eyed girl' named Simone was the perfect gift. That's right. They took turns raping me, Dr. Binet. They raped me," she screeched, in pain.

"I am so sorry, Simone. I know exactly what you're going through. You are brave and strong to have made it this far. I was a coward. I went through the same thing. However, my Sienna ended up paying for their sins. I promise to help you through this. Todd and Robert have to pay for what they did to you. Don't be like me, carrying my abusers' guilt."

"It's too late, Dr. Binet, my daughter is three now. No one would believe me. They'd probably call me fast, just like Mimas did. I just need to know how to move on from here."

"I promise to help you every step of the way. You know I was going to end our sessions today, like I did with the other girls, but I will continue working with you. Please keep it between the two of us. I don't want to hurt any of the girls by them thinking I chose you over them."

"Right now, I will do whatever is necessary. I cannot think anymore, and I need my sanity in order to be what I need to be to Sage. So you have my word."

We embraced, allowing our tears to express our deep thoughts and our pain.

I've spent too many years trying to erase what happened to me, and I have been living a lie. I don't even know who I am anymore. I pretend to be this happy woman who has it all together, when all I really want to do is lie down and let the pain flow through me. I've contemplated suicide, but that's too easy. I am not the one who needs to die. Every time I listened to the girls, I realized how much more I am needed, and me killing myself would benefit only my abuser even more. Simone's story was an eye-opener for me in so many ways. I went to see Dr. Kruk and then Dr. Ness because ethically I had crossed a line. However, after talking to Dr. Ness and learning of Nakita's untimely death, I knew all of this was meant to happen. I have work to do.

"I promise I won't let you down, Nakita," I whisper as I walk out of Nakita's bedroom. I close the door behind me, then make my way to my car.

I am so not in the mood for this right now, I think when I see Jenna and her dad, Dale, walking up the driveway in my direction.

"Brianne, how are you making out? Considering—" Dale begins, but I cut him off.

"I can say I've seen better days, Dale. But in due time we will all heal from this, and Nakita's death will not have been in vain."

"Excuse me?" he says.

"This was a sign for all of us to get our shit in order. We have to deal with all those things we've been keeping inside."

"I agree that counseling and dealing with those deep things do help. Thanks for everything, Brianne. We picked up some food, if you want to stay awhile," he replies.

"No thank you. But thank you for the offer."

"Dad, can you give us a moment?" Jenna interrupts.

"Sure." He removes bags from Jenna's arms and heads toward the front door.

After he shuts the door, Jenna snaps, "How could you act like I wasn't standing here, Brianne?"

"Jenna, it was the wrong time to be discussing anything. Your father was standing here. And it was the wrong time for things to go the way that they did earlier, when we should have been mourning the loss of our friend. Your cousin, for God's sake."

"You're absolutely right. I knew you were upset and didn't mean what you said. Even though it made me think—"

"Yes, it was wrong timing. However, I meant everything I said. This is not for me, and you know deep down inside it's not for you. We can be friends. That's all that I can give you, and that is all you can give, so let's stop beating around the bush and be honest with one another."

"Fine, Brianne."

She brushes past me and storms into the house.

CHAPTER TEN

Until We Meet Again
Candice . . .

My eyes shoot open, and my gaze dances around the room. Breathing short, heavy breaths as sweat beads run down my face and my hands, I jump up from bed. "Alonzo, I had the worst nap. Nakita . . ." My words evaporate in the air as I witness the doleful look painted across his face.

"I'm sorry, Candice. I wish it were just a nightmare. I wish I could bring her back. I am so sorry."

"I need her here, Alonzo. Adrianna needs her mommy. I can never take her place in her life. Why did she do this?"

"No one expects you to take her place. You have always been a second mom to Adrianna, the same way Nakita was with the boys and Amiya."

"We cannot have a funeral. I will not put the kids through that. I wouldn't be any good to them. I've never been to a funeral, and I will not start now. We have to do something different. Alonzo, do you hear me? We cannot have a funeral. I will literally fall apart, seeing her like that. I'm sorry, but I can't do it. If there's one, I am not going, and neither are the kids. We can't. We just can't, Alonzo." He embraces me, and I weep in his arms.

"Did she give you power of attorney, or are you her next of kin?" he asks me when my sobbing stops.

"Y-Yes, I am. After we moved in, we went and had a will and everything drawn up for the kids. She said she didn't want anyone but me to make her last decisions for her or for Adrianna."

"Great. That's a start. You can plan a memorial for her. Whatever you want to do to remember her. We can put our heads together and do something special for her."

"I'd like that. Thank you for being my knight in shining armor, Alonzo."

"I'll be whatever you need me to be, Candice. I love you with everything in me."

"I know, Alonzo. I can feel it. Please give me time to love you back."

"I will love it out of you."

Blushing, I shake my head.

Just then there is a knock on the door.

"Come in," I say.

Ms. Jasmine and Jenna enter my bedroom.

"Hey there, baby girl. We just had to check up on you. Do you need anything?" Ms. Jasmine asks as she and Jenna make their way over to the bed. Ms. Jasmine squeezes herself between Alonzo and me.

"I'm just so lost, Ms. Jasmine. I can't do a funeral service. I just cannot," I confess.

Ms. Jasmine nods. "Well, it's up to you how you want to do this."

"We don't have to have a traditional service, Candice. We can do a memorial tree planting or something like that," Jenna interjects tearfully.

"I'd like that. Can you also do me a favor and ask Brianne and Mrs. Bartlett—I mean Joanne—to make the arrangements to postpone the opening of New Beginnings? I am in no condition to deal with any of that."

"That's what you hired them for, Candice. You don't have to do it all. The opening will be rescheduled. You have all the time that you need," Jenna says, consoling me.

"You're right. I appreciate all of you," I reply.

"You know, if Nakita were here and she walked in and saw you crying, she'd flip out and ask questions later," Jenna muses.

Smirking, I say, "Yes, you're right. She had a temper on her."

"She sure did. Especially when it came to you and the kids," Ms. Jasmine interjects, her eyes tearing.

"How about we go downstairs and get some food in you, Candice?" Jenna proposes. "We can make arrangements, talk, or whatever you want while you eat something."

"Thank you, Jenna. I am not sure how much I'll be able to eat, but I'll try."

Instead of putting off the dreadful day, we have decided to have a memorial for Nakita on the fourth day after her passing. Four was her favorite number. She'd say, "There are four seasons, and on the fourth day of creation, the physical universe was completed." Nakita loved the way the seasons changed, and she thought it was amazing how the weather changed drastically with each season. I, however, find the seasons less desirable because I hate when it's too hot or too cold. There's no happy medium when it comes to the weather. We get two to three good days, and then, *bam*, the weather changes.

Nakita also used to say, "All good things happen on the fourth day. Pay attention." She felt we all got three chances to mess up any and everything in life. But the fourth chance, in her opinion, was always the charm. She just loved the number four. But I just wish this fourth day didn't have to come to pass.

After Jenna mentioned doing a tree-planting memorial, the idea stuck in my head like glue. I did some additional research and learned that a tree serves as a long-lasting memorial for loved ones. Our tree's greenery will symbolize that Nakita's legacy will continue to grow and flourish with us. She will be able to enjoy the different seasons, just the way she loved to when she was here. Well, the tree will, and I know she'd like that idea if she were still here.

Nakita loved lilacs. After Dr. Binet told her about the calming effects of lilacs, she went lilac crazy. From oils to air fresheners, everything was lilac with her. This made it easy to go with a Bloomerang purple lilac tree as the memorial. Purple and lilacs on one tree was the best tree to choose in her honor. Both of her loves on one tree. The tree will bloom twice a year, in mid-May and then again from July to the first frost. What I love most about this particular tree variety is that it fills the air with that lilac scent.

We're going to have it planted at the entryway to her place, which will eventually be torn down and turned into a playground for the kids. I cannot see myself going back in that house after finding her the way that I did. It will just bring back bad memories. I want all future memories of my beloved sister to be good. Initially, I wanted to have the playground done for the memorial service; however, that was pushing my luck.

In any event, we are headed out back to celebrate and remember our beloved Nakita. Our little tree, its root ball still in burlap, is standing by a row of chairs.

Mr. Derek is going to lead us in the tree planting, considering the rest of us don't have a clue about planting a tree. We don't even know how deep the hole in the ground should be or anything. And he volunteered to officiate over the memorial as he is a minister for his church. Either way, it's time to say good-bye or see you later to my sister.

Once everyone is seated, the memorial begins. Mr. Derek approaches the podium that he has erected, then stands in front of us, silent. When a hush falls over us, he addresses us.

"I will start off by reading from the Gospel of Mathew, chapter five, verse four. It reads, 'Blessed are those who mourn, for they will be comforted.' And John, chapter fourteen, begins, 'Do not let your hearts be troubled. You believe in God. Believe also in me.' And Luke, chapter twelve, verse thirty-two, says, 'Do not be afraid little flock, for your Father has been pleased to give you the kingdom.' So, little flock, as we remember Nakita, let our hearts be not troubled. Let us not be afraid. And let us be comforted by the knowledge . . ." He goes on for about ten minutes, and then he looks over at me and says, "Candice will have some words before we give a blessing over the tree."

I stand, walk slowly to the podium, and face everyone. "This is probably one the hardest things that I have ever had to do. I couldn't get my thoughts together, so please bear with me. As you all know, I met Nakita at one of the darkest moments in my life. We all did. She then blossomed into the sister that I never had. As well as into one of the only persons that I know for a fact loved me and didn't want anything in return. She'd rather endure pain before I had to. I wish she were here, so I could tell her one last time how much I love her. I miss her. Sista friends, as we referred to one another, are hard to come by, so when she left, a part of me left with her. Through it all, I vow to love Adrianna and all of you with the same love that she shared. I may not be as blunt as she was, but I promise to be what she'd expect me to be.

"Nakita, I love you *so* much, and you will be missed. There will be a void in my heart, until we meet again. I love you, my beloved sista friend. I just want to add that after reuniting with my dad, I found out Nakita was actually my cousin. So what we had was blood deep." At this moment, I lose control, and Ms. Jasmine has to assist me from the podium.

"It's all right to cry," Mr. Derek assures me as he steps up to the podium. "The Bible tells us there's a season and a purpose for everything. A time to be born, die, weep, laugh, dance, and mourn."

"When can we send our balloons up for my mommy?" Adrianna whines.

Mr. Derek nods in Adrianna's direction and then turns and looks at the little lilac tree. "Let us pray blessings for the tree so we can move to the balloon release. Dear God, creator of life, we come in this prayer of dedication and blessing to dedicate this tree in memory of Nakita Mathews. We thank you, dear God, for her life and come to you in a time of sorrow. May this tree remind us of Nakita and grow full branches as a representation of your love. May we always honor and remember our Nakita, who is a mother to Adrianna, a sister, and a beloved friend to all of us. We ask for your blessings upon this tree and upon us who mourn the passing of Nakita. In Jesus's name, we pray. Amen."

"Amen," everyone utters in unison.

"Now for the balloon release. Each of you will step forward, and Jenna will hand you your balloon. Then I will play a song on this device. Each person can take their time releasing their balloon to our beloved Nakita."

We form a line and receive our balloons from Jenna, who carefully passes them out. I ordered dove balloons for everyone, with note cards attached. Each person in line already penned a note to Nakita on a notecard and wrote his or her name in big letters on the back. Letting go of doves is said to promote healing, as their flight represents a person's spirit going to heaven. So one by one, we release our balloons, and tears and laughter saturate the atmosphere. Everyone instantly reminisces about the impact that our beloved Nakita had on each of our lives. When I release my balloon, my purple dove, I feel I release so much more. I am instantly consumed with a sense of relief and feel like everything is going to be all right. Nakita's not hurting anymore, and I can feel her here with me. For the first time since her passing, I smile.

"I love you, Nakita, and I will always love you. I feel you here with me. I will talk about you to Adrianna until the last breath leaves my body. I won't ever forget you, my sista friend. You will remain fixed in my heart always and forever, until we see each other again. I love you always and forever," I say as my dove sails up, up into the azure sky.

CHAPTER ELEVEN

Disappearing Acts
Simone . . .

It all started around the age of thirteen, when my foster brother Todd went from fondling me to penetrating me. He said if I said anything about it, Mimas would never believe me and I'd end up being sent to another foster family and it'd be worse. I was young dumb and naïve, and I fell for it. He was my big brother. He protected me from the kids who picked on me at school. Todd just couldn't protect me from himself, or myself. I resorted to cutting myself.

I had convinced myself that by making myself bleed, the numbness I felt inside would disappear. If I could see it in red, then I could believe that it was not only in my head. Seeing it made it real, and it made the pressure in my chest fade a little bit. It made the pain and fear lessen.

Long-sleeve shirts and pants were my saving grace. Mimas used to tell me to change out of my warm clothes before I caught on fire, but she never really enforced it. She was too busy cleaning, cooking, talking on the phone, and watching her soap operas. Todd, on the other hand, taunted me and said that I was damaged goods, and that no one would ever want me except him. Every time he uttered those words, death seemed more and more promising.

The day my life changed was when I was separated from the only family that I'd known. It ripped a piece of my soul out, and I thought that piece could never be replaced. Before that day arrived, I had been feeling nauseous for about a month and had been vomiting like clockwork every morning, after or during breakfast.

On the seventh day of this vomiting routine, nausea clawed at my throat during breakfast, which we ate together religiously as a family every morning. I tried to swallow back everything that was forcing its way up, but to no avail. After springing from my seat, I dashed to the bathroom, covering my mouth, trying to contain my partially digested Sugar Smacks. As soon as I graced the toilet bowl, my stomach contracted violently and its contents spewed out.

Terianne rushed to my aid and closed the bathroom door behind her. "Oh, my goodness, Mone. Are you all right?"

I nodded my head no as my stomach turned against me one final time.

After flushing the toilet and then closing the lid, I took a seat on top of it. It felt as if I had just upchucked organs along with my breakfast.

"Here. Take this damp towel and wipe your mouth. How are you feeling?"

"Horrible."

"The phone rang, so Mimas didn't see you, thank God."

"Why are we thanking God? I have a stomach bug or something. I am sick. Why would we thank God for me being sick, Terianne?"

"I think it's a little more than that, Mone. No one has a stomach bug every morning. You need to see a doctor. Unfortunately, you're going to have to tell Mimas that you're pregnant. I know you're afraid, because she warned us to keep our sacred area in the witness protection program, so no one can find it until we are married. Why didn't you use protection?"

"Protection? Are you serious, Terianne? Protection?"

"Um, did I say something wrong? Even though Mimas didn't have that talk with us, you know what you're supposed to do if you're going to be out there having sex, Mone."

"Having sex? Is that what it's called?"

"You're being silly. You know what sex is."

"No, I don't. I only know what rape is."

"*Rape?*"

"Shut up, before Mimas hear you."

"No, I will not. You have to tell her you were raped," Terianne insisted. "Why didn't you tell any of us? Why didn't you tell Todd, so he could take care of the guy? You know he don't play when it comes to us."

"Todd? He doesn't play when it comes to us. No, he just plays *with* us."

"Plays with us? This is serious, Mone." She teared up and brushed her hand across her face. "Who did this to you? When did it happen? I am so sorry. We have to tell Todd. He will fix it."

"Fix what he broke? I hate Todd. He can't fix anything."

"You cannot blame him for this, Mone. He loves you. He will be devastated to know someone hurt you."

"Devastated with himself? How does that work, Terianne?"

"With *himself*? What are you saying?"

"H-He raped me." I burst into tears.

"Todd? You're mistaken. Mone, Todd would never hurt us. He'd never hurt you. Is it someone that looks like him? Listen to what you're saying. He would never hurt you. You know that."

"I used to think that, but I was wrong, Terianne. He has been hurting me for years."

"Why would you blame Todd? I know he is overprotective of us, but to make this up and lie about him like that is unforgiveable. What kind of person are you, Mone?"

"What kind of person am *I*? I cannot believe you're saying this to me! How could you think I am lying? Why would I lie?"

"I live here too, along with everyone else, and Todd has been great to all of us. He would never hurt any of us, and I know for a fact that he didn't do this to you. You probably got your feelings hurt when you told your little boyfriend, and now he wants nothing to do with you. If that's the case, deal with him. Don't go making things like this up. This could ruin Todd's life."

"*His* life? He has ruined me. He has destroyed me. I hate myself because of him. I'd rather die than have him or—"

"Then maybe you should die." She stormed out of the bathroom and slammed the door behind her.

"Are you two at it again?" Mimas shouted from the other side of the door.

"Mone is having one of those days. I cannot deal with her right now. I'm over her," Terianne announced.

"Hurry up in there, Simone, so you can get your tail ready for school," Mimas scolded.

"Ok-okay." I turned on the faucet. With tears blinding my vision, I removed the framed picture from the bathroom wall. I gently placed it on the floor. I pulled a tissue from a hole I had made in the wall behind the picture, and I came eye to eye with my comforter. A mischievous twinkle came into my eyes as I extract my special razor blade from its hiding spot. As softly as I could, I turned on the water in the bathtub and left the faucet on, hoping Mimas couldn't hear the water running. As the tub began to fill, I stepped in, fully clothed from head to toe, to join the water. After taking a seat, I used my buddy to assist me with redesigning the bracelet lines on my wrist. I was not surprised that I felt nothing. No pain. No fear.

After a few minutes, I begin to feel dizzy and faint. As I tried to grip the side of the tub, I felt such heaviness, and my torso slipped down into the water.

After opening my eyes to see Mimas sitting in front of me, crying, I panicked. *Have I died? Is this a dream?* "Where am I?"

"Simone, baby, you're in the hospital. What have you done?" Mimas said, extracting me from my confused thoughts.

Instead of trying to respond, I allowed my fear to be translated into tears. *My reality. My disappointment. I'm still here.*

"You could have come and talked to me, Simone. You know we have an open-door policy. No secrets. I love you. I would have worked with you through whatever it was that you were going through," she said, her voice cracking.

Seeing my shero cry terrified me and wounded my heart even more.

A little above a whisper, I sobbed, "I am sorry to make you cry, Mimas. I didn't know what to do. I was alone and scared."

"You're never alone. If you ever feel that way ever again, please talk to me. We are going to get you some help, so you can talk to someone. Just promise me you will never try to hurt yourself again. I would lose my mind if something were to happen to you."

"I—I promise."

"How long did you know you were pregnant, Simone?" she asked. Her voice had changed.

Startled by her tone, my words lodged themselves in my throat.

"Answer me, Simone!"

"I—I don't know."

"What do you mean, you don't know? Who is this little boy that done did this to you? You know when Todd hears about this, he is going to be very upset and have words with this little boy, don't you?"

I shook my head in disbelief, and fresh tears cascaded down my cheeks at a rapid pace. *Why does everyone continually bring up Todd? He did this*, I scream within.

"You need to start talking, young lady. We need to get all this under control. Do I know him?"

"Y-Yes, you do, Mimas." I felt the air around me evaporate.

"Who is he? I need to call his parents and let them know he is the father of my grandbaby."

"I—I don't know."

"What do you mean, you don't know? You just said I know who he is."

"N-No, I didn't."

"Simone, stop playing with me. We already know you done gone and got yourself knocked up. There's no turning back now. Now, for God's sake, answer me, young lady."

"I don't know, Mimas. T-Todd and his friend R-Robert r-r-raped me."

Her gaze cold, she snarled, "You're talking nonsense. Todd would never hurt you. How dare you blame him after I took you into my home and made my home yours? That is my blood. I know what my blood does, and I didn't give birth to no rapist. Now take it back. Take it back!" She wrapped her hands around my throat.

At that moment, Todd entered the room. "*Mom*! What are you doing to her?" He pulled her off me.

"Let go of me! She is a liar. She destroyed her life, and now she is lying to try to ruin your life."

His gaze hard, Todd stared through me as he and his mother left my hospital room.

That was the last time I saw Mimas, Todd, and the rest of the family. While I was in the hospital, Mimas made arrangements for me to be placed in another foster home. However, since I was pregnant, I was transported to Hope House after a thirty-day stay in a psychiatric hospital as a result of my suicide attempt.

CHAPTER TWELVE

Reunited
Alonzo . . .

When I met Candice at Burger King, I knew she was the one for me. I had to fight with myself and say that such a match was impossible. At that point in my life, I had never paid attention to or been attracted to younger women or women of color. Well, a mixed woman, in Candice's case. At first, I thought it was just a sexual attraction. I couldn't wrap my mind around how beautiful she was without trying. I had an "Oh my God" feeling. But I was wrong. It was more than a sexual attraction. Her innocent smile, her touch, the fear in her eyes—all of those things brought me closer to her. All I wanted to do was be whatever it was that she lacked and put a smile on her face. Of course, I didn't want to come off as some creeper, so I didn't talk to her right away. Instead, I spoke *at* her during our manager-employee conversations. That lasted for about two weeks. During our second time working the late shift, I lost all my willpower. I had to converse with her on a personal level.

As I got to know Candice, I bore witness to the poison that her mom was shoving down her throat, and it infuriated me. Candice is breathtakingly beautiful. Her mom resented her because a blind person could recognize Candice's beauty as soon as she entered a room. I couldn't get past the big clothes Candice draped herself in, along with that banana clip thing she used to lock her coils. And I had no intention of spoiling her innocence. However, the look on her face when she saw herself through my eyes made me want her even more. So soon we were an item. The year we spent together back then was one of the happiest times in my life. But then Candice got pregnant. To this day, I punish myself for what happened next, for listening to my parents, and for allowing Candice's mom to use the same tactics she used regularly on Candice to separate us.

At the time, I was young and afraid. When I came in from work the day my parents found out about the pregnancy, I had so much on my mind. Deep down inside, I had known all along that Candice was pregnant, and when she finally took the test, my suspicions were confirmed. Her confirmation frightened me. I didn't have a clue as to how I was going to break the news to my family. At first I thought I could reason with them, but I knew deep down they wouldn't accept her or our child. And, boy, was I right.

Unfortunately, I underestimated Candice's mother, Camilla. She got to my parents before I returned home that evening from work. As soon as I walked into the home that I'd lived in from birth, an eerie feeling greeted me. I remember that moment now as if it happened yesterday.

"Mom? Dad? Are you home?" I called.

"We're in the den," Dad informed me.

When I walked into the den, my mom was holding a cell phone. She and my dad just stared at me.

"He—hello. What's wrong? Is Grand all right?" I said, my voice dropping.

"Do you mind holding for a moment?" Mom said into the phone's receiver. "I am going to put you on the speaker. Alonzo just walked through the door."

Unable to move or breath, I stood frozen in the same spot as I listened to the voice that came through the phone.

"Hi. Again, I hate to bother you. However, as I stated, I searched my phone bill and was able to find your number. Your son has been spending a generous amount of time with my fourteen-year-old daughter, Candice, and she now finds herself pregnant."

"Alonzo, do you know anything about this?" my dad asked me.

My voice box shut down on me, and I just stood in the same place, silent, as if I were a piece of the marble tile that was beneath me.

"Alonzo, you don't hear your father talking to you? Better yet, Mrs. Whatever You Said Your Name Was, out of all the numbers on your bill, how in God's name did you figure out my son might have something to do with your daughter being pregnant?"

"I know every last number on my bill. It's called the process of elimination. After I asked you if you had a son and if he worked at Burger King, you confirmed my suspicions."

"Again, that does not mean my son is the father of your daughter's child, ma'am," my dad interjected.

"Sir, I am here in a hospital bed, recovering from giving birth to twin girls. The last thing I have right now is time to play games. What I do know is my half African American daughter is pregnant by your son, who is older than she is."

"A black girl, Alonzo? You went and knocked up a black girl?" my dad shouted, then stormed out of the room.

"Do you have anything to say for yourself, young man?" my mom said, her tone menacing.

"I—I'm sorry, Mom. I screwed up. I will do whatever I have to do to be the man you and Dad raised me to be."

"That's not necessary," Candice's mother said harshly. "Candice is being sent away to a home for girls that end up in her situation. I do not want you anywhere near my daughter. If I catch you near her, I will press charges. This is statutory rape." With that, she disconnected the call.

Da made his way back into the den to confront me. "I am extremely disappointed in you. I don't want you anywhere near that girl. For all you know, you're not the only desperate guy she's been with. You don't believe you're the father of that mutt, do you?"

"Dad, with all due respect, Candice is not a mutt. I am the only guy that she's been with. I know that's my child she's carrying, Dad."

"And you fell for the "You're my first" line? Son, it's a game. You were supposed to be her meal ticket out of the slums."

"Dad, how can you say that? Candice has no idea that I come from money. I work at Burger King. No one would think anything like that. I even second-guess it every time I go into that place to work."

"That was a big mistake, it appears. We try to teach you responsibility, and you go and disgrace our family."

"She's not a disgrace, Dad. If you met her, you'd see."

"Meet her? If I see you anywhere near her, you will lose everything, including your inheritance. That is not your child. And I will not repeat myself."

As it turned out, that was the last time that I saw Candice for quite some time. I was forced to quit working at Burger King. And my dad even took my cell phone from me. He finally gave it back when he felt I had come to my senses. But by then he had changed my number. Dad made me work with him in the main office of his construction company. He had inherited my grandparents' company as he was their only child. By then they were no longer physically capable of running the company. It was ranked as the ninth largest privately owned company in the United States. Of course, I was compensated handsomely for my work. I earned pretty much double of what I was making at Burger King.

I blamed myself for not going against my parents' wishes initially and locating Candice. At the time, I thought that if I did that, she wouldn't be sent away. To this day, I cannot understand how Camilla, Candice's mother, the person who birthed her, could feel comfortable ridding herself of Candice, sending her away from the only home she knew. My mom was, in fact, upset and disappointed with me, but she was kind toward me. She said I was too young even to fathom fatherhood. She told my dad I was still learning. And Mom did say that love knows no color and has no color boundaries. She said she could feel the love I had for Candice.

My mom also felt somewhat responsible for the situation, so she did her best to check in with Camilla from time to time. Usually, mom's calls would go unanswered. Except for this one time. I was usually not around when she called. But I was this time. I'll never forget what happened.

"Mom?"

"I'm in the den, Alonzo."

I headed into the den. "Hey, Mom," I said and greeted her with a kiss to her cheek.

"How was work today? You look so tired."

"I couldn't focus all day. My mind has been on Candice. It's a little over nine months since we found out . . ."

"Yes, it has been that long. Why don't we call over to Camilla to check on her? You just be quiet while I talk, so she doesn't get her feathers ruffled." She dialed Camilla.

"I just hope she answers this time."

"Shh." She placed her finger to her lips. "It's ringing." She put the speakerphone on.

"Hello. This is the Brown residence."

"Good evening, Mrs. Brown. I am not sure if you remember me—"

"I know exactly who you are. I thought I made myself clear when I asked that your son have nothing to do with my daughter."

"And he has done just that. I am calling to see if Candice needs anything and if she gave birth to—"

"We are in the process of mourning the loss of my daughter. I would really appreciate it if you stop calling—"

"Loss? What happened to her?" I said, my voice breaking. Then I broke down.

"Candice passed while giving birth. Had you not taken advantage of her, my daughter and grandbaby would still be here. Now please allow us time to mourn in peace. If you continue to harass us, I will get a restraining order," Camilla barked. Then she disconnected the call.

"How is this possible, Mom? She wasn't ill. She's right that this is my fault. I wasn't even there to help her, and now she's gone. Our baby is gone." I wept uncontrollably.

Dad crossed the den's threshold. "What's going on? Is it Mom?"

"It's Candice, Tony. She passed while giving birth."

"And how do we know this?"

"I—I called to see if everything was all right," my mom told him.

"Why, Greta? That is and was none of our business. We have moved past that situation, and now it appears it has moved past us."

"How can you be so cruel, Tony? That was our blood inside that poor little girl."

"My blood is only one color. Now leave it alone, Greta. What's done is done, and what happened is their problem, not ours."

"It is my problem, Dad. It is my problem. She was carrying my child, and because of this, she's—"

His hand connected with the side of my face.

Unable to live under the same roof any longer with Satan's spawn, I took my savings and moved out while my parents were asleep one night. I had been working hard but had had no expenses, so I had saved nearly every dime I made. Originally, I had figured by the time Candice gave birth, she would be back home, and I would be able to help her out. However, it had turned out that I was really saving money for myself. That money enabled me to move out on my own. I didn't need my dad for anything.

But learning of Candice's passing broke me into a million pieces. Over time, I dated here and there, but I wasn't in it. There was always something missing. Candice. On a brighter note for me, one day I met Jenna, and it was one of the best things that could have happened to me. At the time I was in college, studying to become a male nurse, which came with its own set of aggravations. I was feeling alone and somewhat like an outcast, but I didn't allow this to deter me, and I did well in my classes. However, I'd be lying if I said meeting Jenna didn't brighten up my life. After we met, everyone started to look at me differently, and that alone alleviated some of the pressure I was feeling. Without realizing it, I was subconsciously trying to prove my manhood by dating Jenna. I guess I can thank my dad for that flaw.

In so many ways, Jenna resembled Candice to me. I believe that's one of the reasons she caught my attention. Along with her thinking I was gay. Who would have thought that little inquisition she conducted about my sexuality soon after we met would lead to her becoming the sister and friend that I never really had? And never in a million years would I have imagined that Jenna would be the link that would bring Candice back into my life. That day I walked into Jenna's place and saw Candice standing there, I instantly thought preparations were being made for me to go and meet Jesus. It was the scariest and happiest day of my life.

To this day, I have to sometimes remind myself that Candice is really here, and that I have a beautiful baby girl and two little guys to help raise. I still partially blame myself for all that she had to go through in that place her mother sent her to. Had I stood up to my dad back then, things might have been different. Mom has said on numerous occasions that I have no way of knowing that and that I should simply enjoy every moment now. She loves the kids just as much as I do. It's sad that she has to see us behind Dad's back. He is still upset with me, and he still refuses to see or talk to me. Dad pretty much disowned me.

I still struggle with my feelings for Candice. I've vowed to stick it out, considering I have stuck it out this long. However, parts of me struggle with the unknown. Will she ever be able to love me as I do her? Will she ever be able to give her whole self to me? Her mind, body, and soul? How will she ever be able to fully enjoy intimacy after it has been portrayed in the wrong light by Camilla and others for so long? Will she ever be able to share and experience the love, passion, warmth, and connection that encompass sex? I plan to give her all the time that she needs, but what if I am wasting my time fighting a losing battle?

I was hoping my last confession would bring us closer, but of course, my timing was off. Nakita's death sucker punched us so hard. I am just grateful to be able to comfort Candice and the kids. I missed out on all the hard times they had to endure, and I cannot process how Candice is still in her right mind after all that suffering. The kids and Candice mean the world to me, and no matter what does or does not happen between us, I will be there for them.

I've decided to go back to work. I think I have been spending entirely too much time over at Candice's place and I've lost myself in the midst of it. I'm not going to turn my back on them, by no means, but I just need to break my day up and get back to Alonzo. I can't even remember the last time I hung out with the fellas. That's probably what I need right about now.

CHAPTER THIRTEEN

A Mother's Love
Jenna . . .

Even though we had a tree memorial and balloon release for Nakita, it was by far one the saddest days of my life. The others were when my mommy gave me away and then passed away while I was gone. None of this seems real. I keep lying to myself, telling myself Nakita is back at the psychiatric facility. She'll be back. However, reality slaps me clean across the face when I go over to her house. The demolition crew is already in the process of taking the house down in preparation for the park and playground that will be built on the site. Candice has delayed the opening of New Beginnings until the new construction is done. She now wants to have a day-care facility and playground combo built for the new moms to utilize they are in class and in therapy.

The memorial service was heartrending for all of us. The good thing about it is, we were all there to support and uplift one another. Especially the kids. We could not focus on ourselves, because we were so concerned about Adrianna primarily. Every time she cried, we broke down with her and ran for tissues. Amiya catered to her the same way Candice and Nakita did to one another, and it carved holes into each of our hearts. They are miniature versions of Candice and Nakita. I pray everyone begins to see a bigger and brighter picture out of all this. The last thing we need is for any of the other girls to fall into a depression because of all this. Honestly, I cannot even see a brighter picture for myself at all. I am just hopeful. Brianne announced to everyone that she is considering resuming counseling the girls, except for Candice, given that she is now in business with her.

Speaking of Brianne, she's turned into an unfamiliar person. We've spent a lot of intimate time together, and she acts as if we just met. As if she doesn't even know me. One time I broke down in front of her, and she handed me a tissue and walked away — no consoling me whatsoever. I would never have done her like that, no matter what. I know our relationship may not be sexual, but it is in fact on a level higher than friends or what she has with the other girls. Well, perhaps, I am mistaken. It appears she and Simone have this newfound bond, which I am not particularly fond of.

Following the memorial, Ms. Jasmine and Mr. Derek had a reception at their place for everyone to come and unwind and be together for one another. I went from sad and crying to being livid in 2.2 seconds when I witnessed Simone breaking her neck to make a plate for Brianne while she tended to Sage. Since when did Brianne start playing Mommy? I am not saying she doesn't usually bond with the other girls and kids. It was her lighthearted-ness that was unusual. I recall how at one point she and Simone were laughing hysterically.

"Do you two mind sharing what's so funny? God knows all of us could use a chuckle right now," I said, silencing the room.

For heaven's sake, Simone is younger than I am. What the hell does Brianne think she's doing? *I wondered.*

"Simone was just reminiscing about the day she met Nakita," Brianne replied, cutting her eye at me.

"That was quite comical." Candice shook her head.

"Yes, it was. It wasn't at first, though. She caught me off guard. I was so scared when she approached me. Nakita definitely had a way about her. I don't think I will ever again take the last slice of pizza. I have been scarred for life thanks to her," Simone remarked.

Everyone erupts in laughter.

"Are you sure about that?" Ms. Jasmine jested, handing her a slice of pineapple pizza.

Simone loves pineapple pizza, and Nakita did, too. It was Nakita's favorite thing to eat. She could eat a whole pie in a day and be the happiest person in the world because of it. So at the reception Ms. Jasmine and Mr. Derek made sure to have a couple pineapple pizza pies to accompany all our favorite dishes spread across the table.

Nakita scared that girl, Simone, to death on her first night at Hope House. The girls said Simone had arrived during dinner, and when Ms. Nancy invited her to join the girls for dinner, Simone went straight to the pizza box and picked up the last pineapple slice. Everyone knew that was Nakita's pizza, except Simone. Nakita barked at Simone so bad that she dropped the pizza slice. The girls said Nakita was joking, but knowing Nakita's crazy tail, she probably meant some of what she said.

I smirk now just thinking about it. Then I think about one of my interactions with Ms. Jasmine at the reception.

Kneeling to whisper in my ear, Ms. Jasmine said, "Jenna, would you mind helping me bring the desserts out? I want to give my husband a break."

"Of course I'll help." I jumped up from my seat.

"I love what you've done to the kitchen," I tell her upon entering the room.

"Thank you. It gets lonely at times. I find myself spending most of my time over at the girls' place or decorating these days. I am considering taking a culinary class."

"I can see. You could probably be a host on HGTV and help with those fixer-uppers. A cooking class would be great as well. You know I'd be your best taste tester for all the meals without animal products."

"Yes, I know you'd be the first one at the table. Derek, on the other hand, would pass out if I were to get a job."

"Look at you blushing Ms. J."

"Oh, stop it. But seriously, I brought you in here because I wanted to speak with you about something."

"I kind of figured that."

"I know you're fond of Brianne, and things didn't work out the way that you two wanted them to. I personally think you rushed into trying to pursue something with her when you're still unsure of yourself."

"You sound like my dad, Candice, and Brianne right now. Why is it that everyone can see all this and I cannot?"

"You see it, Jenna. You choose to ignore it. I need you to promise me that you will never act out of character or act like a crazed, jealous, insecure woman. You know there is nothing going on between the two of them. Everything that just transpired between the two of them was innocent. We are all family. You two never should have even tried to make things any more than that. It causes problems."

"It's over between us. There are no problems to be caused."

"You just attempted to start some mess by allowing yourself to step out of character. Get yourself together, Jenna. Get back into counseling. This time, do it for you. No one else, just for Jenna. It's time to channel all those deep, hidden things lying dormant inside you."

"I did the counseling thing already, Ms. Jasmine." Tears rushed my face.

"*You went to counseling for your relationship with your sister and your dad. Now you need it for your intimate relationship with yourself, Jenna. You don't need to be chasing women that are old enough to be your mom. If you're looking for a mother's love, I am right here. I love you as if I birthed you. I love all of you as my own. You can call or come by anytime. I am and always will be here for all of you girls—*"

"*I think you might want to call before you come by,*" Mr. Derek interrupted. *We didn't hear him enter the kitchen.*

He tapped Ms. Jasmine's bottom with his hand.

"*Derek!*" *Her face flushed.*

"*I apologize, Jenna,*" he said. "*I was just trying to lighten the mood. You two were crying when I walked in. I just wanted to try cheer you gals up a bit.*"

"*I appreciate you, honey. I was just comforting Jenna, letting her know we are here for her,*" Ms. Jasmine told him.

"*She's right, Jenna. I know you have Dale, and I would never try to take his place. Just know we love all of you as our own.*"

"*Thank you s-so much,*" I said, choking on my words.

Ms. Jasmine just melted my heart that day. I had heard it when my dad and Brianne said I was looking for a mom. However, I hadn't listened, and it didn't sink in until Ms. Jasmine said it. She hit a soft spot when she said she loved me as if she had birthed me. My mom had never even told me she loved me. To hear Ms. Jasmine say that to me . . . Well, it broke a wall that I guessed I didn't know I had erected. It tore something down, because I have been crying uncontrollably ever since she expressed her love for me. I couldn't even eat my food at the reception. I was choked up.

My dad didn't feel comfortable with me being that upset and driving, so he offered to drive me home after the reception. I declined and told him I'd be all right. Ms. Jasmine and Mr. Derek had already offered their spare bedroom to me as we left the kitchen. I am in that bedroom now, making a mess of this pillow. Ms. Jasmine just tucked me, kissed me on the forehead, and told me she loved me, and that caused a tsunami of tears to flood my face. It was just what I needed to feel and hear.

Six Months Later . . .

CHAPTER FOURTEEN

Ethically Incorrect Dr. Binet...

As a result of my training, I am fully aware that injecting my reality into my therapeutic relationships is frowned upon. It's said to have an adverse effect. However, I see myself in Simone. She is me, and I am her. I relate to the hell she escaped from physically yet still battles with mentally and emotionally. I didn't start out this way, and I don't typically comfort a client, as it tends to send the message that therapists in general or I in particular cannot handle emotions. However, my opening up to Simone broke a huge barrier. She connected with me and now trusts me because of my pain. Because of it, Simone has opened up entirely and is comfortable talking about those deep-rooted things that have left her stranded mentally. When she talks, often I hear myself speaking instead of her. It has come to the point where I struggle with fighting back my tears. The more she unloads, the angrier and weepier I become. There's no way Todd should be able to live freely when Simone remains imprisoned emotionally.

Brianne, you have to regain control of this before she gets here, I tell myself. *You're the therapist, not her. You cannot afford to trade places with her. Get yourself together.*

Just then there is a knock on my office door, which is halfway open. From the doorway, Simone says, "Good evening, Dr. Binet. Thank you for rescheduling."

Simone pulls me from my thoughts as she makes her presence known. "No problem at all. Please come in and have a seat. Is everything all right? You missed the last two weeks."

"I am falling apart, Dr. Binet. I hate myself. But I love the part of me that has been blessed with the opportunity to birth my angel. Sometimes, I wish I could trade places with Nakita. Death seems so much safer than dealing with the plague that has consumed my entire being. I cannot sleep anymore. It has come to the point that when I close my eyes, I see Todd's face. No other face. Just Todd's, and that stupid smirk he'd make right before he vandalized my insides. I wish I had never reopened this can of worms. This is all your fault. I hate you for making me talk about it. Are you happy now! You made me relive the most horrific moments in my life. Now it's the only image that plays in my head."

"I understand you being upset. Unwrapping the bandages that have bound you hurts like hell. Although I am not supposed to say this, I can feel and relate to everything you're feeling and saying, but you have to let it out so you can move from this place. You cannot hold on to any of this. It will kill you."

Turn it around, Brianne. Don't allow your emotions to get the best of you, I tell myself.

"Well, that might not be a bad thing."

"Death isn't the answer, Simone. Sage needs you. You've come too far to just give up."

"I feel like I am drowning, Dr. Binet. Almost like I have been hit with a bucket of freezing water. The only time I am or appear to be healthy is when Sage and the girls are around. They are the reasons I have a heartbeat right now. I hate myself and my life. I don't want to be here anymore. I just want it all to go away. Please make it go away, Dr. Binet. Please! I cannot take it anymore." She slides from her seat and crumples on the floor.

Swollen from her tears, her eyes plead with me to rid her of her pain.

Don't get up from your seat, Brianne, I think. *This is her pain, not yours. Separate yourself from this scenario. I ignore your inner self, which wants to join Simone in her wallowing.*

No matter how hard I fight myself, it has been challenging for me to disconnect. The feelings, the depression, and everything else that Simone is experiencing mirror my own experiences and condition. It's as if my skeletons have made their way out of my closet and transformed themselves into a human being named Simone.

I stand, walk over to her, and kneel down. After wrapping my arms around her shoulders, I pull her closer, despite the gnawing heaviness in my stomach.

This is not good, Brianne. You have to try to regain control of this session.

"Please allow me to help you back into your seat, Simone. I know this is tormenting you, but I assure you, you can and will get past this."

"How? You don't really believe that yourself, Dr. Binet. You haven't gotten past any of your stuff. So please enlighten me as to how you know I will get past my issues."

"This isn't about me, Simone."

"I believe it is about both of us right about now. The only reason I've bared my truth to you is that you showed me you're real and not a textbook or scripted doctor."

"Ethically, I was wrong for doing that, and I apologize. I should never have allowed my personal life and experiences to meander their way into our sessions."

"Well, baring it all is how we have made it this far. I need real right now, not what's ethical or nonethical."

"I cannot give you real. Because what I want isn't practical and is actually against the law."

"Against the law?"

"Yes." I pause. "I could do serious jail time if I uttered my thoughts," I confess.

Simone erupts in laughter. "You're hysterical, Dr. Binet. Hell, we'd all go to prison if our thoughts were heard. Thanks. I needed that laugh."

"It's good to see you smile. I know this is rough. But as I said, you can and will get through this. I will prescribe you something to assist you with sleeping. Also, for our next session, how do you feel about hypnosis? I think hypnotherapy would be good to interject into our sessions right about now. It is great for healing the mind."

"Whatever it takes to rid myself of the demons within, I am willing to give it a try. By the way, I want to apologize for earlier. I have so much anger bottled up inside me. I just exploded."

"It's part of the therapeutic process, Simone. I am just happy you let it out here, and not on anyone else or yourself. I know it is getting late. However, I would like for you to do me a favor before you leave."

"Sure. What's that?" Simone says.

"Promise me if you get to the point where death is trying to swallow you whole, you'll give me a call. I changed things around in my life so that I am available at any given moment for my clients. I promise that we will get through all this together."

"I promise to call you, Dr. Binet."

The shrill scream of my telephone cuts the silence during my much-needed bubble bath, startling me. I yank my bath towel off the towel bar and wipe the water from my hands. As I hurriedly grab my phone from its spot next to the tub, I notice the name that flashes across the screen.

"H-Hello? Simone? Are you okay?" I blurt out.

"No. No, I am not okay. Terianne got in touch with Candice and asked her to call me and relay a message. I haven't heard from or spoken to any of them all this time. What could Terianne possibly want from me? Why is this happening? I cannot do this right now, Dr. Binet. I just can't."

"So Terianne got in touch with Candice?"

"Yes, Candice said one of the social workers reached out to her and asked if it was okay for Terianne to call. Candice told the social worker to have Terianne leave her number and a message and she'd relay it to me. The message has been transmitted, unfortunately."

"I see. What we can do is call Terianne on a three-way call, if you'd like to call her. I will be here in whatever way you need me to be. I do feel in order for you to ever have closer, you need to deal with this and her sooner or later. Sooner appears to have sought you out."

"If you stay on the phone with me, I can do it. I cannot do this alone."

"No problem at all," I tell Simone. "Just let me know when you're ready to make the call. We can do it now or even wait until our next session and call together."

"I won't be able to sleep if I don't do it now. Can you hold on for a second?"

"Yes, I can." She places me on hold.

"Dr. Binet, it's ringing. Don't say anything."

"Hello," says a voice on the other end of the line.

"Hello. This is Simone. I am trying to reach Terianne."

"Simone, this is Terianne. How are you doing? It has been forever."

"Yes, it has been. I received a message that you wanted to speak with me."

"Yeah, I thought you'd like to know Mimas passed yesterday in her sleep. They said it was a heart attack that took her. She wasn't the same after she and Todd had to part ways."

"Part ways? She passed in her sleep? That is awful," Simone says.

"Yeah, sometime after you left, Mimas got into it bad with Todd, and she put him out," Terianne explains.

"After I *left*? Is that what you said? I am sorry to burst your bubble, but *I* was put out. I never left. I was thrown away by all of you."

"I—I am sorry about all of that. I didn't call to upset you. I just wanted you to know about Mimas. The service is this weekend. If this is your cell, I can text you the address and everything."

"This is, and that's fine. Thanks."

"No problem. Oh, Simone?"

"Yeah?"

"You're more than welcome to come and stay here with us if you're coming for the entire weekend."

"No thanks," Simone replies.

"Well, the offer is on the table."

The call disconnects. After removing the phone from my face, I nervously press Simone's name in my call log, and the phone rings. She picks up immediately.

"Simone, I know that wasn't easy, but you were great. You handled yourself well," I tell her.

"How could she say I *left*? She knows Mimas threw me away."

"It's hard for some people to take ownership."

"What am I supposed to do? Mimas's passing breaks my heart. I don't understand how when I haven't seen her in forever and what she did to me . . . How can I mourn her?"

"You love her like your mother. She hurt you, and you are hurt by her actions. That doesn't cancel out your love for her," I say.

"Will you come with me to the service?"

Without thinking, I respond, "Yes, I will."

CHAPTER FIFTEEN

Unturned Stones
Candice . . .

It has been six months since my sister left me. There isn't a day that goes by where I don't miss Nakita. Amiya has been great. She won't leave Adrianna's side. They're inseparable. I am almost certain the death of Nakita has played a huge part in her not wanting to leave Adrianna's side. Well, after Nakita's breakdown, I know for a fact the two girls got closer. Amiya has been so good with Adrianna. She is so brave and smart, for she know intuitively what Adrianna needs.

Ms. Jasmine and I are headed to Amiya's bedroom to try to separate the two of them and put Adrianna in her old bedroom, the one she occupied when Nakita was away.

"Amiya and Adrianna, it is time for bed," I announce.

"Okay," they say in the unison.

"Amiya, get in your bed while I tuck Adrianna in her bed," I say.

"Mommy, Adrianna has to sleep in here with me."

I shake my head. "She's a big girl. She has her own big-girl bed to sleep in."

"No, Aunt Candy. I can't go in there. I don't want to." Adrianna throws herself on the floor, screaming and crying.

"Adrianna, please calm down. I will lie down with you and will stay until you fall asleep. It's going to be all right," I say, trying to comfort her.

"Nooo! I can't go. I'm going to die in there. Don't make me die, Aunt Candy," she wails.

Tearing up, I stoop down to her level. My lip quivers as I assure her, "You're not going to die, baby. Please don't say that. I love you so much, Adrianna. It's okay."

Ms. Jasmine intervenes by picking Adrianna up off the floor and rubbing her back. "I know you're scared and feeling very sad, baby. I'm sad too. We both loved your mommy so much, and she loved us too."

Shaking her head no, Adrianna blubbers through her tears, "She didn't love me, Glam-mommy. She left me. Mommy don't want me no more."

My heart caves in.

"She loves you, princess. Mommy didn't feel well . . . She loves you so much," Ms. Jasmine says, choking up.

"I didn't fix her. She's mad at me." Adrianna buries her head in Ms. Jasmine's chest.

"Why would you think that? Who told you those horrible things? Your mommy loves you with everything in her. The doctors fixed her the best that they could, princess. Mommy was sick. It's not your fault," I say as tears run down my cheeks.

"Aunt Kita was in her room by herself, Mommy. Nobody was with her when she died. Adrianna said if she is by herself, she will die like Aunt Kita. I told her Auntie was sick and that she loves her. We all love her. Right, Mommy? I don't want Adrianna to be sad. Can we fix her?" Amiya says, whimpering.

"I promise we will take care of her. She will get all the help and support she needs," I say.

Adrianna wiggles her way from Ms. Jasmine's arms.

"Adrianna, you're not going to die. I won't let you," Amiya declares. The two girls run into each other's arms and cling to one another, sobbing in unison.

After finally getting the girls settled in bed, Ms. Jasmine and I almost fall apart over a glass of wine.

"My heart is bleeding. For Adrianna to think she killed her mother because she wasn't there with her at the time of her death punctures a whole other level of holes in my heart," I say as I sniffle.

Ms. Jasmine nods her agreement, then says, "I cannot even begin to imagine what's going through that baby's mind. She really thinks because she was not with Nakita, she killed her. She is too young to walk around with that type of guilt."

"You're absolutely right, Ms. J. That will have a lasting effect on her, and that won't end well, if we don't do something. I refuse to allow her to grow up with that type of guilt gnawing at her. I am going to do whatever is necessary to find her a therapist."

The next day I get right to work. After researching, emailing, and phoning classmates and colleagues that I've met while in school, I am fortunate enough to find a therapist in New Haven who deals exclusively with children's emotional issues and their impact on families. I will be meeting with her tomorrow, as I'd like to have all the kids take part in therapy. The last thing I need is for them to grow up damaged as a result of our past. My boys are standoffish and very quiet and keep to themselves. I know the older they get, the more they will gravitate to video games and the others things preteen and teenage boys do. They will not be as receptive to an intervention then.

When I was younger, I used to believe that money could solve any problem. Boy, was I wrong. It doesn't matter how much money you have or don't have. If you're crippled on the inside, this will have a profound effect on your life. Guilt and depression are hungry beasts inside of us, and the more they go unresolved, the more they grow. A recipe money cannot alter. I've found myself on the verge of falling into a depression with everything going on.

I used to be able to talk to Nakita when I got to this point, as well as to Alonzo. However, he hasn't been around much, like he used to be. He makes sure to be here before school to get the kids ready and to see them off. But by the time I turn around, he's gone behind the school bus. The same thing happens after school: he's here to help with homework and play with them until dinner, but by the time they sit down for dinner, he's gone. I know he went back to work, but something is just different, primarily between us. When we converse, it's almost as if we are delivering lines from a screenplay. No genuine conversation, unless it pertains to the kids.

The kids should be home any minute now, which means he will be here shortly. Once they're settled, I am going to request a minute of his time. I feel as if he's pushing me away or pulling away. But why? Dad said he might just need time, since everyone deals with things differently, which I completely understand. However, six months is forever to me. Especially when I had thought things were blossoming between the two of us.

Just then the kids race inside the house. Then I hear a car door slam, and Dad walks to the front door to greet Alonzo.

"Alonzo, can we talk alone for a moment?" Dad asks as soon as Alonzo walks through the door, the kids on his heels. Since Dad has beaten me to it, I hope I get a chance to speak alone with Alonzo.

"Sure thing. Dale. But how about a little later? Right now, do you mind helping Dylan with his math for me?"

"Math? Is that a foreign language you speak of?" Dad jokes.

"Dad, you're so silly," I interject as I step into the foyer.

"I feel you, Dale. The math these days does come across a bit foreign," Alonzo says.

"Yes, it does, but I will do my best. Don't leave me too long."

"I'll help you, Pop-Pop," Darren tells him, coming to his rescue.

"Thank you, son." Dad ruffles his curls as he and the boys head to the playroom to hit the books.

I walk warily behind Alonzo as he heads to my office. Once we are inside the room, I close the door behind us.

"How h-h-have you been, Alonzo?" I stutter.

"I am good. Is there something wrong?"

"Honestly, that is what I am trying to find out."

"What do you mean?"

"You seem so distant these days. Did I do something wrong?"

"You've done nothing wrong, Candice. You're perfect. What would make you think you've done something wrong?"

"You aren't the same. We used to spend so much time together. You were always there when I needed someone. When I needed you."

"I am still here, Candice. I haven't gone anywhere. I will always be here when you need me. All you have to do is call me if I am not already here."

"That's the problem. I didn't have to call. You were always here. But it's not just physically. You're not with me *here*." I place my hand over my heart.

"I carry you and those babies in my heart daily, Candice. You don't ever have to worry about not being in my heart."

"We used to lie in bed talking all night. We had breakfast and dinner together often. It just feels like when I lost Nakita, I sort of lost you too."

"I apologize for making you feel that way, Candice. The love that I have for you has not changed. I just felt like somewhere along the line, in the midst of everything, I lost myself. Don't get me wrong. I love spending every waking moment with you and the kids, and I wouldn't have it any other way. With that being said, I had to make time for me. Going back to work is what I needed to do as a man. I have to be able to be a provider to my kids, and I cannot do that without working. As a man, I have to be able to have drinks with the guys and just be Alonzo for a change. Instead, I found myself smothering you, and it didn't feel right."

"You weren't smothering me. I can breathe perfectly fine when you're around. When you're not here is when I have trouble breathing. And you have been a great provider to us, but we don't need anything. We just need you here wholeheartedly. I need you, Alonzo. I don't like not being able to talk to you, lie next to you. For you to hold me. Kiss me. I need it all. I need you."

Before I could utter another word, he slams his lips into mine, nearly knocking the wind out of me. I want to pull away before I lose myself, but I can't seem to. As he breaks our kiss, my heart skips a beat.

With his breathing and heartbeat matching the rhythm of mine, he confesses, "I am going to leave now, before I'm unable to control myself. I want to make love to you, Candice. I know you're not ready, so I have to go."

"You don't have to go, Alonzo. We can just go into the playroom with the kids and finish our day the way we used to."

"Right now I am unable to give you that. I want you right here and right now, but I also want you to desire me in the same manner. I know you're not ready and are unable to give me that, so its best I leave, for now. You can call and text me all night long if you want to. I just cannot be next to you like this."

"I—I understand, and I am sorry."

"Don't ever apologize for being you. I love that about you. Like I told you before, I will wait as long as you need. Just don't stop trying to love me the way that I love you." He kisses my forehead before exiting.

Little does he know, I love him with everything in me. I'm just not ready to take it to the next level of intimacy. In actuality, I am afraid to. Sex scares me. I know it is a result of what was done to me. I promise myself to open that door in my next therapy session with Dr. Raysor. I believe it's time. I cannot allow the rapes to control any aspect of my life any longer. I've come a long way, and I feel better about myself. The only stone unturned is this one. It's time to turn this stone into a polished jewel.

CHAPTER SIXTEEN

The Woman in the Mirror
Jenna . . .

My feelings for Brianne had pretty much turned into an obsession. I found myself thinking about her my every waking moment, along with following her to and from home or work without her noticing. The only time that I'd be over at Candice's was when Brianne was there. I craved being around her all the time. All I wanted to do is soak up her presence. Never in a million years would I have imagined that I'd become obsessed with her.

I hadn't acknowledged my fixation until Ms. Jasmine and Mr. Derek caught me on one of my stakeouts. At the time I had been staying at their place for a while, since I just didn't want to be alone. They had become the Mom and Dad that I longed for. Everything about them, from their chemistry to the way they fussed over me, had had me emotionally traveling back to my younger years. The difference this time was in my head. They were my parents. I was loved and catered to. Mr. Derek and Ms. Jasmine gave me their undivided attention. I devoured the affection they gave me so much that I feigned for more. And they were right by my side, supporting me after my breakup with Brianne.

Ms. Jasmine was so bothered by the way Brianne handled things that I used her anger to my advantage by sending flowers to the house, addressed to me, the card signed by Brianne, supposedly. On the first occasion I sent them, I included a note that said, *I am sorry. Please forgive me* . That ate away at Ms. Jasmine; she felt Brianne was toying with my emotions. She also implied the last thing I need was to try to reconcile with another human being when I hadn't made peace with myself yet. I disagreed with her, but I loved the attention I received because of it. So, I sent more flowers to myself. It got to the point where I sent flowers, gifts, and cards to myself for five days straight.

Shaking my head, I play back one of the most humiliating days of my life.

A smirk danced across my face as the chiming of the doorbell alerted us that we had a guest.

"I'll get it," I announced.

After opening the door to the delivery guy, I shouted, "There's a delivery. Ooh, Ms. Jasmine, what did you do to deserve these long-stemmed roses?"

"He didn't," she said as she came up behind me.

"It looks like he did. Hmm, what did you do to deserve these?" I teased.

"Girl, mind your manners." She took the flowers out of the delivery guy's hands as I signed for them.

"What does the card say? This is so sweet. I love how Mr. Derek loves you," I said.

Ms. Jasmine's usually calm and pleasant demeanor changed dramatically as she looked from the card up at me. With her nostrils flaring and her eyes flashing and closing into slits, she roared, "Enough is enough! I assure you this will be the last day Brianne toys with you."

"Mama, what has you so upset? I can hear you over the television," Mr. Derek shouted from the den.

Storming into the den, Ms. Jasmine threatened, "She has to answer to me now. This is not a game. How dare she toy with Jenna's emotions! This is the last straw. Every single day, Derek? Who sends something every single day, knowing this girl is fragile? To think she's supposed to be this high-profile therapist. From the looks of it, her confused tail is the one that requires therapy."

"Baby, please calm yourself down. You done got your pressure all up. You know good and well that ain't good for your heart."

"Yes, you're right. Let me calm down. Jenna, baby, are you all right? I know this is a lot to deal with and is confusing. Please know it's a trick of the enemy. God is not the author of confusion, baby."

"I'll be okay. I just need air. I am going to go for a drive. I need time to myself to think all this through," I said, laying it on thick.

"We will be here if you need us. You don't have to deal with this alone, Jenna. We love you," Ms. Jasmine said.

"I love both of you more, Ms. Jasmine."

"Are you sure you're all right?" she added.

"Let the girl be, Jazz."

"I'll be fine. I thank both of you for being here for me. I really appreciate it."

I remember now that as I walked out the door, my heart beat hard with excitement. I just loved how they fretted over me. No one had ever really made a fuss over me like that. Dad had pretty much moved in with Candice and the kids, and lately he hadn't had too much time for me. So, the way I saw it, Ms. Jasmine and Mr. Derek had become my saving grace. They were what I needed at that time.

I climbed in my car and headed over to Brianne's office. I was running a little late that day, so I sped. It was a Thursday, so I knew she should be heading to her office for her 1:00 p.m. session with Simone. I liked to get there early and sit in my hiding spot, so I'd be there when she arrived. I just had to get a glimpse of her. Of course, I make it there in record time, as usual. As I waited, I penned another letter to myself, so I could mail it on my way back to the house. Lost in my thoughts, I didn't hear or see Ms. Jasmine standing outside of the car, tapping on the window. I have a vivid recollection of what she said and how mortified I felt.

"Jenna? What are you doing over here? Why do you have on that wig and shades? Why are you over here? What are you doing? Open this door right now!"

I nervously opened the car door, and my love letter dropped at Ms. Jasmine's feet. After picking it up, her eyes stretched as she read the words on the page.

She looked at me. "Are you serious? This is insane. Please don't tell me you've been sending all that stuff to the house too, Jenna?"

"I—I miss her so much. I just wanted her attention."

"This isn't normal, Jenna. This is scary. You could be arrested for stalking her like this. You need to get some help, before it is too late."

"Please don't tell anyone, Ms. Jasmine. I am so embarrassed," I said, feeling frantic.

"I cannot believe you right now. You have me over here looking crazy. What if I had barged in there and given her a piece of my mind, like I intended to? I would have looked nuts. I am so disappointed in you right now."

"Jazz, please calm down. I told you on the way over this isn't our fight," Mr. Derek said and placed his hand on her shoulder.

I hadn't noticed him standing behind her, and now I was even more mortified.

Since that embarrassing day, I have been in therapy. Ms. Jasmine connected me to a therapist, who I have been seeing three times a week for the past five months.

I didn't know how damaged I was until I saw myself through Ms. Jasmine's eyes that day. Therapy has been my solace. I've learned so much about myself in my sessions. It's crazy how you can walk around feeling happy and even accomplishing things and still be a complete mess on the inside. All my actions had been the result of my abandonment issues. Mom's death, Dad breaking up our home, and me being forced to live with Camilla had been traumatic, and little had I known I'd been walking around traumatized because of it.

I can now admit that I was attracted to older women because of my lack of a mother's love. Camilla's verbal abuse just added fuel to the fire, and so did the fact that Dad was not there physically and emotionally for me. He was never around, and deep down inside I took the blame for this and became insecure when it came to the opposite sex. I never allowed myself to get close to a man in that manner because of my lack of trust in my dad. To me, all men were all the same, and the thought of a man is my life was abhorrent. In turn, I told myself that I was a lesbian, and I lived a lie all those years without even knowing it. So, because of my abandonment issues, I stalked Brianne like a nut. Now that I have realized what I did, I have never been so ashamed of myself. Why didn't I know something wasn't right in the first place? All I ever wanted from her was affection, but in the way a mother shows affection to a child. At that time, I didn't realize that's what I longed for. It's clear as day now.

Thank God for Dr. Imberti. She is a genius. I will continue therapy for the foreseeable future, because I want to be able to help other women that are struggling with abandonment, with their identity, or with just knowing who they are. I am a work in progress. Something great will be birthed when I get to the other side of all this.

CHAPTER SEVENTEEN

Temptation
Alonzo...

I had to get out of the house away and from Candice. Lately, just being around her, I'm easily aroused. Thank God, I am meeting up with the fellas tonight. I could use a cold one right about now. I've been able to control myself for quite some time; I am proud of myself. I have slept in the same bed with her and haven't touched her at all. The love and respect that I have for her affords me self-control. I can't believe that I haven't even hung out or hooked up with any of my "female" friends in so long. I've been so consumed with Candice and the kids that I haven't been doing much of anything else. Maybe, I am waiting for her to want me the way that I want and desire her. Deep down inside, I know I don't want to get to know another woman on that level, as my heart belongs to Candice. That's also probably the reason I haven't gone out. I know it's been so long that it might be hard for me to resist temptation.

In any event, I am here at one of my favorite bars, and it looks like all my boys are in attendance as well.

"Hey, what's up, Antonio, Giovanni, Matt, and Dre?" I dap each of them as I make my way to the empty stool next to them.

"You need to catch up," Antonio tells me. He raises his hand. "Bartender, amaretto on the rocks for my friend."

"Tone, you know I don't drink like that," I say.

"Tonight, you do. Chugalug, my friend."

I shrug. "Okay. Just one."

"And another one and another one," Dre say, ribbing me.

"The old ball and chain has him in rehab," Antonio adds, giving me a poke.

I nod my head repeatedly. "Oh, I see. You guys wanted me to come out so you could clown me. Go ahead, Get it out of your system. I can take it."

Matt shakes his head.

"What was that for, Matt? You've been awfully quiet. What's going on?" I say.

"Zo, I love you like a brother, and I mean no harm when I say this—"

I squint at him. "Say what?"

"I think you're in over your head. Don't get me wrong. I think it's admirable of you to take care of your daughter. That's what you're supposed to do as a man. But cutting your life off for her is crazy. You don't owe her anything. The two of you were young and immature. You made a mistake. You don't have to spend the rest of your life trying to make it up to her. It's not your fault what happened to her man. You can't carry that shit, man."

"Are you done?" I ask him, frowning.

He nods. "If I weren't your friend, I wouldn't care."

"I hear you loud and clear. Now I want you to hear me loud and clear. All of you. For starters, the only person I owe anything to is God Himself, and that's it. I will spend the rest of my life making sure my daughter is better than good. As for Candice, she is special to me. I love her. I don't use that word lightly. Neither have I ever professed my love to another woman other than my mom, so that tells me what I have for her is real. I don't feel sorry for her. I admire her. She is strong and brave. Had the shoe been on the other foot, I might have taken my life under all this pressure. Only God in heaven knows how I would have handled what she overcame. I am not carrying anything except the responsibility of being a man to her and a father to all four of those kids if I have to."

Matt's eye grow wide. "*Four*? Man, do you hear yourself?"

"I said it, didn't I?"

"You're biting off more than you can chew. You have my sympathy, man." Matt takes a swig of his drink.

"I don't need sympathy. I'm good and clear on who I am and what I am doing. No, it hasn't been easy. Yes, I want things to be different, but Candice is worth the wait. But what I am really trying to understand is, How the hell are you lecturing me when you have three kids of your own by three different women?"

"And one on the way," Dre says, chiming in.

Everyone chuckles in unison.

Matt looks me in the eye. "Look, I am trying to save you from the hell I am in."

"I'm good, my man," I tell him.

"Are you two done? You're ruining my buzz. Have another drink?" Dre says.

An hour later, I have quite a buzz myself. I head to the men's room. As my feet come in contact with the solid wood floor, I have the sensation that the floor is in motion, causing me to stumble my way into the men's room.

"Zo, you good?" Matt says as he follows behind me.

"Yeah, man. I think I overdid it." I make my way into a stall.

"Not yet you haven't. I have a gift for you."

"A gift? What are you talking about?" I quiz.

Silence.

"Matt? Matt?" I zip my trousers up and make my way out of the stall. I blink. "Excuse m-me, ma'am. You might be . . . be a little lost. This is . . . is the men's room," I slur.

"No, sir. I think I am right where you want me to be," declares a dark-haired, green-eyed, buxom woman who is really tall.

"I . . . I think you're mistaking me for someone else," I tell her.

She pushes me against the wall and sinks to her knees. Then she uses her pouty lips to unzip my trousers. I use all my might to tell her no, but to no avail. Somehow my mouth is working against me, and I push her off me only in my mind.

The sudden ringing of my cell phone sounds like gunshots, and it startles both of us, and we jump at the same time. I suddenly can speak again.

"I apologize, but I cannot do this," I say as I dart toward the door.

"Alonzo, I thought that was you," says a familiar voice. I collide with Jenna.

"Excuse me," the mystery lady says as she exits the men's room, smirking. She deliberately walks between the two us.

"Oh, I got your 'excuse me,'" Jenna growls and grabs her by the hair.

"Jenna, please don't do this," I say and lift her off her feet, forcing her to release the lady's locks. "Lady, just go. Please!" I bark.

Once she is clear out of sight, I put Jenna down, but I maintain my grip on her arms.

Slapping me across the face, Jenna chastises, "What the hell were you doing in there with her, Alonzo? I thought you loved my sister. I thought you was waiting for her. What the hell is going on? I thought you was different!"

"It's not what you think."

Matt and Dre run to my aid.

"Zo, is everything all right?" Matt asks me.

"I'm good. I'm good. Thanks a lot, Matt. You just don't know when to stop."

"I was just trying—"

"Save it," I interrupt. Then I direct my attention to Jenna. "Jenna, can I please talk to you outside?"

"Let my arms go, Alonzo."

"If you promise to keep your hands to yourself."

"As long as there aren't any more surprises."

"I swear, I was blindsided, just like you. Please walk with me outside, Jenna. I can explain."

We walk swiftly side by side and stop at the same time when we reach her car, which is parked out front.

"We're outside. Explain," she says curtly.

"Look, you cannot go around slapping people. Especially men. What if I had slapped you back? Would that have been okay with you?"

"Hell, no, it would not have been all right with me."

"So, what makes you think it is all right with me for you to put your hands on me, Jenna? I had to refrain from slapping you. I've never put my hands on a woman before, and I have no intentions of doing so, but you almost caught one. I had to catch myself."

"I apologize, Zo. I saw that harlot and snapped."

"I get it, but ask questions before you react next time. I was using the john, and she came in behind me. I was tipsy and damn near drunk, so she almost had me. Thank God my phone rang."

"What do you mean, she almost had you? You're a grown-ass man. Can't no one have what you're not willing to give them."

"I wasn't in my right mind. The alcohol had me."

"Maybe it's best you not drink, since you cannot handle your liquor. How would you feel if Candice went out and said some guy almost had her because the drink drank her?"

"Point made. I fucked up. Please allow me to tell her."

"I didn't say to do all of that, now. Candice may not be able to handle all of that or understand."

"What I am not going to do is lie or keep secrets, so it will be what it is."

"You are a great man, Zo. You really are. I am so proud of you."

"Slapping me was your way of showing me how proud of me you are?"

"I am so sorry. I was wrong. I never should have put my hands on you."

"Apology accepted. Please don't ever do that again."

"You have my word," she says.

I squint at her. "Wait a minute. What are you doing up here? I haven't seen you in minute, now that I am thinking about it. Candice said you went back to work. I assumed a new job, because I never see you at the hospital."

"There's something I need to tell you, Zo."

"What happened?" I ask.

"I lost the good sense that God gave me after breaking up with Brianne. And I have been seeing a shrink for the past five months."

"You have? That's not a bad thing. But what did you do?"

"I followed Brianne around. That was my job. I took an extended leave of absence to be wherever she was. I even went as far as having flowers, cards, and gifts sent to myself and pretending she sent them."

"Why?"

"I was trying to fill a hole in my heart. I suffer from abandonment issues, Zo. I'm not even gay either. Can you believe I made myself believe I was a lesbian, because I was looking for a mother to love me?"

I nod. "Yes, I believe it."

"You do? How?"

"The only thing you ever talked about doing with a woman was spending time, going shopping, going to the movies, and just snuggling. Don't get me wrong. Those are intricate parts of dating. However, that was it. For me, when you want or desire something, you want it in every way, shape, or form possible. You, my friend, were limited in your range, so I assumed you might be confused and might need to do a little more soul-searching."

"Why didn't you ever say anything?"

"Sometimes we learn things better through trial and error. You had to turn into a creep in order for you to realize it was deeper than you and Brianne going your separate ways. If I had said something, you might have tried to prove me and yourself wrong, and now you'd be in a nuthouse for stalking people."

"Stop making fun of me, Zo." She shoves me.

"There you go, hitting me again. Maybe you suffer from violent tendencies too," I say, giving her a jab.

"You're so crazy."

I'm glad Jenna is going to therapy. A person never knows how sick they are until they see a doctor. Therapy has helped me understand what Candice is going through and how to deal with it. I am happy that I attended some sessions with her. It made a world of a difference. Hopefully, I won't need further therapy or a heart doctor when I tell her what happened at the bar.

CHAPTER EIGHTEEN

Visiting My Ghost
Simone . . .

"Dr. Binet, thank you so much for being there with Sage and me on her first flight. I don't know if I was more afraid of flying or coming here to Virginia. I am so scared to go inside that house right now."

"Don't allow fear to keep you hostage any longer. This will be therapeutic for you. Keep in mind, I am here with you every step of the way."

"I appreciate you so much. You deserve the Doctor of the Year Award. You've gone above and beyond for your patients, and I personally am forever indebted to you."

"I just want to see you well. Now, let's go inside, if you're ready."

"I am as ready as I am going to be. Also, instead of introducing you as my doctor, I will just say you're a close friend, if that's all right with you."

"Well, I am, aren't I?"

"Great," I say and exhale.

As we cross the threshold, a chill runs along my skin. A bad omen. The faint scent of death, like the smell of a funeral home, is in the air, and I sense that spirits are waiting to torment us.

"My stomach is in knots," I whisper.

"Is that you, Simone? I left the door open when I saw a car pull up. I assumed it was you," a familiar voice shouts from another room.

Without any notice, I get this sick feeling from my gut to my throat, and then the cheeseburger that I had on the way comes spewing out of my mouth and coats Dr. Binet's matte black ballerina flats.

"Are you pregnant again?" Terianne mocks.

Dr. Binet rolls her eyes at Terianne. "Do you think you could get something so I can clean this up?" Then she turns to me. "Simone, are you all right?"

"I think I am going to be fine." But then I drop Sage's hand. I dash toward the bathroom as the ghosts of Mimas's house taunt me.

Running behind me, Terianne taunts, "Are you sure you're not pregnant again? I am having flashbacks."

"Do you mind not doing that!" Dr. Binet snaps.

Terianne gives her the once-over. "I'm just fooling around. I didn't mean any harm. Who are you? Her lover or something?"

"There's a time and a place for everything, and this is definitely not the time or the place. I am her friend, and she is not pregnant, so please do her a favor and do not ask that again."

"My bad. Don't be so uptight," Terianne responds.

"How about we try to have some sympathy? Maybe this is a little hard for Simone. Did that ever cross your mind?"

I emerge from the bathroom and hear everything they are saying as they stand in the living room. As I enter the room, I interject, "Thank you Dr. Binet . . . I mean Brianne. I don't think Terianne meant any harm."

"You don't have to make excuses . . . ," Dr. Binet tells me.

"I don't know what's going on here, but I was just joking with my sister. Lighten up. It's bad enough we have to bury Mimas tomorrow. We don't have to be so uptight. I haven't seen you in forever, for God's sake." She turns toward Sage. "Oh my God, she is beautiful, Simone. She looks just like"

"Go ahead and say it. Like Todd," I bark, my blood boiling.

Terianne stares at me. "Why would she look like Todd? I was going to say she looks just like you."

"You can't be serious right now, Terianne. You know what? I think it'd be best if we met you at the funeral home later. I cannot do this or put myself through this again. I refuse to." I burst into tears.

"Good idea." Dr. Binet grabs Sage's hand. "Let's go, Simone."

"You really don't have to leave. There is more than enough room here, Simone. I apologize for whatever I did to upset you. Please don't go."

After stopping in my tracks, I turn to face her. "Honestly, I am not sure I'll be able to stay here. Too many memories, and it still hurts just thinking about it."

"You act like it was so bad here. We had it good. Mimas did good by us. It's no one's fault except your own that you got knocked up. It's bad enough Mimas, Todd, and everyone else fell out because of you. It was like a domino effect after you left. Now, to make matters worse, Todd is in the streets somewhere and Mimas died from a broken heart. All because of you."

With tears blinding my vision, I raise my hand, pull it back, and thrust it forward with as much force as I can muster, and it connects with her face. "You evil bitch. I hate you." I charge her and knock her off her feet. "You let him rape me. You knew what was going on." I pound on her, landing blow after blow.

"Mommy . . . no! Mommy, stop it!" Sage squeals.

Sabrina and Kathy race through the front door just then.

"What's going on? Get her off her," Sabrina yells as she tries to pull me off Terianne.

"Get off me! I am going to kill her!" Terianne shouts.

"Please calm down," Sabrina pleads, her face wet with tears. She manages to pry me off Terianne, and then she wraps her arms around me.

"What happened?" Kathy says.

"All of you knew what Todd did to me. None of you helped me. I hate all of you. You were supposed to be my family," I snarl. "Let me go, Kathy."

"Don't cry, Mommy. Let my mommy go," Sage whines.

"Why did you just stand there and let this happen?" Kathy asks Dr. Binet.

"I—I had the baby. No one was hurt. Sometimes, we need to do whatever we have to do in order to channel our anger," Dr. Binet told her.

"I can't believe I allowed myself to step out of character like that in front of my daughter. I am so embarrassed," I tell Dr. Binet as I pace back and forth in the hotel room we share.

"Don't be. She deserved it."

"Dr. Binet, I cannot believe you just said that."

"I am your friend right now, and as a friend, I am telling you she got what she had coming to her. She was completely out of line. Evil and hurtful, for no reason."

"If Sabrina didn't pull me off her, I think I would not have stopped until I saw blood. I wanted her to suffer the way I did."

"She deserves to suffer. Especially if she knew what was going on. She really knew, huh? You never told me that."

"Yes, she knew. I am not certain Kathy and Sabrina knew, but I know for a fact Terianne was well aware of what was going on, and she did nothing. She turned against me."

"You know this for a fact? How?"

"I saw her." A single tear escapes one of my eyes. "Mimas was at a doctor's appointment. She always made appointments while we were in school or were off from school during holidays. I can recall it exactly as if it was yesterday. I was in the kitchen, doing my chores, and Todd came up from behind and stripped me from the waist down. He used his free hand and pushed my face into the sink. I begged and pleaded for him to stop, but he ignored my pleas and shoved himself inside me. My head dropped into the sink and fell to the left. When I lifted my head and opened my eyes, in the reflection of the refrigerator, I saw Terianne standing there, watching. She never said anything to me about it. Instead, she'd make sly comments and call me names under her breath."

"I am so upset with her right now. You should have killed her. She deserves to pay just as much as Todd does."

"I know you're saying that in anger, but parts of me wish she could pay for standing by and doing nothing. She treated me just as bad as Todd did. He raped me physically, and she raped me verbally and emotionally."

"Yes, she did, and she needs to pay for her sins," Dr. Binet insists.

"It's too late now. I don't even know why I came here. This just made me relive everything. I feel like I was just raped all over again," I say and begin to weep.

A sudden knock on the door frightens us.

"Who is it?" Dr. Binet jumps to her feet.

"Ka-Kathy. It's Kathy."

"You can let her in," I say.

Dr. Binet opens the door and allows Kathy to enter.

"I hope you don't mind. I followed you back to your hotel to make sure you were all right," Kathy tells us.

I nod. "I guess I will be all right eventually. Thanks for checking up on me, Kathy."

"Can we talk?"

Dr. Binet shakes her head. "Now really isn't a good time. She just got Sage settled down for bed."

"It's fine, Dr. Binet. Come and have a seat, Kathy."

Kathy takes a seat, but her eyes never leave Dr. Binet. "Doctor?"

"Yes, she is my therapist. She came down here with me because she knew how hard this would be for me," I explain. "Right now, I am beating myself up, wondering why I even bothered to come."

"Because you're so brave," Kathy responds. She pauses for a long moment, then blurts out, "I blame myself. Even when I was old enough to tell someone, I just allowed it to continue. I guess I must have liked it or something."

"No matter how old you were or were not, *rape is rape*," Dr. Binet tells her, clarifying matters.

I can't quite believe what I just heard. I look Kathy straight in the eye. "So . . . Todd hurt you, Kathy?"

Through a thunderstorm of tears, she nods her head yes.

"I am so sorry. I had no idea," I say, my voice barely above a whisper.

Staring blankly, fixated on the brownish-beige carpet, Kathy begins rocking back and forth as more tears escape her eyes. As she rocks, she says, "Do you remember I was the house alarm clock? Mimas sent me into everyone's room to wake you all up for school. Every time I went into Todd's bedroom, he'd touch my private parts and threaten me not to tell a soul. I was five years old. At a time when kids my age are living carefree lives, I was being fondled and molested. By the age of ten, he started penetrating me. My only escape was going to school. That bastard raped me up until the day Mimas threw him out. You're so right about Terianne. She stood guard every day after school while he raped me. She's no saint either. Since I was younger than her, she made me do things to her, Simone. She wanted me to be gay, just like her."

I step over to her, lock my arms around her, and hold on to her for dear life. "I am so sorry, Kathy. I had no idea."

"It's good to get it out. Is this your first time talking about it?" Dr. Binet says.

Kathy nods her head yes.

"You're off to a good start. What happened with Mimas and Todd?" I say.

"I was in bed, sick with the flu. It was my senior year. I'd been ill for five days straight. We'd run out of Theraflu and ginger ale. Those two things and toast were the only things that I was able to keep down. In any event, Mimas hadn't been feeling well for quite some time. She'd been seeing a cardiologist. They said she had acute endocarditis. At the time I didn't know it was severe and that her health was failing." Kathy took a deep breath.

She went on. "Terianne stayed by her side at all times, so the two of them went to the store together. Todd, on the other hand, thought he'd pick up were Mimas left off in taking care of me, and used his penis to take my temperature through my vagina." Her lip quivers. "While he was on top of me, Mimas walked into the room. Of course, he tried to say I pulled him on top of me, but Mimas knew better. She would always say how she should have done better by you, so I knew that deep down inside she knew you were telling the truth."

"What did she do when she found Todd raping you?"

"She pulled him off me and beat him until he was black and blue. Todd may have towered over Mimas, but she was much stronger. She pummeled him with all her might. After putting him out, Mimas called the police, and no one's seen or heard from him since."

"He was never arrested?" Dr. Binet asks.

"No, he wasn't, Dr. Binet. Mimas called the police after he was long gone. She wasn't been the same after that.

She'd stay in her room in the dark and cry all the time. Thank God for my scholarship, because I escaped the misery and went off to college. I work and go to school, and I hope I never come back here. If Mimas hadn't passed, I wouldn't be here now. That house, this town . . . they are haunted by the ghosts of Todd and Mimas."

CHAPTER NINETEEN

The Funeral Service
Dr. Binet . . .

Last night was extremely difficult for me. I had to
stay calm and remain the professional that I am in this
situation. I did the best that I could. In all honesty, I
wanted to help Simone beat Terianne into another life.
After leaving, in my mind, I went back over to Mimas's
and gave that Terianne just what she deserved. There
is a customized place in hell for people like her. She is a
screwed-up individual. What kind of person sits by and
allows something like this to happen to a child? Then,
to make matters worse, joins in and sexually abuses the
poor girl as well. Thank heavens, Kathy was able to bury
her childhood in work and school. This is similar to how
I had to entomb myself in my practice to escape my bare
bones.

My hands tremble now as I think back on last night.

Even though Mimas had walked in on Todd violating
Kathy, Kathy had never spoken a word about any of it
until last night. The comforting prospect in all this is that
she currently attends college on the border of Connecticut
and has agreed to come down on her breaks and days off
for counseling. She'd also like to reconcile and rekindle
her relationship with Simone. Even though the two of
them had resided under the same roof and endured

the same pain of Todd's actions, they had drifted away from each other. Afraid and ashamed, they had kept to themselves and had shied away from everyone, including one another. I've even taken the liberty of agreeing to travel to see her weekly for counseling.

We are now headed to the service, and my gut is telling me we should reconsider attending. However, I promised Simone that I'd be by her side. Kathy was too worked up last night to go back to her room, so she ended up staying with us. Right now Terianne is the last person that I need to see, but she is the first person I catch sight of in the parking lot of the funeral parlor when we pull in. She deserves to be in that coffin alongside her precious Mimas. While they're at it, lay Todd right on top of them. Alive. Then have the coffin nailed shut. Experience is the best teacher. That alone will teach him the true essence of what it feels like to suffer and have your innocence and freedom stripped from you.

A malicious grin prances across my face as I get out of the car, but within seconds, it evaporates as we walk through the doors of the funeral parlor. *Of course, Terianne is standing at the podium,* I tell myself. I sigh.

"I just want to get this done and over with," Kathy says and squeezes my hand.

"Thank goodness it's a closed casket," Simone mumbles.

As we take our seats, Terianne steps up to the podium. Searching the room, I notice there really isn't a vacant seat in this place. Mimas appears to have been truly loved. If Simone and Kathy weren't considered family, we'd be standing.

Looking at Terianne, you'd think she was one of the sweetest persons in the world.

Terianne stands about five feet nine and has a tinted vanilla complexion and a tiny frame. Her eyes appear to be the most significant part of her body, and they complement her beauty. She is a beautiful girl. Looks can be deceiving, because her behavior makes her hideous.

As I study her, Terianne opens her mouth and begins to speak. "On behalf of Todd and myself, I would like to begin by thanking everyone that is here today and those who have sent their condolences. We've received countless phone calls, flowers, meals, visits, thoughts, and prayers. They have been comforting during this difficult time. As most of you know, my name is Terianne. I am one of Marguerite's children. Mimas to Todd and me, but Marguerite to most of you. After Todd, she wasn't able to have any children of her own, so she took me in and made . . . me . . . her . . . own . . ."

The sounds of chatter suddenly invade the air, making it hard for Terianne to continue and for anyone to hear her. Which is fine with me, since I have been doing my best to ignore Terianne, as her words pierce me. As I do everything in my power to focus all my attention on Sage, I hear Simone's voice loud and clear.

"You evil witch! Now Mimas will be mourned by one less child," she shouts. I look up as Simone leans forward to wrap her hands around Terianne's neck.

"I didn't even see her get up from her seat," Kathy blurts as she stares, dumbfounded, at the scene before us.

Frozen, unable to move from my seat, I shield Sage's eyes to prevent her from witnessing her mother give Terianne what she deserves. It feels as if I am having yet another out-of-body experience. Simone is up there, but I see and hear myself inflicting much pain on Terianne.

As Simone's hands slide around Terianne's throat, Terianne's eyes widen in surprise. Simone tightens her grip as Terianne flails her arms and tries to pry Simone's hands off her neck.

"You don't deserve to take in the same air as the rest of us!" Simone yells as she tackle Terianne to the floor.

Seemingly out of nowhere, Candice and Tracy appear and try to pull Simone off Terianne.

"Where'd they come from? I didn't know they were here," I say to Kathy.

With her chest heaving up and down, Simone breaks Candice's and Tracy's hold on her arms and knocks the two of them down. Then she attacks Terianne again. "I won't stop until there isn't any breath in your body," she shouts as she kicks and punches Terianne.

With the help of Kurt and Patrick, the nephews of Mimas's deceased brother and Mimas's plus-sized family members, Candice and Tracy get Simone under control, and she is carted out of the grieving area. She puts up a fight on her way out; however, she is no match for Kurt and Patrick, the family's "bulldozers," as they refer to themselves. The name is fitting since they are six feet five and weigh around 300 pounds. Still, the two of them aren't rough or harsh with Simone, or with Kathy and me when they ask us to leave, though we know they mean business. Terianne also makes sure that we are told that we aren't welcome back at the house for the repast either. So instead, the five of us—our little group now includes Candice and Tracy— find a diner a couple of blocks away from the funeral parlor so that we can have a bite to eat.

"What came over you in there, Simone?" Candice asks, badgering, once we are all seated at a table in the diner.

"Terianne is a monster. She deserves to be six feet deep, alongside Mimas," Simone responds.

"You don't mean that. You're angry right now. Take a moment to calm down," Candice tells her.

"I'm calm right now, or I'd be trying to get my hands around her throat again."

"Simone!" Candice rolls her eyes.

"Look, everyone please settle down, before we get kicked out of this restaurant. It's bad enough Simone got us put out of a funeral," I say, chiming in.

"That was humiliating. I have never seen anything like that before in my life. I am mortified," Candice acknowledges.

"I appreciate you coming, Candice, but you don't have to be here," Simone snaps. "Everyone can't be perfect like you. Terianne humiliated me and the rest of us up there, talking about how she and Todd were Mimas's only children. How do you think that made me feel?"

Candice frowns. "For one, I am far from perfect. Yes, Tracy and I came unannounced, as we wanted to surprise you, but most importantly, we wanted to be there for you. We got on an airplane for the first time in our lives for you. Does that mean anything to you, Simone? I get you're upset, but you don't have to take it out on us." She looks to Tracy for assistance.

Tracy nods her head in agreement.

"Like I said, I appreciate you coming all this way for me. I really do. However, if you went through what she put me and Kathy through, you'd understand," Simone says.

Candice's frown deepens. "Understand? That would be difficult, no matter what. The last thing I wanted was to see you fight. What if you had gotten hurt or something? It was scary and shocking to walk in and see you choking the life out of someone. So, forgive me if it's taking me time to wrap my head around what just took place, Simone. We got put out of a funeral, for God's sake."

"All right. Settle down, everyone," I say, trying to restore the peace. "I understand where both of you are coming from. However, this isn't about you, Candice. Simone did what she needed to do for her own closure. It might not have been the traditional or peaceful way for someone looking for closure, but it was her way of obtaining it."

"Dr. Binet, I cannot believe you're saying this right now." Candice's eyes grow wide.

"Everyone has their own way of handling things. That you have to understand," I tell her.

"You know what? You're right, Candice. You did come here for me, and to see me like that should have bothered you. Please forgive me if I scared or upset you. What I won't do is apologize for what I did. If I could have killed her, I would have," Simone says.

"What about Sage? You're not thinking clearly right now," Candice responds.

Simone shrugs. "I would just have to cross that bridge when I get there."

"When?" Candice shakes her head.

"She's upset right now, Candice. Let's try to change the subject," I say, attempting to steer the conversation in a different direction.

After lunch we pick up some snacks and fast food to hold us until the morning, and then we all go back to my, Simone, and Sage's hotel room. Our flight is at 6:30 a.m. Candice and Tracy were able to get set on the same flight back that Simone, Sage, and I are taking. God in heaven knows when I made the plans for this trip, I had no idea all this would go down the way that it did. The last thing I wanted was for Candice and Simone to go at it with one another. But, on the other hand, Candice needs to see both sides of therapy. She's familiar with only the comfortable stuff.

These two days have worn me out. I am as tired as Sage is, and I cannot keep my eyes open. The girls spend the entire afternoon and evening talking, rekindling ties and catching up. By eight o'clock, I am ready to get my beauty sleep, but they are still going strong. I am a little older than they are, and there's but so much of their conversation that I can tolerate these days. So instead of losing my mind with their chatter, I take Sage around the corner to the hotel room that Kathy reserved, and Sage and I spend the night there.

CHAPTER TWENTY

Open Wounds
Candice . . .

"Hey, Jenna. Thank you for helping Dad with the kids. I know you're not asleep. Stop pretending like you are." I throw all my weight on the bed to give her a hard time.

"You're such a big kid sometimes." She smirks with her eyes still shut. "This bed is so comfortable," she adds and pulls the covers over her head.

"I know it is. It's like it sucks you right in, making it almost impossible to want to get up from it."

"Now you understand my dilemma."

We laugh.

"Trust me I do."

"What just happened?"

"What do you mean?" I say.

"Your voice drifted off, and you sound a little sad. Did something happen? How was the funeral? How's Simone doing? I know it must have been rough for her to go back there after all this time."

"I don't even know where to begin, Jenna."

"Was it that bad? What possibly could have happened?"

"For starters, on a bright note, I think I am in love with flying. At first, I was anxious and scared, but once we were in the air, I couldn't stop looking out the window. I am just in awe of God. Only He could have created something that amazing. It's mind blowing how there aren't any street signs, roads, or anything up there, just clouds. And the pilot is still able to get us from one end of the world to the other."

"It's called GPS, Candice."

"No, that's God. You can call it what you want, but only God can orchestrate something of that magnitude."

"Here we go, Joeline Olsteen. I don't have any offering money on me. Do you accept credit cards?"

"Real cute, Jenna. I am serious, though."

"So am I."

We giggle.

"But seriously, flying is amazing . . . until the turbulence," I tell her. "That scared the living daylights out of both of us. I never prayed so hard in my life."

"I know that's real. Anyway, are you going to tell me what happened at the funeral?"

"Honestly, Jenna, it was like Nakita was there."

"Nakita? Maybe you should consider grief counseling, unless talking to your therapist will help. You do know Nakita wasn't there, right?"

"I said it was *like* she was there, Jenna. Not that she *was* there. Simone transformed into a clone of Nakita. The plane was late taking off, so we arrived at the funeral late. When we walked through the doors of the funeral parlor, there was a lot of commotion. By the time we managed to see what was going on, we witnessed Simone on top of her foster sister Terianne, with her hands wrapped around her throat."

"Are you serious?" Jenna says. "Simone is so sweet. I've never even seen her get upset before. What the hell happened?"

"Tracy and I ran to the front to try to pull Simone off Terianne, but Simone knocked us down and went back to punching and stomping on that girl like she was in a wrestling match."

"She clearly was. Oh my goodness. I cannot believe that happened. What made her flip like that?"

"*You* can't believe it? *I* can't, and I was there. Well, after we got escorted out of the funeral and went back to their hotel room, Simone filled me in on what happened. We missed the beginning of the match."

Jenna's eyes get big. "*Escorted* out of the funeral? Who the hell gets kicked out of a funeral, Candice? That is unheard of."

"Evidently, we do and did. But, anyway, Simone opened up to us last night and said Terianne knew about the rapes, and she humiliated them during the eulogy by leaving out the other foster kids, as if they didn't exist."

"Wow! That's cold-blooded. I probably would have tried to knock her out myself."

"Now you sound like Dr. Binet. She was someone else yesterday. I don't think I know the lady that accompanied Simone to the funeral service."

"What do you mean, she was someone else? She was probably relaxed and not in therapist mode."

"I don't know who or what she was, honestly, and a therapist was definitely not one of them. She talked with so much malice and condoned Simone's actions."

"I just condoned her actions, so am I too unfamiliar to you now?" Jenna says.

"It was different with her. Even her eyes appeared unfamiliar. I cannot put my finger on it, but something was off with her. Let me ask you a question. How have things been with the two of you? Have you noticed anything different about her?"

"Speaking of Brianne, there's something I haven't been completely honest with you about—"

"Oh no! I don't think I am ready for this. What happened?"

"I have been seeing a therapist for going on six months now. After we parted ways, I began stalking Brianne, and it didn't end well," Jenna confesses.

"Stalking her? It didn't end well? What are you saying, Jenna?"

"Long story short, remember when you said I need to be sure of what I really want, because I sound confused and unsure of myself?"

I nod. "Yes."

"Well, you were right, and I have been searching for a mother's love, so I searched out women to try to form a motherly bond with them. Ms. Jasmine caught me on one of my stakeouts and lit into me really good. I am a better person because of her and therapy. For the first time in my life, I am actually really happy and comfortable in my own skin."

"I am so proud of you, Jenna." I push back the covers and pull her into an embrace.

"Stop manhandling me. I am fragile."

I crack a smile. "Stop being silly. But seriously, I am so proud of you, Jenna."

"Thank you. God in heaven knows I needed it."

"Yes, you did. I believe everyone in some way, shape, or form can benefit from counseling. I am an advocate for it."

"I bet you are, considering you are one."

"Almost, but I am at the threshold," I say, beaming.

"You know what? Something just came to mind."

"What's that?"

"The day things went sour with me and Brianne, she shared some things with me. I know I am probably not supposed to repeat it, but if you're saying you think something is wrong, I think I might know part of the reason why."

"You do? Why? What is it?"

"That day she was at Nakita's old place, she broke down badly. I've never seen that side of her. She no longer epitomized the strong woman that I was so desperately fond of. She actually appeared normal and weak, sort of like me. Not perfect, with all the answers and solutions. I actually felt sorry for her and kind of still hurt for her."

"*Hurt* for her? What are you trying to say?"

"She told me she too was raped and impregnated by her rapist."

"That cannot be. We did background checks. I've spoken to her on a professional level in order for her to work at New Beginnings. None of that came up at all. Are you sure you heard her right?"

"I am positive. I can recall it as clear as day. She said I could see past her facade, and she isn't as perfect as everyone thinks she is."

"This isn't good."

"Maybe not, because she also said she's been where Nakita was, and sometimes finds herself there now. Oh, and that no one deserves to be treated the way that the girls have been mistreated. Someone deserves to pay, and it should not have been Nakita."

"This is really bad. She sounds too damaged to be counseling anyone. You know what? That's the look she had in her eyes."

"You saw that she shouldn't be counseling in her eyes? How? That doesn't make sense."

"That's not what I am saying. I saw anger, hurt, and despair in her eyes. It's hard to explain, but what you just shared matches her appearance."

"Now I am afraid for her. Maybe I should not have said anything."

"No, you needed to have said something. I cannot have her working with these girls. She might need time, because I know for sure if she is still covering it up, it is still a bleeding open wound."

"I have to admit, you're right."

We sit in silence, pondering all this.

This is going to be a challenging task. Probably one of the hardest things that I've ever had to do. There's no way I can keep this to myself. I have to say something to Dr. Binet. It sounds like she is still struggling with her past. How was she able to listen to all our stories? We are probably the cause of her relapse. I cannot believe she went through the same things that we went through and was able to keep a straight face while listening to us relive our pain. That is probably why we gravitated to her in the manner that we all did: the pain in our spirits connected. I know the majority of therapists have their bag of issues and suffer from depression. I've had my share, but I also know I am not ready to have or do one-on-ones. I still have some open wounds that need to be stitched up. It sounds like Dr. Binet bypassed the stitches and has been using Band-Aids to conceal her open scars.

CHAPTER TWENTY-ONE

Honesty, the Best Policy
Alonzo . . .

I've literally been avoiding Candice. You'd think we were in this full-blown relationship and I actually cheated, the way I have been ducking her. The last thing I want to do is break her heart. I know I didn't do anything wrong and the alcohol impaired my reaction and reflexes, but will she believe or understand that? I'm standing outside her house, at the kids' bus stop. They are all ready for school and are jumping up and down. This school bus needs to hurry up and get here. I thought she was coming back tomorrow. Why is she back so soon? I wonder. I need more time.

"Hey, Alonzo. Did you miss me?" she asks as she approaches me and the kids.

"Shit," I grumble.

"What was that?"

"Shit yeah. Shit yeah," I said.

"Sure you did. What have you been up to? I called you the other day, after our talk, and I haven't been able to catch up with you since."

"Just working and catching up with the fellas."

"Is your phone broken?"

"No, it isn't. Didn't we just talk the other day?"

"When I called you? No, we didn't."

Just then the bus pulls up.

"See you later, Mommy and Daddy," the kids interrupt as they board the bus.

I'm just going to be straight up with her, I decide at that moment. I can't do this any longer.

"Hello?" she says when I remain quiet and watch the bus pull away.

"I am here. I apologize. Do you want to go inside and talk, or are you busy with getting things set up for the grand opening?"

"Nope. I am all yours."

"I hope so," I say and wink.

She smiles. I love that smile. And the blushing drives me and my other brain crazy. I shake my head as we walk back into the house.

"What's going on?" she asks, getting straight to the point, as we take a seat in the den.

"You know that you and those kids are my world, right?"

"Oh boy. What happened? Did you meet someone? You're tired of waiting for me, aren't you?"

"Slow down, beautiful. I am a man of my word. I said I will give you the time you need. I just would like for us to progress a little further than we have, if that's possible."

"I know sex plays a big part in relationships, but I am not there just yet. I'll understand if you have to do what men do and handle your business. This is just hard for me right now, but I will do what I need to do to get there."

"Sex doesn't define a relationship. Yes, it is a part of it, but there is so much more to building a relationship with someone. Don't get me wrong. It has been hard as hell not being able to make love to you. Just the little things you do, like the way you smile or even just walk past me, stimulate me. But I know there is a time and a place for everything. Especially after everything you've been through."

"You are an amazing man, Alonzo. I will do whatever I need to do to make you and me work. I love you and have loved you since I was a teenager. You were and still are my first and only love outside the kids."

"I love you more," I say, and then I taste her lips.

Pulling back, she confesses, "I haven't felt like this since the first time you kissed me like that. Can you do it again?" She closes her eyes.

"How about we talk a little more? If you still want to inhale and exhale each other's essence afterward, we can."

"Okay." She turns her head to prevent me from seeing how flushed she has become, but she cannot hide the rosiness of her cheeks.

"The night you called me and I didn't answer, I was out with the fellas, having a few drinks—"

"That's not a bad thing, is it?" she interrupts.

"Not at all. Although, I did get pretty wasted, and when I went to the men's room to alleviate myself, some woman came in the bathroom behind me."

The color in her face diminishes.

"Please believe me when I say that I have no idea who that woman was. When she pushed me against the wall, I was caught off guard and buzzed, so everything was off. You phoning me snapped me back to reality."

"You were having sex with her when I called you?"

"No. Hell no. She was trying to put her mouth on me. But nothing happened. I swear to you, nothing happened."

"Did you *want* something to happen?"

"At that time, I don't believe I processed fully what was going on, to say I did or didn't want something to happen. Honestly."

"So, you wanted to have sex with her? Is that what you're saying?"

"It did feel good to have a woman touch me, but it's not what I wanted or who I wanted it with. I didn't go out looking for her or anyone else."

"I hear you, Alonzo, but it sounds like had I not called, things would have turned out different."

"I was so drunk. I am not sure what would have happened. I am not drunk now, and I can assure you that's not what I want. I want you."

"Maybe you shouldn't drink if being intoxicated causes you to black out and makes you unaware of things that are going on or happening to you."

"Candice, it's not like that. I wouldn't be telling you this if it was. To be honest with you, I have not been with a woman or touched a woman like that in months. Probably close to a year. I've committed and devoted myself to you. It ate away at me that any of that happened, which is why I've been avoiding you. The last thing I want to do is hurt you."

"Alonzo, if you feel the need to sow your royal oats, then do so. You don't have to worry about hurting me if that's what you really want to do. I might be younger than you and may not have experienced all that there is when it comes to really being in a relationship, but what I do know is I cannot keep a man that doesn't want to be kept. Especially if I am unable to satisfy all his needs. Well, your needs."

"You're only hearing what you want to hear. Nowhere in anything that I just said did I say I wanted that woman, that I wanted to sow anything, or anything else that you just twisted around. Listen, I am telling you this because I don't want there to be any lies or secrets between us. If we are going to do this, let's do it. And I am not just talking about doing the bus thing and me sleeping over and staying up talking all night long. We can do all of that. Maybe not the sleeping over for a while. But we need to go to dinner, just the two of us. The movies, walks on the beach, or whatever romantic things couples do. We need to start being a couple, and not just saying or thinking we are. Wait, are we a couple? All this is so confusing."

"Are you asking me to go steady with you, Alonzo?" she asks coyly.

"If that's what needs to be done so we can progress, then yes, I am."

"Thank you for being up front and honest with me. I apologize for jumping the gun. I am afraid that another woman is going to come and whisk you away because of the lack of sex in our relationship."

"I'm here with you, where I want to be. As long as we communicate and take our time, I will wait and go as far as you want to go, until you're ready." I pause. "Please don't leave me stranded for too long, though," I tease.

"I promise I will do what I need to do so that I can give you my all. I want everything you just said and then some. I'd love to court you. Now please kiss me and take my breath away again."

Little does she know, I am going to marry her someday. This is where I want to be and where I am supposed to be. I'll do my part by giving her the time she needs. It might result in me taking more cold showers then a man could ever want, but Candice is worth the wait.

CHAPTER TWENTY-TWO

Out of Control
Simone . . .

"Simone, I must say, this is a different side of you," Tracy tells me as she stands in the middle of my bedroom.

"What side? My backside? I know I am getting wider and wider by the day."

"I am not talking about your size," Tracy says and chuckles.

"Oh," I giggle. "You walked in while I was bending down. I thought you were talking about this wide load of mine."

"There is nothing wrong with you at all. People pay to have a body like yours. If they're not paying for it, they're starving themselves to get it."

"Well, maybe I need to join them on that starvation diet. I most definitely can afford to miss a few meals."

"You're so silly. But seriously, I know you are and were upset about the things Terianne said, and also what she did to you was incomprehensible. However, you went to the funeral to pay respects to your Mimas. I am sure there was a better way to deal with Terianne."

"Please do not lecture me, Tracy. You don't know what you would have done or how you would have reacted if you were in my seat. It's easy to pass judgment and say what you would or would not have done from the other side of the door. Anyway, speaking of the funeral service, did you or Candice take the cardigan that I had on? I cannot find it. It was the last thing that Mimas gave to me."

"No, I haven't seen that sweater since the funeral. But you know what? You're right. I don't know what I would have done if I were alone, but in front of all those people and my child, that would not have ever happened."

"Just like a volcano erupts through cracks or weaknesses in the earth from pressure and has no control over the magnitude of the eruption, I cannot and will not justify, try to control, or apologize for how I react when pressure is applied."

"You're not a volcano, Simone. You have complete control over your life. Don't ever allow anyone to change that. I would have died if something had happened to you."

"Trust me, nothing was going to happen to me, unless I was able to put her in that casket with Mimas."

"Don't talk like that, Simone," Tracy says as she plops down in the chair in front of my desk. "Perhaps you should see if Dr. Binet could give you something to help you channel and control your anger. I don't think I've ever witnessed you this vexed. Even when we were going through all that we did with the evil brothers that took advantage of us, Paul and Anthony, you weren't this mad."

"I was a ticking time bomb. *Tick. Tick.* Time is up. It was long overdue after holding all this in for so long. It was only natural that I exploded."

"But it's not good to let yourself get that upset. You lost complete control of yourself. Look what happened with Nakita when she lost it on Ms. Nancy, Paul, and Anthony."

"So, you're saying that was a bad thing? They got what they deserved, and so did Terianne."

"What about Sage? What would she get if something were to happen to you? You really should ask if you can take something to help you with your anger, Simone. It is dangerous to be that upset."

"I'm already taking something, and it clearly agrees with how I feel, because my thoughts have not been altered. In fact, I think I get upset a little faster these days. Usually, I have a delayed reaction, and everything goes over my head. Not anymore. I am taking heads off now."

"Simone, stop it."

"You don't understand, Tracy. You weren't there when she disregarded my existence and acted as if it was just her and Todd. She knew what he did to me, and she acted like it was my fault. I hate her just as much as I hate Todd. Thank God he wasn't at that funeral service. There's no telling what I would have done."

"Please do me a favor and talk to Dr. Binet and tell her all this stuff."

"I talked to her already. She knows, and she understands. You and Candice are the only ones on this imaginary high horse."

Tracy puts her hands on her hips. "High horse because I am concerned and want the best for you, so you can be your best for Sage?"

"As I said, you don't understand. Agreeing to attend Mimas's home-going service was the worst decision I've ever made in my life. Terianne is a wicked individual. She got what she deserved. I don't feel contrite or remorseful. If I could have split her neck in half with my bare hands, I would have. I have never hated someone as much as I despise her. I truly hate her. If I were ever to see her again, I'd hurt her in so many ways never thought of. Then I'd bury her where no one would find her. I'd love to watch her die in a fire. Just seeing her sizzle and crying for help would be a gift from God. The perfect image, her burning like she was in hell, where she belongs."

"You're really scaring me, Simone."

"Both of you need help. I am so over all this," Judith says, cutting in, as she walks into my bedroom.

I roll my eyes.

"Where'd you come from, and how do we need help?" Tracy returns as she fiddles with the stapler on my desk.

"I was in the hallway, and I just heard the tail end of your conversation. And for starters, Tracy, you're sitting here, going on and on about how Simone needs help and how she's scaring you. The last time I checked, none of us are in the clear and could use some form of help. Which is why we constantly live in some form of fear, no matter how much we try to cover it up."

She's right. I take in a big gulp. The truth got me, and I blank out for a second. I can feel my mouth trying to move, but to no avail. Time decides to stop in my head.

Are you okay over there, Simone?" Judith snaps me out of my stupor.

"Y-Yes. I'm good—" I answer, but Judith interrupts me.

"Good to hear." She looks us up and down. "In other news, two weeks from today, me and Chandler will be moving out. I will assist with the bills for the rest of the month, so I don't leave you guys stranded."

"Moving out? How? Where did this come from? Where are you going?" Tracy quizzes, in a panic. She places the stapler back on the desk.

"I'm in love," Judith reveals.

Tracy has more questions. "In love? What in the world are you talking about? Are you joking?"

Judith knits her eyebrows. "What's with all the questions, Tracy? Better yet, why in the world would my happiness be the butt of any joke? I am confused."

"First off, please calm down," Tracy says. "Secondly, when did you start dating? The moving, I get it. It was bound to happen sooner or later. We have to move on one day in life. Yes, it's sudden, but I get it. However, I had no idea you were involved. And it's that serious where you're moving Chandler, your son, in with this person?"

"This person? His name is Elliot. Another thing, I didn't know I was required to report to you or anyone else every intricate detail of my life."

"Where is all this hostility coming from? It's me, Judith." Tracy's lip trembles. Then tears flood her eyes and course down her cheeks, unchecked.

Judith just shakes her head. "I knew you'd be the one to have something to say, when you should be happy for me."

"You caught us . . . well, me . . . off guard. You just dropped several bombs on us, so you cannot expect there not to be some kind of hysteria," Tracy says through her tears.

"Both of you are getting on my nerves," I tell them. "I don't need anyone to speak for me. However, I do agree with erupting and taking action when bombs are detonated. Whether it be at the time they are released or after you've pulled yourself together, I am all for the hysterics."

"Simone, can you please stop? No one said anything about *you* being hysterical. I was talking to Judith," Tracy says.

I wag my finger at them. "Y'all are in my space. You are free to take the rest of this conversation upstairs, to your areas of the house, by all means."

"All I can do is shake my head. You two have magically transformed into persons I do not recognize," Tracy tells us.

"You don't recognize me, because I am moving on with my life and refuse to be stuck in my past. I thought that's what all the therapy and sisterhood was all about? We have been striving to better ourselves so that we can move past the abuse and not only love ourselves but also be able to love someone else wholeheartedly." Judith shakes her head.

"I don't know why I keep crying." Tracy uses the back of her hand to wipe the tears from her eyes before continuing. "You are a thousand percent right, Judith. We are in the 'process' of bettering ourselves. I stress the word *process*, because we're still taking steps toward being able to fully love ourselves without the shame and guilt."

Judith crosses her arms over her chest. "Speak for yourself, Tracy. I talked to Dr. Binet about all this already, and she is perfectly fine with me moving on."

"She said those exact words to you?" Tracy answers, posing yet another question.

Judith looks down at the floor. "Well, not exactly. She said I am still in the process of embarking on the journey of loving myself. If I'm still struggling with accepting myself and my flaws, I cannot and will not be truly happy with someone else."

"Nothing you just said sounds like she gave you her stamp of approval," I note.

"I thought you removed yourself from this conversation, Simone?" Judith says.

"And guess what? You're still in my space," I remind her.

"Anyway, like I was saying, she did say she is in no position to stop me and that I must make sure I know what I am doing, because she wouldn't recommend that I make this commitment right now. But, like I told her, I am happier than I have ever been in my life, outside of giving birth to Chandler."

I shake my head as my thoughts consume me. Judith heard nothing Dr. Binet said, and she doesn't hear herself at this point. I just told her nothing sounds like a stamp of approval, and she proceeded to repeat and confirm how Dr. Binet isn't in agreement with any of this. I don't have any idea what Judith is doing or thinking. But it's her business, not mine. I am just nervous for her, because I don't understand why she felt the need to keep the love of her life a secret. I am no expert on relationships, but I do know when you love something or someone, you can't stop talking about it or them. I go on and on about Sage because I love her and am in love with my baby girl. Hopefully, Judith knows what she's doing, because it's not just about her. Chandler will be pulled out of the only real home and family he's known.

"I don't think I like any of this, honestly," I say, my thoughts seeping through my lips.

Judith squints at me. "What is there for you to like or not to like, Simone? The way I see it, you don't like anything these days unless it involves you getting hot under the collar and flipping out on someone."

"Judith, you can project all this on me and Tracy all you want. All I know is, when you're in love, you want the world to know. Yet you hid it. As far as me flipping out, I dealt with what needed to be dealt with the way I saw fit. Period."

"Now we are on the same page. I dealt with getting to know Elliot and building a relationship with him the way I saw fit. Period," Judith retorts.

I sigh. "I am not one to judge and would never pass judgment on you, Judith. My concern is Chandler. This is the only stable home and family that he's ever known, and it is being ripped right out from under him."

"You act as if we're moving to West Africa, Simone. I am not ripping anything out from my son. I am affording him a better life. I cannot give him what a man can. I am a woman, not a man."

"I hear you, but not every man is equipped to be a father, the same way not every woman is fit to be a mother," I tell her.

"Whatever, Simone. Worry about you and yours, and allow me to worry about mine."

Tearfully, Tracy pleads, "At this point, I don't know what to say anymore. I love both of you and want what's best. I don't want to argue. Judith, all I ask is that you listen to what Simone and Dr. Binet said. They both have made some points. And, Simone, please do whatever you have to do to channel your anger, before it channels you."

"Since we're making requests, can you two do me a favor and get out of my space, so I can put my child down for a nap? Thanks." I cut my eye at them.

CHAPTER TWENTY-THREE

Sometimes Your Words Just Hypnotize Me
Dr. Binet . . .

I am on edge right now as I think about my upcoming session with Simone. It is the conversation that I just had with Candice that has me uptight and unnerved. Candice left my office just a few minutes ago, and I was so furious that my heart pounded practically through my chest. I try now to shift gears and think about my session with Simone, which will start in about fifteen minutes, but I am just a wreck. My hands feel clammy against my bouncing knees. I can't sit still. I decide to stand to calm myself down. That doesn't work. I end up pacing back and forth up. I take a deep breath.

I should have known the conversation wasn't going to be a pleasant one when Candice came in here, her eyelids raised in a blank stare, as if she were unfamiliar with her surroundings.

Shaking my head, I sigh as a flashback of the conversation comes to mind.

A fist tapping at the wooden door to my office startled me. I was not expecting anyone for another two hours. Who could it possibly be?

C-Come in," I called from my seat behind my desk.

Candice stepped through the door. "Good evening, Brianne. Can I have a word with you?"

"Sure. Please have a seat, Candice."

"Thank you," she said, her tone too formal, and took a seat on the other of my desk.

"Is everything all right? You look like something is bothering you."

"I am a little scared and nervous. I'm having a difficult time understanding what's going on."

"Now you're frightening me, Candice. Did something happen to the kids? The girls? What's going on?"

"The last time I checked, everyone is as best as they can be. They're not my concern. You are, Brianne. I'm worried."

"Please share what it is that has you worried about me."

"Your behavior, for one."

"My behavior, Candice? The last time I examined myself, I was a grown woman. My behavior is none of anyone's concern, honestly. I am not a child, and I don't need to be disciplined with regards to my behavior," I told her.

"Perhaps I used the wrong term, or it came out the wrong way. Although it's fitting. I am just going to say it." She exhaled. "You are completely out of line with the way that you're advising Simone. You're encouraging angry outbursts. Not to mention how unethical it was for you to attend the funeral with her. What happened to boundaries?"

"I appreciate your concern, Candice, but what you will not do is come into my office and tell me what I should or should not be doing. I have been doing this for years. I know exactly what I am doing. When you're done with school and actually have a practice, then and only then we might be able to have a conversation of this nature.

You can't possibly have any complaints concerning my practice, because I am reputable therapist. If I am not mistaken, you can vouch for me yourself." My nostrils flared.

"I may not have completed my master's or have a practice, but I do know one thing. What you're doing is dangerous. When you and Jenna had your thing, you admitted how unethical it was for you to continue counseling us, because, and I quote, 'It is impossible and wouldn't help for a therapist to form a relationship outside of the consulting room.' How and why did that change with Simone?"

"Like I stated, I know what I am doing. You're textbook driven. I know what it is to have a thriving practice and a successful turnaround rate within that practice. Which is how I have been around this long," I reply.

"If you keep going at the rate that you are going, you're not going to make it in this field much longer. You've crossed every line that there is. Including lines that haven't even been drawn. No matter how successful your practice has been, you're not only putting Simone's progress in jeopardy, but you're jeopardizing everything you've worked so hard to build as well. Also, I will be as textbook driven as you stated and will also stand on the premise that psychotherapy will not work and is dangerous without boundaries. Period!"

"Excuse me, little girl. Everything, and I mean everything, that you preach to me, I taught you. You have your sanity because of me. You aren't sitting in someone's nuthouse, because of me! Now, show me some respect! Money doesn't give you a right to waltz yourself in here and speak to me any kind of way. I am helping Simone the same way I helped you. If anyone's crossing a boundary right now, it is you."

"Wow, Brianne. That was a low blow. Money didn't change me one bit. I came here as a friend, before all this spirals out of control. What I do see is transference and countertransference in your and Simone's relationship. That same anger she has was just displayed right here by you. You're turning her into a mini Brianne, minus the practice. You're using her to avoid dealing with the things that are metastasizing inside you."

"Metastasizing inside me? Yes, you've swallowed one too many of those textbooks, sweetheart."

"Jenna told me, Brianne. You should get some help. I don't think you're fit to counsel or help anyone right now, in the state that you're in."

"Get out of my office, Candice. I am fine. Jenna had no right to tell you anything. Don't you sit there and judge me. Get out of my office. Now!"

"I am sorry, Brianne. I really am. Please talk to someone. You're spiraling out of control. And another thing. I am sorry, but I don't feel comfortable with you counseling the girls at New Beginnings. I would never judge you. I want what's best for you, and this decision is what's best for New Beginnings," she said. Then she stood up, walked to the door, and left my office. A pair of tears raced down her cheeks as she went.

I am perfectly fine with not working at New Beginnings. Focusing on my practice is what I need to do. None of these things were an issue before I met Candice and Jenna.

That's enough, Brianne. Let it go. That is just what I will do, I tell myself. Right now, I have to erase it all from my thoughts. I'm fuming all over again from revisiting that meeting in my mind. *Meditation. That's it. I will meditate until Simone gets here,* I think. Meditation heals the wounded places in our minds. I have to rid myself of all negativity.

After retrieving my yoga mat from under my desk, I place it on the floor and take a seat on top of it. Sitting with my eyes closed, I put my right hand on my belly and focus on my breathing. I concentrate on allowing myself to breathe naturally through my nostrils. After taking a deep breath, I hold it and count to four. I exhale for a count of four while still concentrating on my breathing. My main focus is on forgetting everything. I refuse to submit to the temptation of reviewing my meeting with Candice once again. I take another deep breath.

Finally, after repeating my breathing routine, I feel great. Haven't felt this calm in several weeks. As I pull myself up from the floor, Simone barges in without knocking.

"Hey, Dr. Binet."

"Good evening, Simone. Is everything all right?"

"Yes. Why do you ask?"

"You didn't knock, and there's a strong negative and angry presence here with you," I say as I tuck the yoga mat under my desk and take a seat in an armchair in my office sitting area.

"I am just annoyed. I cannot explain why. But I love it. I'm usually timid and soft spoken. Not any longer. I speak my mind, and it feels good."

"What has transpired since our last session, when you were forced to speak your mind?"

"Tracy thinks she knows everything."

"How so? Please explain."

"She said I was wrong for what I did to Terianne, and for what I said I'd do to her if I had a chance to. The crazy thing is, in my mind I did it, but I know I didn't, unfortunately."

This is a good time to take her to that point and time in her mind, I tell myself.

"Do me a favor. Have a seat, Simone."

"Oh, my goodness," she says, gurgling. "I am so fired up that I didn't even realize I was still standing." She takes a seat in one of the other armchairs.

"Try to relax and bring yourself down some."

"Why does your voice sound like that?" she asks me.

"Do me a favor and loosen up." I rise to my feet and make my way over to where she is sitting.

"I'm loose as a goose."

"Look up without moving your head upward and try to focus on my two index fingers," I instruct, holding my index and middle fingers in a V shape above her forehead. While her eyes are fixated on my fingers, I ask her to breathe in and out as I move my hand up and down.

It's working. I celebrate inwardly as I witness her breathe in as my hand moves up and breathe out as my hand moves down.

"Close your eyes," I instruct, then move my hand down in front of her face.

After instructing her two additional times to breathe in and out, I see that she's complying. I ask Simone to open her eyes on the count of three, and I inform her that once her eyes are open, a wave of relaxation is going to flow across her body.

"Simone, when I click my fingers, you will see yourself back in Virginia, at Mimas's house, after the funeral service. The repast is over. What happens next?"

"The front door is slightly ajar. I walk in. I can see Terianne sitting in the living room, sniffling. Please hold my sweater, Dr. Binet." She hastily removes it. "'Is someone out there?' Terianne shouts. 'Your worst nightmare,' I say, and then I charge her. Instead of trying to defend herself, Terianne tries to save herself from falling. She tumbles to the floor. Catching my balance, I spring upward and use my feet as if they are weapons of mass destruction, kicking and stomping on her face until the color of blood becomes her new skin tone." She is silent for a moment.

"Look at her, Dr. Binet," she continues. "She doesn't have much to say now, does she? But then she says, 'Maybe we should go, now that you've proven your point.' And I reply, 'Maybe we shouldn't.' I am not done. She needs to pay for her sins and the sins of her brother. Just like you've always said. So then I leap my way into the kitchen. I retrieve the sharpest knife I can find, and then I gallop back into the living room. 'Not so fast. We're not done,' I tell Terianne, and then I kick her back down and sit my body on top of her. Sliding my bottom forward, I position comfortably across her stomach. Hand me my sweater, Dr. Binet."

I hand her the sweater.

"Thank you. So I take it and wipe the blood from Terianne's face. 'That's better,' I say. 'Now let's see what's behind this evil face of yours.' I place the knife under her right eye, swiped it underneath her eye, and then bring it down to the bottom of her chin. 'Look how pretty you are now,' I tell her, and I admire my homemade makeover."

Feeling nauseated by her words, and by the images from my own thoughts and my own skeletons, I regain control by commanding, "On the count of three, I will snap my fingers and you will wake up. You'll be fully awake and alert. You will remember pieces of what you said under hypnosis." I pause. "One, two, three."

Simone blinks her eyes. "Oh my God, did I do something wrong?"

"Why do you say that? What do you recall?"

"I am not sure. My heart is racing, and images of a bloody Terianne are flashing in my head."

"I believe it is and was your anger talking. Try increasing the dose of your medication. Instead of taking one capsule, take one and a half. Cut one in half. It'll help you sleep and clear your mind. This was a great session. I will see you in four days."

"That's the grand opening of New Beginnings. I have to be there for Candice. You'll be there, right?"

I nod. "I'll try."

CHAPTER TWENTY-FOUR

Wolf in Sheep's Clothing
Jenna . . .

At the recommendation of Dr. Imberti, I've faithfully been attending a recovery program geared toward different traumas, and they're digging into abandonment at the moment. I joined at the perfect time. I've learned on a deeper level how abandonment has inflicted a deep personal wound within me. Without knowing, I have been silently suffering, and I can now say that for the majority of my life, I've felt as if I'd been stabbed in the heart by my mother and father—a penetration through the spirit that has left me to suffer, confused and alone. My one-on-one sessions with Dr. Imberti have been enriching. I've learned so much about Jenna. Those deep, dark places that I've avoided all my life have had the curtains drawn on them, and I've been discovering what's been festering there.

Group therapy, on the other hand, is allowing me to realize I am not alone and to find my voice. It's a safety net where I can relate to others and myself in healthier ways. Listening to members of the group recount how far they've come gives me so much hope. However, I spent my first several group sessions in tears. In the beginning, I wasn't comfortable with the setting. At first, I was intimidated by hearing everyone's stories, but I quickly learned the benefits group therapy provides that individual therapy does not. For instance, in my sessions with Dr. Imberti, it is just the two of us, and after each session I have found myself struggling with feeling like I am the only one in the world confused about her sexuality because of her mommy issues. Oftentimes I have second-guessed the benefits of counseling, other than pinpointing and nailing down all my issues. Both of these issues are reasons why Dr. Imberti suggested group therapy.

During the last group session I attended; I believe I shed some layers. Despite an overwhelming flow of tears, I openly confessed my issues. Just acknowledging them helped me face myself. I never realized all the things that I have been harboring on the inside until I started talking about the things I went through as a child and how my mother throwing me away because of her hurt had scared me. A work in progress, I am, but I am so much better and further along than I was.

My sponsor has been a godsend. Omarion checks on me two to three times a day. He's become the friend I need during this season of my life. Naturally, since I am thinking of him now, he calls. I smile as his name flashes across my phone's screen.

"Good afternoon," I answer on the first ring.

"Did I catch you at a bad time?"

"Not at all. I am at the supermarket, trying to get some healthy foods. I've put on a couple pounds over the past six months."

"I wouldn't know, but I will say either way, it is working for you."

"Thanks, but I am uncomfortable. My clothes don't fit right, and I refuse to purchase a new wardrobe in a bigger size."

"So, what are you going to do about it?" he asks.

"I'm going to be conscious of what I put in my mouth and get back to my morning run. I haven't run in God knows how long."

"You run?"

"I do. Lately, I have been so caught up in everyone and everything else that I have not."

"Right now, you need to focus on Jenna. You're no good to anyone if you neglect your most valuable player, which is yourself."

"You're so right about that. Finding out my sister is still alive and learning of the things she went through shook my world to the core. I made it my business to make up for lost time and be the family that she or I never had."

"That is great, and what you should have done," Omarion says. "Although, you gave so much, you sucked yourself dry. You avoided dealing with yourself and your stuff by focusing on your sister. Not that you should not have been there for her, but you just needed to balance everything out. Her world and her problems became yours, and you got lost in the thick of it all."

"You're absolutely right. Especially when I learned the things she endured at the hands of those men in the home, which was supposed to nurture and train her for motherhood—"

"I take it you get off telling everyone's business," says a familiar voice right behind me.

I had been staring at the contents of my shopping cart, but at the sound of that voice, I look back. "B-Brianne." I stop myself from backing into her with my shopping cart.

"I've been behind you for some time now, and I cannot say I am shocked to hear you on the phone, telling your sister's business, because you did the same thing to me," she declares.

Placing my phone in the shopping cart, I retort, "I spoke to my sister because I was concerned about you,

Brianne. She was scared of how you reacted to Simone, and it made me think of how you responded to Nakita's death, as well as the things you shared with me at that time. The last thing I was doing was being malicious. I wanted to help you."

"Help me? *Me*?" She points to herself before snapping, "Let me help you out for the last time. I am a renowned therapist. Your sister, the one whose business you were just sharing, yes, her . . . She, along with her house sisters, was referred to me because the attorney representing Nakita knew if anyone would be able to get Nakita off and help her, it'd be me. And what did I do? My job. Nakita didn't go to prison, where she should have gone for what she did, according to the law. However, she was sent to a rehabilitation center due solely to my recommendations. She got out early as well. Why? Because of my direction and counsel. My word, my decisions, and my practice hold weight in this community. If they didn't, your sister would probably have taken her life while Nakita rotted in prison. None of that happened because of me. So, before you go around thinking you know me and adding more to what I've experienced than what you should have, let all of that marinate."

"Yes, you helped my sister and her house sisters. That does not mean in any way, shape, or form that you don't need help yourself—"

Preventing me from finishing my sentence, Brianne's hands grasp at my neck, I can hardly breathe, and my eyes widen from fear as small, ragged gasps escape my throat.

"Uncomfortable and scary to be caught off guard and have someone gripping you by the neck, cutting off your life support, isn't it?" Brianne snarls.

I do the best I can and nod yes through tears.

"I know it is. That's exactly how I felt when your sister elbowed her way into my office and threw my past in my face. I too couldn't breathe. How about you do both of us a favor and stay out of my business?" She releases her grip and then stalks away.

Gasping for air, I wrestle with trying to breathe.

"Jenna, are you there? Is everything all right?" Omarion's voice echoes through the speaker of my phone.

Coughing and sputtering, I grab my phone, open my mouth to speak, but only a sick gurgle escapes.

Suddenly, as if by magic Omarion appears at my side. "There you are. Here. Drink this water," he offers.

"Th-thank you," I say, my words muffled.

"I heard what was going on through the phone, and I was close by, so I raced in here. Are you all right?"

"I am better now. I think she has completely lost her mind."

"Was that Brianne? The doctor?"

"Yes, it was her. She appeared from out of nowhere and grabbed me. I know I mentioned to Candice what Brianne shared with me, but it wasn't done viciously. I swear it wasn't," I say. I sniffle and sob.

"Here." He hands me a tissue to wipe the snot and the tears that trickle down my face. "Clean your face up."

"Thank you for being here for me. My hands won't stop shaking. I suddenly have lost my appetite. I just want to go home."

"I think we need to go down to the precinct. You need to file a report to take to the courts to try to get a restraining order against Brianne. There's no telling what she's capable of doing. She assaulted you. In broad daylight, and in a public place at that. I don't trust her, Jenna."

"That's not the same woman I met. Her eyes were so cold, and her voice dripped with disdain."

"Look at your neck." His face glows red. "Her finger-prints are still on you," he says, his temper about to boil over.

"I cannot believe Brianne did this to me." My hands develop a mind of their own and quake uncontrollably.

"You're in no condition to drive. You're really shaken up. I will do you a favor and drive you to the precinct myself."

"Thank you, Omarion. I really appreciate you."

Following our trip to the precinct, where I filed a re-port, Omarion chauffeurs me to the diner so we can grab a bite to eat. My nerves are all over the place, and the last thing I want to do is eat. So when our food arrives at the table, my eyes watch him eat while I pick at my food. The whole time my mind replays Brianne trying to cut off my air supply. I am in no mood or condition to spend time at my place alone, so Omarion and I decide that he will take me over to Candice's place. I call her to let her know that I will be on my way over after we eat, and I let her know that ran into Brianne and that she lost it on me. After our conversation, Candice is worried sick, so she texts and calls me nonstop.

After Omarion and I finish eating, he drives me to Candice's place. He puts the car in park and turns to me.

"Well, we're here, Jenna. Are you sure you don't want to come stay with me? I have a spare room."

"No thank you." My face turns an embarrassing reddish hue.

"Seriously, it's no big deal at all. I have the room. You won't even know I'm there. Besides, you won't be able to relax and clear your mind with the kids and everything else you mentioned your sister has going on."

"You have a point. I don't want to bring any negative energy in there. Those babies have been through enough sadness." I fumble through my tote bag in search of my phone. "Just a minute," I say, and then I scroll through my call log on my phone and locate Candice's number. I write her a text.

Hey, Candice. I am going to take a raincheck. I've decided to go home. I'm off tomorrow. If you're still up to it, come by in the morning, after the kids are off to school, and we can go for a run. I press send.

Are you sure? If you change your mind, you know where the key is. I love you, Jen .

I love you more. After sending this text, I place my phone back in my bag.

"Is everything all right?" Omarion asks me.

"Yes, it is. I was just letting Candice know I've changed my mind, so she's not worried and calling and texting me every second. However, I do have a question for you."

"Ask away."

"Do you think it's a good idea I go to your place, with you being my sponsor and all?"

"If you don't have a problem or see anything wrong with it, I don't either. I might be your sponsor, the vehicle used for us to cross paths, but if I'm not mistaken, we've outgrown that part of our relationship and have developed a friendship. A bond, wouldn't you say?"

"You're right," I tell him. "You remind me so much of Alonzo. He might get jealous you're trying to steel his best friend." I giggle. "Seriously, though, he and I always hang out until all times of the night and the morning at times. So, yeah, you have a point. We have become good friends. Thank you for being the friend I need right now."

"No thanks needed. I believe that's what friends are for," he says as he pulls away from Candice's place.

"Oh, my God, Dionne Warwick. You and Zoe are twins. He too makes the same corny jokes," I say, and we both crack up.

Omarion is a darker version of Zoe, but they don't look alike physically at all. They just have identical personalities. From day one, I have been able to talk to Omarion about any and everything, the same way I do with Zoe. Omarion appears to be a certified ladies' man, however, and that is something Zoe is not. He is six feet of smooth brown skin over a muscular physique. His smile is mesmerizing. So, I guess I can see why women do a double take when they see him. Now that I am thinking about it, it looks like all my male friends have that double-take effect on the ladies. And I can safely say I am not interested in either of them in that way. I won't lie. Sometimes Omarion does make me blush, and I often get butterflies when I see him. I do know it isn't anything serious, so I ignore it. From what I've learned so far, he appears to be a great guy. I, on the other hand, am a mess still trying to find herself.

"Earth to Jenna. Earth to Jenna," he says and extracts me from my thoughts.

"Yes, I am here. Just thinking, that's all."

"About? You want to talk about it?" he says as we drive.

"It's nothing. I'm just anxious to get off this road to recovery. It's as if I have been lost for so long. I just want to be found already."

"Unfortunately, Jenna, there is never an end to the journey to self-improvement. The more we grow, the more we realize there is always something about ourselves we can improve on. It isn't humanly possible to reach a point of no growth. Whenever we think that we are good, that we've made it, we can be even better."

"I never thought about it like that, but you have a point. You're the positive motivational force that I so desperately need in my life, Omarion."

"O to the rescue. And we are here." He pulls up to a condo complex similar to the one I live in.

After he parks in his designated spot, we head inside. Omarion's condo is breathtaking. It's a trendy two-bedroom loft adorned in black, white, and gray throughout. The decor has the scent of a woman's touch, though there is a male feel to it. The best part about his place for me is the view of the harbor.

"You have to put me in touch with your interior decorator. Your place is exquisite," I tell him.

"I believe you met him already."

"Really? Who was it? Dabien, from group? I can tell by the way he dresses. His taste is impeccable."

"No, you're looking at my decorator," he answers.

"No! Are you serious? You did this yourself?"

"What? Because I am not dressed to the nines like Dabien, you're having a hard time believing I am capable of piecing my place together?"

"I never said that. You just don't look like the type that has the patience for something like that."

"Looks are deceiving."

"It appears that way."

"Are you in the mood for a glass of wine?" he asks me. "I know I can use one."

I nod. "That might be what I need right about now. This was a pretty interesting day."

"Say no more. Make yourself comfortable. There are some sweats and T-shirts in the back bedroom. Along with a face towel and a washcloth. Before you ask, my little sister leaves the clothes here for the days I have to pick her up after she's had one too many drinks." He heads over to his bar area.

"I wouldn't feel comfortable wearing your sister's clothes. I'll be fine wearing this. Wait! Sister? You never mentioned you had a sister in any of the talks we've had."

"Are you sure? I am sure I have. I talk about her more than I talk about myself most of the time."

"I guess I missed that in our conversations."

"It appears that way." He hands me a glass of wine. "By the way, the clothes are new. Every time we go out, she picks up a pair of sweats or two, because she ends up leaving with whatever's here. I think it's OCD."

"Well, I think it's rather smart. And thank you for the wine." I take a sip.

"You're more than welcome."

"Since you put it that way, I will take my wine into the bedroom and change, if you don't mind. I'm exhausted as well. I think I am going to call it a night. Thank you for everything, Omarion."

"It's okay. You can call me O. And no trouble at all."

"Thanks, O," I say, blushing. I head to the guest bedroom, feeling a little light headed. Maybe I should have eaten more. I think this wine is going straight to my head. Hopefully, it will aid in giving me a perfect night's sleep.

"Did you find everything you need in there?" Omarion shouts from the other side of the door about fifteen minutes later.

"Yes, I did. I have already changed and am about to bury my head in the pillow. By the way, your sister has great taste," I call as I shut out the lights.

"Great. Good night."

"Night-night, O."

A few hours later I awaken suddenly and feel disoriented. As my eyes adjust to the dark, I scream in pain from the pounding to my insides. Omarion is now *inside* me.

"Please *stop*! No, *don't* do this to me. Please get *off* me. What are you doing?" I yell.

"Don't play coy now. You knew you wanted it when you decided to have a sleepover." He digs deeper into my insides.

"You're hurting me!" I do my best to get him off me.

"See? You're no fun, you confused slut. You're making this harder than it has to be," he growls, and then he strikes me across the side of my face, causing everything around me to fade to black.

CHAPTER TWENTY-FIVE

Your Pain Is My Pain
Candice . . .

During my last few sessions with Dr. Raysor, I've been discussing my fear of sex. It is a long overdue topic of discussion. I guess, like they say in group therapy, the first step in recovery is admitting you have a problem. Group therapy is another recommendation of Dr. Raysor, along with exposure therapy. She advised that I might want to consider joining a support group for trauma survivors. When I spoke to Jenna about it, she raved about how beneficial the support group she's been attending has been for her. I have been considering it; however, I cannot even envision group therapy being more rewarding than my sessions with Dr. Raysor.

Just recalling our last meeting brings tears to my eyes.

"Tell me what occurs if and when you think about sexual intercourse," Dr. Raysor asked me.

"I am ashamed, scared, and I feel dirty and weak. Why would someone want me? I am used-up, damaged goods."

"No matter how you feel right now, it is essential to remember that you are not to blame yourself for what happened. You did nothing to bring any of this on yourself. You have nothing to be ashamed about. It is not abnormal to feel this way. Just remember,

you don't have to stay there. It is possible to recover everything you've lost emotionally, and that includes your safety and trust. When you feel you're losing touch with your present, and the flashbacks consume you, talk to yourself. Tell the inner you that this or that is no longer your reality. Pinch yourself if you have to. No matter what, do whatever it takes to regain control of your thoughts, because you hold that power."

"Wow." Tears flooded my eyes. "Something that appears to be so simple could be one of the remedies to my deep issues."

"Please explain what you're saying," she replied.

"When a flash from the past consumes me, I get stuck there, and my mind travels back to each time they violated me. I stay in that moment for weeks and days. I walk around with a smile plastered across my face, as if everything is perfectly fine. It's a cover-up. I am dying on the inside. Never would I have thought to pinch myself to snap me into the present, to prevent my mind from wandering completely away. And something that simple could help prevent me from drifting into a deep depression."

"It can aid in helping you not get lost in your head," Dr. Raysor tells me. "Lastly, it is scary to start all over again and learn to love your body after being assaulted. To a high degree, rape puts you at odds with your body, and it becomes your adversary — something you despise. Because you've been violated, you tend to feel contaminated. Reconnecting with your body and feelings is scary but not dangerous. Avoiding your feelings is where the danger lies. Some approaches can assist you with reconnecting with your body. One, in particular, is massage therapy."

"A massage, Dr. Raysor?"

"Yes. However, it isn't the traditional massage. This is massage and bodywork therapy. Bodywork can help *survivors learn to trust their bodies and not view any form of human contact as degrading or a violation."*

"This is so what I need, Dr. Raysor. I just want my body back."

I will have my first bodywork session next week. It sounds extremely promising, and I am excited to undergo this. I am a work in progress. That's why I am anxious to start running in the morning with Jenna. I am on my way over there now. With all this freedom of not living out of a room, like we used to do at Hope House and pretty much at Ms. Jasmine's, I have been eating as if the food industry is going out of business.

"Not any longer," I say, my thoughts seeping from my lips, as I pull into a parking space in Jenna's complex.

I climb out from behind the wheel. It's getting hot out here. I remove my fleece jacket and place it the back of my SUV. As I close the door, I look at my reflection in the window, and I notice Jenna's car next to mine.

Turning around, I say, "I didn't even realize I parked next to you." I reach out to open her car door, but it is locked. "Jenna! What's wrong? Unlock the door. Why are you in there crying? What's wrong? Please unlock the door, Jenna. What's wrong? What happened? Are you okay?" Hysteria sets in.

As she lifts her head and turns its completely in my direction, a picture of grief, loss, and devastation sucker punches me. Her eyes and face radiate a familiar pain.

"Please open this door," I say frantically. "What happened to your face?" My eyes burn as the car door opens.

I kneel before her, and my chest feels heavy, as if it is being filled with lead. Jenna's arms make their way around my neck.

"What happened? Please talk to me," I say. After a minute or so, I break our embrace.

She attempts to hide her face and breaks down entirely. "H-He . . . I—I . . ."

"Take your time. I am right here," I tell her. Her face sinks deep into my chest as I put my arms around her. "Please talk to me, Jenna," I blubber.

"O-Omarion . . . r-r-raped m-m-me. He raped me." Her chest heaves up and down.

My words lodge themselves in my throat, but finally, I say, "Your . . . your counselor?"

I try not to panic any more than I am on the inside. I cling to my sister, trying my best to absorb some of her pain. There's no script for this. I don't know what to say at all. I do know there aren't any words to comfort her or make her feel better at this moment. My heart is bleeding right now.

God, if your listening, I need your help, I pray silently. *I cannot find words, because I am hurting for my sister. Why is this happening? Why would you? How could you let this happen, God?*

"Jenna, I need you to know this isn't your fault. We have to call the police. There's no way he's getting away with this. No, Jenna. No, I will not let you go through what I have been through internally," I tell her, on the verge of breaking down myself.

"I—I can't go to the police. I'm not even sure about the exact details. They won't believe me, Candice. I went to his house. I slept there. It is my fault." She shakes violently.

"You trusted him, and he took advantage of you. You did not give him consent, Jenna. He assaulted you, and he has to pay."

"Okay," she whispers.

I raise myself up off my knees and then lift her to her feet. I can feel my heartbeat, every single pound in my chest. I daren't breathe or move. I am frozen to the cement. Then I catch sight of Alonzo making his way toward me.

"Candice, this doesn't look the—" Alonzo stops in his tracks before he reaches me. Noticing what has me glued to the ground that I stand on, he becomes alarmed. "What happened to her, Candice? Is she hurt? Why is the middle of her pants saturated with blood?"

Burying her head deeper in my chest, Jenna weeps like an inconsolable child.

Raising my eyes to look at Alonzo, I shake involuntarily. I can't speak.

"We need to get both of you to the hospital," he gasps, flipping out.

CHAPTER TWENTY-SIX

Trauma: Past & Present
Brianne . . .

I heard stories of this happening to other parents. I counseled countless parents. I also found myself questioning their judgment, which prompted me to push my practice in another direction. Every time I heard a story, the words floating in my mind surprised me. *That's extremely irresponsible of them. There's no way that you can do that.* Until it happened to me. I still ask myself every day, How could you leave her? How could you have forgotten her? I remember exactly what happened to this day; it plays back in my mind daily. Now more so than ever before. Deep down inside, I will never forgive myself. Sienna didn't ask to be here, and God in heaven knows she didn't ask to be taken away from me.

Regardless of all the training that I had undergone, I didn't realize I was suffering from a bout of depression. Without question, I chalked it up to new mother syndrome, mixed with a little postpartum. Nothing serious, though. I did find myself extremely tired at the end of my day, but it all appeared normal to me. The only unusual and uncomfortable thing I noticed was that when I lay in bed at night, I tossed back and forth, fighting images of Mason and Chuck brutalizing my body.

In addition, I tried in the wee hours of the night to figure out who Sienna looked like the most, and I was haunted by the question of whether Mason fathered our daughter. If he did, even though I didn't consent to the sex with either of them, I would never have turned my husband down. In my eyes, Chuck raped me, and the last thing I wanted to do was give birth to my rapist's child. I hated Mason for what he did to me; however, I would not have made my child suffer because of it.

Giving birth to Sienna was supposed to save my marriage. I thought it was a sign from God that I was supposed to forgive Mason, that we were supposed to undergo therapy and patch things up. No matter how much I fought it and tried to convince myself, deep down inside, I knew the truth the moment I laid eyes on Sienna. It ate away at me day in and day out. Mason and I both have blue eyes, so it's only natural that our child has blue eyes. Not Sienna. She was born with green eyes. She had yellow-brown hair, which is where her name derives from. The same color hair and eyes as Chuck, as if he had spit her out of his mouth. I couldn't give her back; she was my child. I carried her for nine months.

I attempted to do everything in my power to take my mind to another place on those sleepless nights when those thoughts and images plagued my mind. I tried taking a hot bath, reading a book, as well as drinking some warm milk. I did whatever I could think of. But none of it worked. When things became unbearable, I consulted my therapist, who prescribed sleeping tablets and antidepressants. I took Ambien and Seroxat, but they were hopeless. Until I incorporated a bottle of pinot noir into the mix. The images evaporated, and I went from unhappy to bubbly, in conjunction with getting a perfect night's sleep. At times, I'd see things that may or may not have been present; however, as a mental health professional, I knew it was merely a side effect, and that prevented me from becoming alarmed or panic-stricken.

There's no way I didn't take Sienna out of the car. I bathed her and put her to bed. I didn't leave her in the car. I would have never done anything of the sort. Forgotten Baby Syndrome is what they call it, when the parent loses awareness that the child is in the car. I know I did not have postpartum or Forgotten Baby Syndrome. I brought her into the house.

I cry convulsively. This pain is like no other. Natural death can be worked through over time. Not this pain. It's dogged, and it never goes away.

I pop half of a Seroxat and chase it with a glass of pinot noir. I didn't follow instructions and attend therapy back then. Maybe if I had, things would have turned out differently. My mind rewinds, and memories of the day Sienna was taken from me invade my thought process.

"Good morning, my beautiful Sienna I know you're hungry," I said, soothing her, as I strapped her to the front of me in her baby carrier as I prepared both bottles for feeding. "Aw heavens, Mommy is out of her happy pills and low on her friend pinot." I poured the final glass with a twisting motion of my wrist.

Shortly after her feeding, we headed to the CVS drive-through for my happy pills. Then we went to the wine and spirits store for a bottle of pinot noir, and on the way Sienna was out like a light. I admired her peacefulness through the rearview mirror as we reached our destination. Considering the temperature had reached ninety-nine degrees today—eleven degrees above average—and I was parked right in front of the store, I decided to run in and leave her in the air-conditioned car.

I will be right out. I can see her from the counter. What I need is right next to the counter, *I told myself silently, and I was thoroughly convinced.*

I bought what I came for, hopped back in the car, and pulled away from the curb. As I made my way across the bridge, my thoughts consumed me, and I became so distraught that driving off the bridge appeared to be the only logical thing to do at that moment. Gripping the steering wheel, I stared at Sienna through the rearview mirror and gathered myself. Refocusing my eyes on the road, I heard a loud bang. Thinking there was something wrong with my car, I signaled to pull over.

After inspecting the car and realizing there wasn't anything wrong with it, I drove to the exit and pull over near the lake not far from my house. Unable to escape my taunting thoughts, I removed the bottle of wine from the bag. I needed a drink right now. My nerves were all over the place.

"Damn, I don't have a corkscrew," I said aloud. "Wait a minute. The tree method." I beamed at the tree to the left of the driver's seat.

After stepping out of the car, I grabbed the hand towel that had been catching the sweat from my face from the front seat. As I approached the tree, I wrapped the towel around the bottle of pinot. Then I hit the bottom of the bottle against the tree, which forced the cork to spring up. I chuckled hard.

"Thank God, Sienna is asleep," I declared aloud as I grasped the exposed edge of the cork and pulled. It popped out.

After taking a seat on the ground, beside my new best bud, I removed my happy pills from my pocket and tossed two back, then followed them with a swig of my pinot. Unable to remove images of Mason's and Chuck's face from my mind, I took another pill and then downed half the bottle in three separate gulps.

"Oh, yeah, I'm feeling good," I said as I rose to my feet into a hip shuffle.

It's beautiful out. I think I will drive around a little more. That way, Sienna will sleep well while I try to enjoy my day, *I thought as I walked over to the car. She loved car rides; they were like a sleep aid for her. No matter what, she couldn't seem to keep her eyes open when I drove around with her. Now that I was thinking about it, all she did was sleep. I guessed that was what babies did. What else could they do anyway?*

By the time I made it back on the highway, I could feel my happy pills taking effect, as my eyelids were growing heavy.

"Home, sweet home," *I said out loud as I pulled into my garage ten minutes later.* "But how did I get here so fast? I don't even remember driving here or in this direction. I must have fallen asleep in the car. Maybe I came back out for something. I am not sure." *I got out of the car and tried to walk into the house, but my legs had a mind of their own. They swayed left and right. No matter how many steps I attempted to take, it appeared I was not getting any closer to the door. Then I stumbled and landed on the floor of the garage, and everything went dark.*

"Mrs. Binet. Mrs. Binet," someone called, pulling me from my stupor.

"H-Hi, Helen. Where am I?" I said, slurring.

Helen, my neighbor, looked concerned. "I was walking Mannie when I saw your garage door open and noticed you on the ground. Are you all right?"

"Oh my God! Sienna is in the house, alone." I got up and raced inside.

With my head pounding at the same rate as my heart, I searched the house frantically.

"Mrs. Binet! Oh my God, no!" Helen shouted from the garage.

After running as fast as I could back to my garage, my heart stopped when I witnessed Helen attempting CPR on my Sienna.

"What have I done?" I sobbed as I raced back inside for the telephone.

Once I had the phone in my hand, I dialed 911 as I scurried back to the garage. When the dispatcher answered, I wailed into the receiver, "My baby is hurt. She isn't breathing! Please hurry. She's unresponsive. Please don't let my baby die. Please hurry! Oh my God! My baby isn't breathing."

Helen continued performing CPR until the ambulance arrived, and the whole time I felt my soul leave my body. It was like watching a terrible movie, but this wasn't a movie—it was my daughter's life. The EMTs arrived and attempted, unsuccessfully, to help my baby. They pronounced her dead before we got to the hospital, and I passed out before the EMT got to the end of his first sentence. By the time I came to, I was handcuffed to a hospital bed. Thankfully, with the help of my therapist and the jury, which heard the panic and horror in my voice in my 911 call, I was found not guilty of manslaughter, but I was devastated.

Following my baby's death, I underwent an extensive amount of therapy and was granted the opportunity to continue working in my practice. I was permitted to keep my practice open while I recovered. Technically, I was supposed to be working only at the hospital while I recovered. However, I knew I was better before everyone else did. After all, no one knows me better than I know myself. And so I took on patients on the side. My license to practice remained intact, and I was able to continue prescribing medications to patients. Which meant, I was not a danger to myself or anyone else, or therapists would have deemed me such.

And that is why I am so upset with Candice for using her textbook knowledge to tell me what I can and cannot do. I am more bothered by Jenna for repeating what I shared with her. I should have known better. Running into her in the grocery store was perfect. But I didn't set her as straight as I should have, which is why I am headed to her place now. If she never learns anything else, she will learn what it means to preserve the secrets and the loyalty of a friend or an ex-lover.

As I approach Jenna's complex, I am startled by the deafening sound of sirens, and this sparks a flashback of the EMTs arriving to work on my Sienna.

"That's Jenna! They're putting on the stretcher," I say aloud as I slam the car into park and jump out. "What happened to her?" I yell as I rush through the crowd that has gathered.

Locking eyes with Candice, I see her pain-stricken face, and it is interchangeable with every rape victim that I've ever counseled, and this stops me in my tracks. As I gaze around, I take notice of my surroundings, and then Candice practically leaps into my arms and buries her head in my chest.

"H-He r-r-r-raped her," she blubbers.

"Who?" I catch sight of Alonzo, and my eyes pierce through him. "You will pay for this," I snarl at him. "You will not get away with any of this. I promise you will suffer dearly for this."

"You're barking up the wrong tree," he shoots back.

I refocus my attention on the situation at hand. "Candice, I need you to be strong. Get into the ambulance with Jenna. I will meet the two of you at the hospital," I say.

Who did this to her? This cannot be happening right now. The girl was a virgin. Whoever this coward is, he must pay severely for his sins, I tell myself.

My adrenaline spikes. This perpetrator deserves to be tortured for what he's done. Chuck got away with raping me, just like all the rapists the majority of my patients have encountered. This time should be different. It has to be. If we know who he is, we shouldn't leave it up to the authorities to rectify the situation. I jump behind the wheel and accelerate as I head down the street in the direction of the hospital.

When I reach the hospital, I park and then run toward the emergency room. As I dart through the emergency-room doors, I run smack-dab into Alonzo.

"My bad. Where is she? Is she all right? Who did this to her?" I say, all in one breath.

"You owe me an apology, Brianne. How dare you openly accuse me of doing something like that!"

"I don't owe you a damn thing." I brush past him and race toward the receptionist. "Hello. Can you tell me where they have Jen—"

"Brianne, she's this way," Candice shouts from the door.

"Where is she? Is she all right? What happened? Who did this to her?" I ask.

"She's in that room over there." Candice points over her shoulder. "Omarion hurt her really bad, Brianne."

"Omarion? I don't know him. Where did she meet him? Where did he come from?"

"He's her sponsor from group."

"You have to be kidding me," I say, fuming.

"I wish I were. Dad and the detectives are in with her now. I called Dad from the ambulance. Well, texted him . . . to meet us at the hospital. They still have to do a rape kit on her. She is in a bad way right now. She keeps shaking and won't talk."

"Is she at least talking to the detectives?"

"No. She's writing it down the best that she can in between crying. Why is this happening, Brianne? She is the sweetest person in the world. Why would someone want to hurt her like this?"

"Candice, we all . . . I mean, no one deserves anything remotely close to this happening. These cowards play on women's vulnerability and take advantage of them. I had no idea Jenna was going to counseling or group."

"She started after things went left with you. Is there *anyone* that we can trust? Are all men like this, Brianne?" She burst into tears.

"You can trust me, Candice. I would never hurt you or anyone like this," Alonzo remarks as he walks up behind us.

"I am going to go and see if I can be of assistance," I announce and then I head in the direction of Jenna's room.

I make my way to the room, and my heart skips several beats as I open the door.

"Get *out*. I *don't* want her in here," Jenna growls when she sees me.

CHAPTER TWENTY-SEVEN

It's My Fault
Simone . . .

Can this be happening? We are trying to move on and recover from our rapes, and this happens to Jenna. My heart aches for her right now. It is as if we are having a déjà vu moment while riding in this van with Ms. Jasmine. Well, and with Mr. Derek this time as well. Silence and sobs mix as we make our way to the hospital, and this reminds me of the drive back to Hope House when we first met Jenna. That was one of the scariest days of my life. I didn't know what to expect when we arrived at Hope House. Nakita being hurt was all that played in my mind. But when she walked out in handcuffs, full of blood, my heart became jumbled. Ever since that day, I've admired her and looked up to her for her bravery. Unfortunately, this ride doesn't look like it'll result in such a happy ending.

When Alonzo phoned Ms. Jasmine, we were having a little after-school barbecue outside with the kids. It was beautiful out and too hot to turn on the stove, so Mr. Derek offered to throw a few things on the grill. Everything was going great, and the calm atmosphere was just what I needed. But it didn't last long. The screech that came from Ms. Jasmine while she was on the phone stopped everyone in their tracks. The music, laughter, and peace faded away instantly. It was as if the world came to a standstill the moment she screeched, and it was not set in motion until after she shared with us what had happened to Jenna.

Right now, I think if I go inside the actual hospital room where she is being treated, I might lose it. There's no way I will be able to look at her and not recall each and every time Todd hurt me and not want to strangle every male in the hospital. I have to calm down. It would be better if I kept my anger in the reception area.

"We're here," Ms. Jasmine informs us, her voice a little above a whisper, when we arrive at the hospital.

"I'll stay in the van with the kids," I say. "You guys go in and give Jenna my best. The kids don't need to see any of this. Just tell Candice, her little ones is out here with me, so she isn't worried."

"Are you sure? I can stay back with the kids while you ladies go inside," Mr. Derek offers.

"I think Ms. J needs you, Mr. Dee," I tell him.

A tear slides down Ms. Jasmine's face at the mention of this.

"Yes, she does." He cradles her.

"You know what? I think I will stay in the car and give you a hand," Tracy volunteers.

I stare at her. "A hand with what? Every last one of these kids is knocked out."

"Well, I'll keep you company. I don't think I can handle seeing Jenna like that. If they even let us in the room. Either way, I don't want to go in there. I'll fall apart, and that's so not what she needs right now."

"That makes two of us," I say as Ms. Jasmine and Mr. Derek step out of the van and close the van doors.

"I'm aching for Jenna right now, Simone," Tracy tells me when we are alone with the kids. "She was a virgin, for goodness' sake. Why would someone take advantage of her like this?"

"At some point, a lot of us had our innocence ripped from us, and we will never understand why these things happen. I think I would try to kill the person if I were to see them. All this has me on ten, and coming down is nowhere in sight."

"You're right. Each and every one of us shares the same pain, and it's the type of suffering that I wouldn't wish on my worst enemy. On another note, did you talk to Dr. Binet about all this killing and strangling you keep talking about doing? You're no longer a Nakita clone. You've bypassed her rage."

"Hell, I just picked up where she left off," I reply with a snicker.

"That's not funny, Simone. I hope you don't talk like this around Sage." Her eyes widen.

"I don't, because she's too impressionable right now. You can walk around, trying to mimic everything Candice does, thinking you have the answers to everything, because you're now following in her footsteps, going to school. She's not perfect, and neither are you. It's okay to get upset and not allow people to walk all over you. I am sure that televangelist that you two love so much would agree if you sat down and talked to him. Better yet, if it happened to his wife or daughter."

"No one ever said it was wrong to get upset and allow people to walk over anyone. You've surpassed being upset and have stepped into being enraged at any little thing. Your face is all flushed and tense just from this conversation. I didn't hurt you, Simone. I would never do anything to hurt you. I love you like the sister I never had."

"Would you please stop with the one-on-one interventions, Tracy? Please! Jenna was raped! That doesn't bother you at all? You're going to sit here and tell me that you're not the least bit upset? None of this triggered anything in you? You went through the same damn thing. How are you calm? I don't care how much therapy you've undergone or what you're learning in those textbooks. You're human. You cannot pretend like it didn't happen."

"I am not pretending anything, Simone." Her lip quivers.

"Look, I might have anger issues. It has gotten to the point where I actually recall or relive hurting Terianne the night of the funeral. Like I went back there and gave her exactly what she needed. If the police came and arrested me today, I'd probably plead guilty, because you cannot tell me I didn't carve her like an apple. However, with all that being said, I acknowledge what happened to me. After all this time, not once have you said your abuser's name or recounted what happened to you. I know I kept pieces locked away because I was hurting, but guess what? I talked about it. You need to talk about it. You're walking around diagnosing everyone when you're the one that needs a diagnosis. Did you even talk to Dr. Binet or another therapist about your rape?"

"Stop saying that," she squeaks, her voice shaky, as she reached for the door handle.

"Where are you going?"

"I can't sit in here."

"It's hot out there."

"I don't care," she says as she climbs out of the van. As she closes the door behind her, I hop out too.

"You have to talk about it eventually, Tracy," I say as I follow behind her.

"Why? I told Dr. Binet what she needed to hear. I don't want to keep reliving that time in my life. You already know what Paul and Anthony did to us. What more do you need to hear? Why is it so important to you? Do you want to hear it so you have another reason to become enraged? So you can dream of cutting up another person? Maybe Dr. Binet needs to have you put in inpatient therapy, like they did Nakita. It helped her. It might do you some good. You're a danger to yourself and Sage, judging by the way you talk."

"That was cute, what you just did. Now that I think about it, you always do that."

She looks back at me, her brows knit, then marches back over to the van so that no one sees us having this heated conversation. I follow her. "Do what?" she says.

"You deflect. Anytime the spotlight is on or near you, you spin it in another direction. Well, guess what? It's not going to work this time. And you might be right. Maybe I do need additional help . . . or maybe I don't. What I do know is, holding everything in is no longer eating away at me like a flesh-eating virus. I got it out. Now I will get the rest of this anger out, even if it means carving someone up, as you said."

"That's not funny, Simone. Stop saying that."

"If you talk, I'll stop."

"Why is this so important to you?" Tracy asks.

"Because you're important to me, and if something were ever to happen to me, I'd want you to care for Sage the same way Candice does for Adrianna."

"Nothing's going to happen to you. Don't say that." She dissolves into tears.

"Look, as you can see from what we've been through and now with Jenna, anything is possible. I am just being realistic, Tracy. Tomorrow isn't promised to us, nor is it scripted to be pleasant for us. We're living witnesses of that one."

"He was so much bigger than me, Simone. I was helpless. I tried pushing him off each time, but I knew physically I couldn't stop him. So, I stopped fighting and let him do whatever he wanted to do to me. I let it happen, so it's my fault. I cannot cry rape when I allowed it to happen. I knew it was wrong. He said I had to look out for him the same way he looked out for me. What was I supposed to do?" She pauses to wipe her tears with the backs of her hands.

After catching her breath, she continues. "Mom would never believe me. She didn't believe me with the previous boyfriend, who used to touch me. Do you know what she did then, Simone? She beat me instead. So why would I tell her that for a year, when I was between the ages of fourteen and fifteen, her new boyfriend had sex with me? He even went as far as threatening me, saying if I ever got pregnant, I would have to have an abortion. He said if I refused to, he'd beat it out of me, so I ran away. I couldn't kill an innocent baby when it was my fault that it was here. I went to the ER and told them I'd been raped and was pregnant and I didn't know who had done it. Neither did I have a place to live. That's how I ended up at Hope House," she says, still sobbing.

"Tracy, listen to me and hear me good. You were raped, just like you told them in the ER. He was a grown man. He had no business touching you, period. You didn't do anything wrong. He was wrong. He raped you. You did not consent to anything. Now, I am going to ask you the question you're always asking me. Did you tell Dr. Binet any of this?"

"No, because I didn't want them to say I was a liar."

"Why in God's name would you think that? That man messed your head up. He raped you, Tracy. You just said he was too big to fight. That's rape."

"Yeah, but I stopped fighting after a while."

"Did you tell him no? Did you ask for it? No, you did not. That is rape. Did you ever tell your mother?"

"In the beginning, yes, I told him no. I knew Mom wouldn't believe me. She said I never wanted her to be happy. When I told her about her other boyfriend, she confronted him, and he put us out of his house. Mom blamed me. Things between us were never the same after that. She hated me. She'd say, 'As soon as you're of age, I can live my life. We have to live here with my sister because your fast ass wants everything I have.' Why would I tell her anything after that?" Tracy took a deep breath to collect herself.

She went on. "She was happy when she met Calvin. At first, he was cool, almost like a big brother at times or even a father to me. Now that I think about it, it was a setup. He had a hidden agenda. Mom moved him in after three weeks of dating. Calvin jumped to my defense when mom was enforcing her law. He had a way of getting Mom to do whatever he said. When my friends would come over, Calvin would sneak alcohol to us. We loved him. We thought he was the most relaxed adult ever known. Everything changed when he pretended to work the night shift and sneaked back into the house through my window.

"It started on the weekends, when my best friend, Monica, would sleep over. Her mom did doubles on the weekends, which included overnights. She was never home. Of course, Calvin talked Mom into letting Monica stay with us on the weekends, since we were always at one another's house anyway. He'd come fully loaded with food and alcohol. As soon as we started feeling the alcohol hit us, he'd invite us to play spin the bottle. In this game, well, his game, with every turn, an article of clothes had to be removed. He'd touch himself while we removed our clothes. Later on, he graduated to feeling a part of our bodies with each spin. Eventually, he, of course, initiated physical contact. The first time he had sex with us, he made us hold hands while he took turns with us. It was the most humiliating and scariest time in both of our lives. After that, Monica stopped coming over and talking to me. She . . ."

"What, Tracy?"

"She hurt herself. It's all my fault. If I had said some-thing, she'd still be here. She kicked and screamed, but he covered her mouth. When she tried to run while he was on me, he hit her so hard that she passed out. I thought she was dead. After that, whenever he'd come through my window, I'd just lie there. I was so scared, Simone." Tracy looks like she is going to vomit.

"I am so sorry, Tracy."

"This is something you should have shared with me, Tracy," a familiar voice says behind me.

I turn around. "Oh my goodness. Dr. Binet." A rush of adrenaline consumes me as the blood drains from my face.

Standing behind us, as if she had appeared from nowhere, she scolds, "That's the problem. Anyone could have been here listening to you two and taken full advan-tage of both of you. I have been standing on the side of this van since you two stepped out of it. Neither of you had any idea I was here. Simone, you are in no place or condition to be talking about any of this or trying to help Tracy. You're in dire need of help yourself."

"I was being a friend," I retort.

"Neither of you need friends right now. You need ther-apy. You might need more than that, because something isn't working for you. I do my job one hundred percent. So it has to be you."

"That was cruel, Dr. Binet. I know what we need. However, I was what Tracy needed right now. If you were doing your job right, you would have known all this already. You're just salty because, without any training or a license, I did your job better than—"

Dr. Binet raises her hand and brings it down hard on my face. My cheek is on fire from the slap.

The sound of the slap echoes in my ears, and I lose it. "How dare you hit me!" I charge her.

"Stop it. Please stop it," Tracy pleads.

Simone, *get off* her! What in the world is going on!" I hear Candice scream as Mr. Derek yanks me off Dr. Binet. I didn't see them approaching.

"What the heck is going on? Where are the kids?" Ms. Jasmine asks, clearly upset by the scene that just unfolded.

"They're in the van, asleep." Tracy looks over her shoulder. "Well, they *were* sleep. Dylan and Darren are up now."

"Dear God, hopefully, they didn't see this fiasco." Ms. Jasmine rushes over to open one of the van's back doors. "Dr. Binet, you should be ashamed of yourself," she says as she jumps in the van. She pokes her head out. "I am not sure what's going on out here, and right now neither do I want to know. Jenna is in there, hurt. She needs us to be here for her, all of us. And you're out here carrying on like a bunch of animals."

"She attacked me. Don't you dare call me an animal, Ms. Jasmine. I am a highly decorated therapist. All you people need help," Dr. Binet replies, indignant.

"You people." I rush toward her again.

"Mommy, please stop it," Sage whines through the window, stopping me in my tracks.

CHAPTER TWENTY-EIGHT

Stolen Voice
Candice . . .

"Alonzo, something is going on with Brianne. I get she was upset because Jenna kicked her out of the room. That by no means gave her the right to attack Simone and Tracy verbally. It's like no matter what's going on, she has to be the center of attention," I tell him as I pace back and forth across the hospital waiting room, my phone pressed up against my ear. "Then, whether she's wrong or right, she tosses around the fact that she's a highly decorated therapist. From what I've seen this past year, she needs to be stripped of any and everything that is 'highly' and 'decorated.' They carried on like schoolgirls out there, in front of the kids. I am so disgusted with all of them. More so with Brianne. She doesn't deserve to be recognized as anyone's doctor. I am going to see if I can talk to someone. That woman is dangerous. Look what she's doing to Simone. Simone never acted like this. She is a new-age version of the old Nakita."

"I know you're upset, Candice. I want you to do me a huge favor and calm down. I need you to be there for Jenna. Right now she needs you. We can deal with the nutcase therapist at another time. Jenna is the priority, not her."

"You're so right. Thank you so much for taking the kids back to the house. How are they doing? Are they upset? I could barely talk to them after all of that. I was too emotional. Crying and sniffling all over them. Upsetting them even more."

"They're fine. I was honest and explained to the boys that Simone and Brianne were upset and they acted out their anger. I did let them know that, that is not the way you handle your emotions, and that if they ever find themselves upset, to take a moment to calm down. No one deserves to be hit, the same way they wouldn't like to be hit."

"You are an amazing man, Alonzo. I love you so much for being our protector and superman."

"I love you more, Candice. Now, do me another favor. Give Jenna a kiss for me and tell her I love her and I understand. I am going to hang up now. The boys are at each other's throat again. My pep talk must have run its course." He chuckles.

"Okay. I will call you later," I say and then disconnect the call.

Taking a deep breath, I head back toward Jenna's hospital room. Dad left with Alonzo. Jenna didn't want him to see her like this. She asked that everyone go except for me. Well, she wrote it down. The only time she has spoken since she got here was when she told Brianne to get out. No male nurses or doctors either. Dad's heart is crushed into a million pieces. He is trying to understand, because he wants to be there for her, but she won't allow it. He said the only way for him not to try to find Omarion—in order to teach him the biggest lesson of his life, as Dad threatened to do—was to try to occupy his mind by tending to the kids with Alonzo.

"Can I get you something, Jen?" I offer upon entering her room.

She shakes her head no in response as new tears cascade down her face.

Using the back of my hand to wipe her tears, I plead, "Listen to me, okay?"

She nods her head yes.

"If anyone knows what it feels like to have somebody reach inside your soul and to have it ripped away from you, it is me. Everything you're thinking I've thought, and I sometimes struggle with those thoughts to this day. It is like every pain and horrific thing imaginable coming at you that you all at once, and you can't even muster up the words to describe what is happening. You feel worthless, like you did something to make this happen, but you didn't, Jen. You didn't. You didn't do anything to deserve this. I am so sorry he did this to you." I climb into the bed with her and cradle her. "God in heaven knows I wish I could turn back the hands of time."

"I feel so dirty, like there is something wrong with me now. Can you tell that I've been raped?" she says, her voice faint, almost inaudible.

"No, Jen. No. You're beautiful. There's nothing wrong with you. No one can tell anything," I assure her, my voice cracking.

"He took my worth, my privacy, my confidence, and my voice. I am disgusted with myself. I'm just worthless."

"These feelings are temporary. You will get past this. I promise you will. Look at me. I am not all the way together, but I am better than I was. You will be too. I promise you will, Jen. I will make sure of it. You are not worthless. *He's* worthless."

"The damage is done. No one can undo it."

"God knows, I wish I could. But we will get through it. We cannot let any of this destroy us. I say *us* because we're in this together. You're not alone. We will face this head-on, and he will be punished for this. We won't stop until they put him under the jail," I tell her.

Emotional pain flows out of her every pore as tears race down both of our faces.

Unable to utter another word, considering I am tired of hearing my own voice, I drift deeper into the heartache. Right now, I am to the point where I am not sure I even believe what I just said to Jenna. So in silence, I hold on to her as if we are on a roller-coaster ride. Well, now that I am thinking about it, aren't we on one? I just want to know, When do we get off?

Closing my eyes, I silently petition my Heavenly Father. *Dear God, I know I am wrong for questioning you, and I ask for your forgiveness. Today is one of those days when life doesn't make sense. How can I be positive and uplifting when the world seems so unfair? Please help me understand, because I cannot comprehend how something good is supposed to come out of this. My sister is hurting, and I don't have anything left in me to console her. I'm to the point where I myself might even be inconsolable. This cannot be the life you destined for us to live. You're supposed to be a loving God, and yet nothing but hate has been poured into us. I am beginning to doubt everything. I want to understand. I want to see the brighter picture, but the only thing that has been displayed over and over is darkness.*

Suddenly the silence is broken. I am pulled from my prayer when the lyrics to Michael Smith's "Open the Eyes of My Heart" pierce the air. It's the ringtone on my phone. Bothered by the interruption, I slip my arm from around Jenna, who has fallen asleep, reach in my pocket, yank out my phone, and hurriedly answer the call.

"Hey, Ms. Jasmine," I whisper into the receiver.

"How is she?"

"She's asleep right now. She cried herself to sleep."

"Okay. I will call back, so we don't wake her."

I slip off the bed, making sure not to awaken Jenna, then head for the door. "It's okay. I am walking out of the room right now, on my way to the lobby area," I whisper.

"That poor baby. She was just getting herself on the right track, in the right head space, and that coward does this to her. I am so upset, I cannot think straight."

Taking a seat in the lobby, I confess, "Ms. J, I am beyond angry. I am not sure if I am angrier with Omarion or with God. Like, why would God let this happen to her? Why does this have to keep happening to us? Are we cursed or something? Is there a hex on us?" I break down.

"God loves you, Candice. He loves Jenna. I completely understand you feeling this way. I can't event fathom how something like this could happen. But keep in mind, we live in a cruel world, with a loving God. Some people are monsters, no matter how loving God is. No matter what, I know He will never leave you or forsake you, Candice. You cannot give up. It might look and feel like He doesn't love you, but I know you, if no one else, can attest that something good always come out of our suffering."

"How can I believe that? Where was He or His love when this was happening to Jenna? When it happened to me and the other girls? Honestly, right now, I feel the same way I used to feel while at Hope House. Hopeless and in doubt, thinking that God doesn't care about me or anyone else."

"I am so sorry, Candice. I don't have all the answers. I just know the faith I have in God. I know and believe He will bring you out of this and will continue healing those wounds of yours, as well as Jenna's. You know, that doubt you had at Hope House gave you the energy to do what you needed to do."

"I'm not understanding," I say.

"Doubt got you out of bed every morning. Doubt pushed you to go past the odds that were stacked against you, and doubt sent you straight to college. Doubt propelled you to be an amazing mom, friend, sister, and daughter to Dale, Derek, and me. So . . ." She sniffles. "If doubt was your muse to accomplish and overcome all that you have thus far, I cannot wait to see where it propels you to this time."

"I—I guess if you put it that way, you have a point. Thank you for being the mom I never really had, Ms. J. Blood doesn't make you a mother. Love does. The love you pour into us girls, who were once strangers to you, is the same love I pray I'll always have to give and pour into the kids."

"You're already doing it, Candice. You're already doing it, and I am so proud of you. You're so strong, whether you feel it or not, and that strength comes from everything you've witnessed and experienced. God in heaven knows I wish you didn't have to endure so much to become the amazing woman that you are, but you did, and look at you know. I love you, the girls, and all my grandbabies with everything in me. The moment you girls fully entered my life, my life was complete."

"I think I have to disagree with that, Ms. J." I giggle.

"Disagree? How is that?"

"I think Mr. Dee completed you. We had nothing to do with that."

"Hush, child. Derek was there long before you girls."

"Oh, I know. I remember the early morning strolls down the lovers' path back home. I saw you," I tease.

"You're too much. That was for you girls. After everything that you'd been through, my Derek didn't want to make you girls feel uncomfortable if you were to awaken in the night and see him there. It was too much too soon, so we opted to spend time at his place. You know, we were considering adopting right before we took in Micah. Now we have five daughters and ten grandbabies."

"Ten?"

"Yes. Samantha's twins make ten."

"Lord, I completely forgot. How are things with her?"

"She was in rehab but signed herself out. We have court the day after New Beginnings' grand opening for temporary custody of them. So keep your fingers crossed that everything goes well."

"I'll pray instead. That will go further than crossing my fingers."

"That's my girl."

"Ms. J, I think I am going to put the opening off for a little while."

"Why would you do that, Candice?"

"I want to be there for Jenna. I don't want to be focusing on that when she needs me."

"I am sure if you mentioned it to Jenna, she'd get upset with you for even considering it. You'll see."

"I'm not going to even mention it to her. That's the last thing she needs to worry herself about," I say.

"You won't have to. I know my babies, and although you two aren't twins and don't have the same mother, your blood is identical, and you two are one of a kind in many ways. Now, get back in there with her. I will check in with you when I get to your place."

"My place?"

"I am going to check on my grandbabies and give your dad and Alonzo a break. Now get in there and kiss my baby for me. Tell her I love her. I love you, Candice."

"I love you more, Ms. J."

CHAPTER TWENTY-NINE

Why Does It Hurt So Bad?
Jenna . . .

No matter how hard I try to relax, sleep will not come to me. I think I rested my eyes a little better in the hospital, at least up until my "rape kit." Filling out the paperwork was bad enough, but having swabs taken in areas where I never want to be touched again made me feel like I was being assaulted all over again. I thought I'd be able to sleep in this spare bedroom and be all right, but I was wrong. It is clear that it doesn't matter where I am, where I seek refuge, because my thoughts are always with me, and images from that awful experience have been engraved on my mind, to be replayed over and over again.

I wish I had never gone to Omarion's place. Why was I so stupid? Did my choice lead to my rape? This is all my fault. I stayed, when I should have left. Why was I so dumb? I should have just come here, like I had intended to do.

"Jenna, is it all right for me to come in?" Candice says as she peeks her head in the room.

"Sure. I can't sleep. I was just lying here thinking."

"Would you like to talk about it?"

"I know Omarion will get away with what he did to me. I hate myself so much for letting this happen."

"Jenna, you are the victim. You didn't *let* anything happen. You didn't do anything wrong. Omarion is to blame, not you. He's solely at fault. He took advantage of you and played your vulnerabilities against you."

"But I went to his place, Candice. I changed my clothes there. I put his sister's clothes on and slept in his home. I asked for it. It's all my fault."

Candice shakes her head. "One of the hardest parts in all this is beating yourself up. I want you to know you did not ask him to rape you, Jenna. You fought him off you. You told him to stop, and he didn't. That's rape."

"I did. I really tried to fight him, Candice, but he held me down. He turned into a monster. 'You're no fun, you confused slut.,' he taunted. I guess I fought a little too much, and that's when he hit me."

"I hope he rots in prison. He deserves to be put underneath the prison."

"Hopefully, he doesn't get off. I don't know what I'd do if he does. That'd really show it was my fault," I say.

"No matter what does or does not happen, it isn't, wasn't, and never will be your fault. I am going to retain the best lawyers money can buy if I have to. He will not get away with this. Enough is enough. We will fight until the last breath is in our bodies. Do you hear me? No one will get away with doing anything like this to any of us ever again. No more, Jenna.

"And I want you to know, even though it feels like it's your fault, the world is against you, and every harsh thing you have floating in your head, it's all a lie. It will get better. You have a support system like no other. The girls and I have been in the same confused, hurt, vulnerable, and angry frame of mind that you're in right now, and just like we are progressively healing and moving past it, you will as well. Dad, Ms. J, Mr. Dee, and Alonzo love you with everything in them. You are not alone in any of this."

"I know. I just need time. Right now I don't want to be around Dad and Zoe. I can't look at them."

"You do know they would never hurt you, right? They love you. Take your time with it all, and like I said, we will be here every step of the way." She pauses. "Do you want to sleep in my room with me? You know you love my bed."

"I do love your bed," I agree. "But I want to just lie here for now."

"Well, in case you change your mind, I will leave your side of the bed open for you."

"Thank you, Candice."

She kisses my forehead before leaving.

I remain in the spare bedroom, but time appears to get the best of me. I cannot sleep, no matter how hard I try. In the middle of the night, with my eyes closed, I try to force myself to sleep. But the snapshots in my mind of Omarion on top of me won't fade away. I've tried thinking of other things, and the only thing I can think of are the images I am trying to delete from my mind. Although I am trying to go to sleep, I am afraid to drift off. I'm sure that's why it's so difficult for me to do so. I thought Omarion was different. How could I have compared him to Alonzo? Zoe has never looked at me seductively or made me feel uncomfortable. We've slept in the same bed, I've had to change my shirt in front of him, and he never once made me feel uncomfortable.

Tears slide from behind my closed eyes.

I grab my cell phone, I search for Zoe's number and text him.

I know. And thank you.

He texts me back right away. I love you, Jen, and there's nothing you can do about it.

I didn't have the words to respond. I knew he'd understand what I was saying. I'll talk to my dad later, I decide. This is just an awful feeling. I'm so afraid. The pain is unbearable. It hurts so much. Dr. Kirby said that beast ruptured my hymen. I may or may not require surgery. I have to wait until my follow-up gynecologist visit to find out. If it's not necessary, I am going to decline, in hopes it heals itself. He prescribed antibiotics to reduce the risk of an infection. Right now, I have a tampon-like device, called a dilator, inserted in my broken vagina to keep the hole open as it heals. I was hoping he could prescribe something for the growing hole in my heart.

The most challenging part of all this is having to go to my place of work as a rape victim. I don't want anyone looking at me funny or treating me differently if and when I return. So many things have bombarded my mind recently that I feel like my head is going to explode. I despise taking pills, but they appear to be a part of my new life. Besides, this headache is going to take me out. I have to take something for it. Dr. Kirby also prescribed Valium and Motrin for the pain, considering I refuse to take anything stronger. My mind is weak right now, and I don't want to self-medicate my worries away, though I am in the lowest place of my life. I think sleep is really what I need right now. I am going to take this melatonin Candice left here for me. Supposedly it's a soporific.

Boom! A loud noise pulls me from my sleep just after I doze off.

Opening eyes, my heart pounds in my ears, and I open my mouth to scream, but I am unable to utter a sound. I find myself paralyzed too, unable to move, and then I see this menacing shadow hovering over me.

"Listen to me and hear me good," the shadow says, its hand over my mouth. I realize it is a woman. "I don't appreciate you rejecting me when I ran to your aid. I was nothing but good to you, and you push me away and embarrass me like that? How dare you! I am going to remove my hand. You better not make a sound."

I remain still, and she takes her hand off my mouth. But the moment she does,

"Dad . . . Alonzo . . . Candi—"I muster everything in me and shout, "Dad! Alonzo! Cand—" before she jumps on me and slaps her hand over my mouth.

Somehow Alonzo heard me, and he races into my room.

"I have had enough of you, Brianne." Alonzo tackles her to the floor.

"Dr. Binet! How did you get in my house?" I gasp.

"Get off me, you coward!" she yells as she fights Alonzo.

Suddenly Dad appears in the doorway.

"Dad, call nine-one-one!" I shout. "She broke in. Dr. Binet broke in!"

"How can I break in when I know where the key is? You invited me in," she screams, trying to break loose of Alonzo's hold.

CHAPTER THIRTY

You're Fired
Brianne . . .

"I am a doctor. I have patients who need me. I'm the hero. You crooked cops are not! I don't have time for this. I have to get to my patients," I say. Then I burst into tears and throw a fit as they attempt to handcuff me.

"Ma'am, we need you to calm down. And please stay still," one of the two officers says firmly as we all stand in the living room.

"*You* calm down. I am calm," I retort.

The other officer tightens the cuffs on my wrists.

"Loosen those things. You're hurting me."

"Ma'am, we need you to calm down," the first officer repeats.

Candice catches my eye. "Brianne, calm down and listen to what they're saying. You're making this harder than it needs to be."

"Shut your whining up, Candice. Now, one of you crooked officers, loosen these damn cuffs." I kick my foot back, and the heel of my tennis shoe lands in one of the officers' midsection.

"You just assaulted a police officer. You have the right to remain silent. Anything you say can and will be used against you in a court of law. Do you understand these rights?" The officer I kicked shoves me toward the front door. I can tell I angered him.

"I am not illiterate. I am a highly decorated therapist. Do *you* understand your rights?"

"Well, now you can decorate a jail cell," the angry officer tells me as he and his partner escort me to the squad car.

What have I done? I panic. "Mr. Officer, I am so sorry. Please listen to me. If you put my name out there, I can lose everything," I plead.

"It's too late for that. You should have thought about that before you broke into that home and assaulted my partner," the first officer tells me. "Now do us a favor and shut up." Then he opens the back door to the squad car, puts his hand on the top of my head, and I sink down onto the backseat.

"Don't you dare talk to me like that. I know my rights. Help! The police are assaulting me!" I scream from the backseat as I kick my legs.

"It looks like the shrink needs some shrinking herself," the first officer taunts.

"Brianne, this is serious. They're charging you with unauthorized entry, resisting arrest, and assault. What the hell happened?" my longtime friend and attorney, Deborah Tompkins, says.

"I didn't assault, resist, or enter anything unauthorized. I have no idea what they're speaking of. Maybe I blacked out, because I don't recall any of that."

"Listen to me and hear me good. This is serious. For heaven's sake, you attacked someone who was just raped! What in heavens came over you? I hope you know you won't be able to get around any of this with your psychotherapy. If you want me to help you, I need you to be honest with me about everything, if you plan on ever seeing the light of day again."

"Rape? She's not the only one that has been violated. I didn't hurt her. I asked her a few questions. That's it."

"Well, it is your word against hers, and you were in that house, unwelcome."

"I knew where the key was. Candice told everyone where it was."

"That's great, but did she invite you in at that time? And you said she wasn't the only one that was violated. Is there something you'd like to share with me? This could possibly help with your case."

"I really don't want to talk about it, Deborah."

"Maybe you didn't hear me clearly. You could be facing jail time. Jenna is pressing charges against you for attacking her. The owner of the home confirms Jenna's statement, and the officers put in their report that you assaulted her, kicked one of them. And to add insult to injury, everyone in the house confirmed these allegations."

"After all I've done for those ungrateful sons of bitches."

"Brianne! What has come over you? I have never seen you like this before. What's going on?"

"I don't want to lose everything. I've worked so hard for all this. They will take my licensure away from me. You have to do everything in your power not to allow that to happen. I don't care what you do. You cannot allow them to strip me of everything. Do you hear me, Deborah? You work for me. Now please do your job," I snap, coming apart at the seams.

"As your friend, you're scaring me."

"That makes two of us, and that's not good. I need you to be fearless and to save my livelihood. It's all that I have left. They took everything else away from me."

"*They*? Who is this *they* that you speak of, Brianne? Look, if you want me to do my job, I need you to help me. How can I stand before a judge and shed light on anything if you leave me standing in the dark? Now, please talk to me."

"So you can judge me? Everyone isn't equipped to handle the things I've gone through or the things I help others overcome. I'm a professional at all this, so I can handle it. I just need you to be the attorney you aspired to become and do your job."

"Maybe you need other representation, as it appears you're not comfortable being open and honest with me."

"While you were fulfilling your dreams in law school, I suffered from a mental breakdown. I underwent a significant amount of therapy, and yet the pain is still present. It appears no matter how hard you try, you never get over the loss of a child, especially when you're the sole cause of it. I struggle every day, wondering if it was negligence and if knowing who had fathered Sienna prompted me to be negligent. Either way, I cannot live with myself because of it. My practice is the only thing that has been my saving grace. So, as I have been saying, I need you to do everything in your power to save me from losing my other baby. My firstborn. My practice."

"Brianne, I am not a doctor, but it sounds like the last thing you need to be doing is to be worrying about and practicing anything right now. You're no good to yourself right now without the proper healing, so there's no way you'll be what any of your patients need at the moment. I am saying this to you as your friend."

"Right now I don't need or want you as my friend or my attorney. *Guard*! Please get this woman away from me. And, for the record, I've helped the woman whose house I was in, and she is doing great. I am a highly decorated therapist. An award-winning therapist. How dare you pass judgment?"

These past few days, I've learned the hard way that you have to be selective and cautious as to whom you consider a friend. Deborah is the last person whom I'd consider a confidante. She should be disbarred for violating attorney-client privilege. She petitioned the court about my case, saying it would be a conflict of interest if she stayed on as my attorney, and somehow she recommended that I undergo a mental health evaluation. Which is a barefaced lie, considering I fired her. How she was able to do this and not be stripped of her credentials to practice as an attorney is beyond me.

My new attorney, Jeffrey Scardingo, informed me Deborah did everything ethically and legally. He also suggested I take advantage of the opportunity to have a mental health assessment, as it could be vital to my defense in the case. He asked that I be open and honest, so that I can win this case and save my name. I wonder if he handed me a bag of bull. In any event, after I listened to the charges in depth, opening up to a court-appointed therapist might be my saving grace.

"Good afternoon, Brianne. Nice to meet you. I am Dr. Javier Reid."

"Nice to meet you. I am Dr. Binet."

"Excuse me. My apologies, Dr. Binet. Please have a seat. I am aware that you have been practicing for quite some time now, which makes you fully aware of how this works. So instead of trying to pick your brain to get you to talk, how about you try to take your Dr. Binet hat off and tell me about Brianne? I know it's tough being both, so tell me about it."

"Finally, someone that understands me. Usually, I decline male representation, whether its therapy or legal counsel. However, it appears I struck gold this time."

"Do you want to tell me why you decline male representation?" Dr. Reid asks.

"The men that I've encountered use their power as a man to diminish and belittle a woman in order to assert their authority."

"Do you mind elaborating?'

"I will get there. Don't you worry."

"Please continue."

"You know, I often describe myself as a high achiever who wants to do everything right. Because of my profession, I am aware of the early signs of depression. However, despite me knowing the signs, I ignored them when I exhibited them myself. For instance, I'd talk to patients about being depressed, how they're struggling with sleeping, and how waking up saddens them, because death appears more promising. As their therapist, I advised them to challenge their negative thoughts, and as a result, I have had great success stories with my patients.

"Naively, I thought I was immune to any mental challenges myself, and I didn't know I'd succumbed to depression the way that my clients have. That was the situation I found myself in several years ago. I thought I'd recovered from being raped by my husband's friend, up until I began seeing patients outside the facility I was practicing out of. Without realizing it, I crashed, and I have been in a sunken place ever since. All I ever wanted was for every person that caused harm to a woman sexually to pay for their sins. Death was my wish." I take a deep breath.

I go on. "I hate men because none of you can be trusted. The only reason I've opened up thus far to you is that I know it will help my case. If it weren't for this case, I wouldn't say a word to you. I'm sure if we weren't here, you'd try to use what I've shared with you against me and play on my weaknesses. That's all you cowards are good for. Because of the male species, I lost a child, and if I had my way, every one of you would pay, whether you committed the act or not. The simple fact that you're a man makes you responsible."

CHAPTER THIRTY-ONE

Enough Is Enough
Candice . . .

I have to say if it isn't one thing, it's another. Brianne put the icing on the cake. I am still speechless concerning her behavior. Honestly, I am just happy she is getting the help she needs, because this could have ended tragically. She could have taken her life, or someone else's, in the state that she's been in. I hate that she had to go to prison to get the help that she needs, although in the same breath, I'd say it is the best thing that has happened to her. The detective said they have her on suicide watch. She has been placed in a facility because of her mental state. Ironic as it is, we met her through the same type of facility. She was a fantastic therapist. Dr. Binet was a lifesaver for me.

That goes to show just because someone appears to have it all together doesn't mean they do. The ones that appear to have all their i's dotted and t's crossed are the ones that we should check on the most. My heart aches for her right now. I pray she gets the help that she needs. If and when visitors are allowed, I will go and visit her. I plan on going to her trial for support. She's going to need it. Maybe she would have gotten off a little easy had she not assaulted the police officers.

With everything going on, I was still able to work things out for the grand opening today for New Beginnings. Jenna has been here since being released from the hospital and has chipped in tremendously. She's the reason why I am going through with the opening today. It has helped her get her mind off everything that she's dealing with. I am grateful for this, because I've been a nervous wreck with everything concerning her. In actuality, focusing on the opening has been a distraction for me as well.

Dad and Alonzo have been on eggshells around Jenna. Both of them want to hurt Omarion badly and give Brianne a taste of her own medicine. Thank God they're allowing the courts to do their job. I don't think any of us could handle any more heartache right about now. It's bad enough the kids have been sleeping in the bed with Alonzo and me, thanks to Brianne's performance. She really did a number scaring them. Especially having the police officers escort her out of here in cuffs. This added to everything they appear to be dealing with.

I didn't notice how much Dylan's and Darren's behavior had changed until we got a call to come to the school because they'd been in a fistfight with two other little boys. Apparently, they'd been acting out in school for quite some time. If they didn't get their way, or if someone did something they didn't like, they'd respond physically. Their teacher said that they'd talk to them and given them time-outs, less playtime, and so on, and that this would calm them down, until something else happened. The problem that I have with all this is, Why did it take a fistfight for me to learn any of this?

When Alonzo and I spoke and met with the school social worker, Mrs. Hilton, she pointed out that when children think they are in danger, they may become sad, angry, or afraid. The only way some cope with those feelings is to engage in physical altercations. Confused as to where this was coming from, as I didn't understand why the boys felt they could be in any imminent danger, I asked 407 questions, until I received something concrete. It was as if she was beating around the bush or I wasn't asking the right question. I remember the conversation now.

"I understand that when a child feels they're in danger, they react to those feelings," I said. "However, what I don't understand is what danger the boys felt they were in. Is there a piece of this story that I am missing? If I am not mistaken, you said the altercation came about because the little boys called me ugly?"

Mrs. Hilton nodded. "Yes, that is what it stemmed from."

"Well, I am confused about how that would make them feel as if they were in danger. Oh no. Brianne and Jenna."

"I am unsure what you're referring to," Mrs. Hilton replied. "However, if the children have witnessed any type of conflict, when they act out themselves, they tend to mimic what they've heard or seen."

"We don't in any way exhibit any violence in front of our children. But a couple of our family members had an altercation. However, the boys were shielded from it all, and we had a long sit-down with them, where we explained right from wrong," Alonzo interjected.

"Research shows that when children see someone get hurt, it makes them feel unsafe," Mrs. Hilton said patiently. "Right now, the best thing you can do is work at showing them that they are safe by asking questions. Ask them what would keep them safe. Help them come up some with ideas. If at all possible, try to leave the place where the conflicts occurred. The beauty in all this is we are catching it now. I will work with you and your husband—"

"We're not married," I said, correcting her.

"We are not married yet!" Alonzo added, clarifying the matter.

"My apologies. As I was saying, I will work with you and your family and will provide you with the assistance that you need. Here's the name of a child and family therapist that I highly recommend." She handed us a business card.

"I never thought about it like that. I have Adrianna in counseling. I had every intention to do the same for the boys and Amiya, but I just never got around to it. Dear God, my poor babies. The last thing I ever want is for them to hurt or suffer silently," I said and broke down.

Needless to say, I didn't wait for us to get into the car before Googling and then calling Dr. Chambers. Looking at the testimonials on her Web site gave me the confirmation I needed that she was talented, and I called her immediately. We will have our first session next week, and I am eager to attend. In the meantime, Alonzo and I will practice the communication exercises that Dr. Hilton recommended.

Right now, my nerves are all over the place. The grand opening is an hour or so away. After everything that has transpired, although I'd love for my babies to be in attendance, Alonzo and I thought it'd be better for the kids if they stayed home today. Alonzo, Dad, and Ms. J offered to keep them occupied. At this point, the way things have been going, I'd prefer they missed this one. I don't want anything to go wrong. I'm just being cautious and protecting my children. You know, only in case something doesn't go according to plan. I want them with me. However; I don't trust having them here right now. Mr. Derek will be here, so that's just like having Dad and Ms. J in attendance. They're all one of a kind.

Alonzo gave me a silver heart locket necklace earlier today. He said that since they won't physically be there, whenever I feel nervous, I should clutch the locket, and it would ease my anxiety. That way, I will have them with me every step of the way. The necklace is engraved with the words *Always in My Heart*. When you open the locket, on one side you see this picture he and I took while we were lying in bed one day. On the opposite side, he paired it with a tiny photo of all four of our babies.

This isn't the official first day of business, but I have been advised that we're having a "soft opening." Honestly, according to Mrs. Bartlett, that is, Joanne, all this is, is an opportunity for me to meet the press, draw public attention, and become acquainted with our local officials, who will be conducting the ribbon-cutting ceremony. Joanne has gone above and beyond to make today a success. She assisted with advertising by sending press releases to everyone. Because of the negative press Hope House received when the community became aware of the reasoning behind Paul's arrest, the local community is excited about something positive coming from such a horrible place.

When the guests arrive, they will receive champagne and hors d'oeuvres up until the opening comments. I am a nervous wreck about speaking in front of everyone. But I wanted this. Just like the good book says, "To whom much is given, much is required." Following my opening remarks, Joanne will lead an hour-long tour of New Beginnings for our guests.

I am so excited about the tour. The playground came out fantastic. We also did such a tremendous job with the place. I am anxious to show it off. Each room has been set up like a studio apartment equipped with all the necessities. There are now four studio rooms on the premises. I want the girls to get used to having space for themselves in preparation for their unborn children. I think by having us in the same rooms after everything went left at Hope House, we became too dependent on one another and not self-sufficient, as we should have been.

Without question, there will not be any men living on the premises. When and if we need things done around the house, a local handyman that I've contracted with will assist. Background checks and fingerprints have been done on everyone that will step foot in this place, including everyone that I've contracted with. My job is to keep these girls protected, and I promised myself that I will do just that. I will do everything in my power to make sure I live up to that promise.

Well, forty-five minutes until showtime. I admire the woman standing in my master bath admiring the woman in the mirror before me. I have come a long way and am proud of who I am blossoming into.

"Candice, are you ready to knock them off their feet? You look beautiful," Jenna says, complimenting me.

"I'm as ready as I am going to get. My nerves are all over the place. You know, I am perfectly fine with you hanging out with Ms. J, Alonzo, Dad, and the kids. This might be too much for you, especially the speech that I have prepared, in which I share some of the things I've overcome."

"No matter what emotions I encounter today, the last thing I will allow myself to do is to miss this day. I haven't jumped off a bridge because of your strength. Don't get me wrong. I still cry myself to sleep at night, but something on the inside won't allow me to sink as low as my mind is leading me to go. I believe it's you. Your courage, strength, and humility are contagious. I pray one day I will be able to look back at all this and see the good that has come out of it. Because right now, every time my mind reviews what happened, I end up vomiting."

"Aw, Jen, you're making me cry. I love and appreciate you so much. Your pain is my pain. My strength is your strength. *We* have no choice but to get to the other side of all this together. I love you with everything in me. Always remember, no matter what, you are not in this alone, and it is not your fault. That coward is locked up where he belongs. I'm sorry. We won't waste our breath or energy any longer on thinking about him." I embrace her.

"I love you so much more, Candice." Then she shifts gears. "The girls are here."

"I guess it's time to get this show on the road." I grab her hand and lead her out of the room.

We run right into Tracy and Simone, who are being escorted around by Alonzo.

"Congratulations, Candice. Everything looks amazing," Tracy and Simone exclaim in unison when they see me.

"Thank you, guys. Where's Judith?"

"I haven't spoke to her. I suppose she's on her way," Tracy replies.

"I cannot fight back these tears. None of this would have been possible without all of you," I blubber.

"I don't know why any of us bothered putting on any make-up. We look like a racoon family right about now," Simone jokes.

"She's right, you do. But you're a good-looking racoon family, I must add," Alonzo jests.

"What's wrong, Alonzo? Are the . . . the kids all right?" I stumble over my words.

"I need you to do me a favor, beautiful. Please relax and calm down," Alonzo tells me.

"Aw," the girls tease.

"The kids are great. You're beautiful and great. You have an amazing sister, and amazing sista friends, as you call them, along with an untouchable and unstoppable support team. Everything is and will be outstanding.

Take a deep breath and exhale everything contrary to the spectacular day you're going to have today—"

The sudden ringing of the doorbell stops him in mid-sentence and instantly jangles my nerves.

"Who could that possibly be? They're early," I say, and my stomach churns.

"I'll get it on my way out." Alonzo kisses me on the cheek. "The world is yours. All you have to do is prove it to yourself."

I blush as Alonzo heads to the front door.

Less than a minute later, we overhear a male voice say, "Good afternoon. My name is Detective Stone, and this is my partner, Gloria Donovan. We're looking to speak with Simone Gibbs."

"Simone," Tracy whispers.

"I am Simone," Simone shouts as we make our way to the front door.

"Simone Gibbs?" Detective Stone says.

"I am she. How can I help you, Detective?"

"Simone Gibbs, we have a warrant for your arrest for the murder of Terianne Knowles. You don't have to say anything. Anything you say or do will be given in evidence," Detective Donovan announces. Then she cuffs Simone.

"Murder? She didn't murder anyone," I say in her defense.

"Are you serious, Officer? I didn't murder anyone. How could I? She lives in Virginia," Simone remarks, becoming frazzled.

"Simone, don't say another word. I am calling our attorney, Mrs. Bartlett's husband, right now. We will fix this," I tell her.

"Sage. I need to see my baby," Simone whimpers.

"She shouldn't see you like this. We will fix this. You'll be back, like nothing happened," I assure her. "This can't be happening right now. Please call whoever needs to be called and tell them the opening is being postponed," I add.

"You can't do that, Candice. Like you just said, I'll be back before you know it," Simone tells me. Fresh tears join the existing ones on her frightened face.

"I am in no condition to do this," I say.

"Do it for me. Do it for everything we've overcome," Simone urges. Her lower lip quivers as the detectives escort her out the door.

As the door closes, I lose it. "I can't do this. How can I when my sista friend was just carted out of here in cuffs? For murder. How?"

"Well—"

"Well, what, Tracy? Finish what you were going to say," I snap. I am fuming.

"I don't think Simone did anything. Well, at least I hope she didn't. I know I am not the only one who heard all the crazy things she's been saying lately. Especially the things she said she'd do to Terianne if she could. Candice, you saw how enraged she was at the funeral."

"Are you *crazy*, Tracy? Are you losing everything God gave you?" I exhale before continuing. "Let me calm down. How in the world could Simone have done anything of the sort if she's been here? Virginia is not around the corner, Tracy. They're wrong, and so are you. How could you even think something like that?"

"You have a point. But the police don't just come and arrest you from another state without probable cause. You don't have to be an attorney to know that."

"How about you do Simone the biggest favor in the world and not talk anymore to us or anyone else about this? If her freedom were left up to you, she'd be in prison," Jenna snapped.

Ms. Jasmine hurries in at that moment and tries to calm everyone down. "Girls . . . ladies, please try to settle down. Candice, right now you have no choice but to proceed with the opening. The guest, public officials, and community members are more than likely en route here. Derek is going to take me down to the precinct. Tracy, I need you to assist Dale and Alonzo with all the kids. Remember, we've been through worse, and just like then, we will see that there's nothing too hard for God to fix. He will show us His grace and mercy once again. Now, please do me a favor and clean your face up, Candice. It's your time to make us and yourself proud. We've come too far to turn back now. We will not give the devil the satisfaction or the recognition. Do you hear me, baby?" She tears up.

CHAPTER THIRTY-TWO

I'm Innocent!
Simone . . .

"I apologize. I got down here as fast as I could. I was on my way to New Beginnings when Jasmine phoned me. How are you holding up?"

"Mr. Bartlett, what is going on? I am falling apart. I didn't murder anyone. I've dreamed of hurting her. I know I did not touch her. Did I?"

"That's what you need to tell me," he replies as he loosens his tie.

"It's physically impossible. She's in Virginia, and we're in Connecticut."

"Where were you May twenty-first?" he asks as he takes a seat across from me at the table.

"May twenty-first? Isn't that the day of Mimas's funeral? Yeah, that was the day of Mimas's funeral. I was in—" My eyes widen, and I stop in mid-sentence.

"Were you anywhere near Terianne Knowles?"

I shake my head. "This isn't going to look good or even sound convincing."

"I am here for you and will do everything in my power to get you out of here. I cannot do that unless you're open and honest with me. I need you to tell me everything."

Dropping my face into my hands, I can feel the sweat on them against my flushed face. Shaking my head again, I murmur, "This can't be happening."

"This is serious, Simone. I need you to talk to me. Were you anywhere near Ms. Knowles?"

"Yes! Yes, I was. I attacked her at Mimas's house and at the service. I threatened her in front of everyone. I even wished death on her. I did not, and I repeat, I did not murder her. In my visions and dreams I did, but I know I didn't. Did I?"

"You don't remember?"

"The images in my head seem real. I just don't recall actually doing it, though," I reveal.

Mr. Bartlett leans forward a little. "I am not going to beat around the bush. You could be facing serious time. This is felony murder. Ms. Knowles was stabbed to death. Although the police do not have a murder weapon, they do have a sweater with your hair and the victim's blood on it. Have you ever seen this sweater?" He pulls a folder out of his briefcase and displays a photo of the sweater Mimas gave me as a gift. There are bloodstains on it now.

It feels like my stomach jumps into my spine. With tears blurring my vision, I confess, "Yes, that is my sweater. It was a dream. I thought it was a dream. I didn't think I actually did it."

"Tell me about this dream."

"I took the knife with blood on it from Terianne's face and wiped it on my sweater after Dr. Binet handed it to me. I had just carved Terianne's face as if I were peeling an apple. That was my dream. Pieces of that dream have been haunting me. There's no way I did it. I thought it was from the hypnosis. Even though I went only four times, I just thought it was from that."

"Ms. Knowles was found with multiple stab wounds at three-twenty-four Alexander Street at about one fifty p.m. eastern standard time on Monday and was declared dead half an hour later, according to local authorities."

"That's Mimas's address. And I wasn't there on Monday. We left on Sunday."

"She was found on Monday. However, she expired eleven hours prior," Mr. Bartlett informs me.

"There's no way I could have done it. I was in the hotel room with the girls. We stayed up talking all night long. None of us went to sleep that evening except Kathy. The reason I remember so vividly is that we painted her face while she was sound asleep. I didn't do this. My dreams and talks with Dr. Binet don't even mirror what you're saying. With the exception of the sweater. That probably played in my head because I lost it and she made a joke about me leaving it behind after I handled Terianne. I don't know. All this is making me feel and seem crazy. I didn't do that to Terianne. I wouldn't be able to function without throwing up just thinking about it. That's how I know it was just a dream or my mind playing tricks on me. Ask the girls. I was there with them. Yes, I wished death on her, and I even dreamed about it, but I didn't kill her."

Mr. Bartlett thinks for a second before saying, "I will speak to the girls. Who can vouch for you?"

"Candice, Tracy, Kathy, and I were up talking . . . until Kathy fell asleep. But Candice and Tracy will tell you, we stayed up all night talking, drinking wine, and watching television. In fact, *The Temptations* was on really late. It was my very first time seeing it. Actually, none of us had seen it before. It is what kept us up all night."

"This is good. I will have my team look into all this. This might be the piece or pieces of the puzzle that we need to get you out of here."

"It's the truth, Mr. Bartlett. I swear to you. I am not lying."

He waves his hand. "No need to swear. I believe you. What I need you to do now is tell me everything you recall from the hypnosis sessions with Dr. Binet."

"Just what I told you. Days after each session, pieces of me going to Mimas's house and attacking Terianne with a knife replayed over and over in my mind. Up until now I wasn't able to piece it all together, because I hadn't really thought about it. I believe Dr. Binet recorded our sessions. It will confirm everything I am saying. She even asked me questions while I was under. Yeah, she did . . . And that's when she made the joke about my sweater, now that I am thinking about it."

"This is good. Now, there's a hearing in the morning. I am going to see if I can find a loophole in the paperwork so you're not extradited, and then we will work our way backward."

"Extradited. What is that?"

"In English, because the crime took place in Virginia, the authorities want you in that state, but they cannot take you there legally without a court order."

"Mr. Bartlett, I cannot go back there. I did not do this. Please don't let them take me. Please help me," I plead.

"My job is to do everything in my power to see that you stay here and your name is cleared of any wrongdoing. I will do everything I can to make that happen."

"But how? If the Virginia authorities sent for me, isn't it a done deal?"

"My task at hand is to find a technicality in the paperwork, and I will do just that."

"What if that doesn't work, Mr. Bartlett? Oh, my God! They're going to throw me in some jail with criminals, when I didn't do this."

"I will petition the court to waive extradition, which would allow me a week or so to get this straightened out. Right now, I need you to try to remain calm and to get some rest. I know it's easier said than done. I just need you to try. I will get you out of here. I promise."

***

Mr. Bartlett is the best attorney hands down. He was able to postpone extradition. As crazy as it sounds, there was definitely a technicality in the paperwork. Thank God for miracles, and for God looking down on me, because the state of Virginia neglected to include the governor's authenticity certificate in the paperwork. I am now in the car with Mr. Derek and Ms. J, on my way home to my baby girl. Well, to Candice's. I cannot believe that all this happened and that Mr. Dee and Ms. J stayed at the precinct all night, waiting for me. They got to the court when I was being released.

CHAPTER THIRTY-THREE

The Confession
Dr. Binet and Brianne . . .

I cannot believe they have me in this shithole. After my session with the court-appointed therapist, I was placed in a hospital. How is this even legal or possible? Mr. Scardingo is on his way up here now. There's no way that they can expect me to stay here. I've probably counseled most of the patients here. These morons have the nerve to have me in a separate part of the facility. I know my rights; this unlawful imprisonment is illegal.

"Good day, Brianne," Mr. Scardingo says as he enters my little cell.

"You're late, Jeffrey." I roll my eyes.

"My apologies. I got held up in court today. But I have some good news for you."

"That's what you get paid handsomely for. Do tell." My mouth twitches as I try to fight a smile from forming.

"The court-appointed therapist found you to be mentally ill, too ill to stand trial or appear in court. He recommends you undergo competency restoration, meaning you take antipsychotic medication and attend therapy to stabilize you enough so that you're able to stand trial. On average, this process takes about three months. Which means you won't have to sit in a jail cell until the court proceedings."

The smile on my face dries faster than superglue. "Are you kidding me? I'm no rookie. I know how all this works. The courts send hundreds of people to mental hospitals. I am a member of the team that diagnosed these people and helped get them off. I don't need a drill. I create and implement the drills."

"I understand all of that. If that is the case, then you're aware that by the time this makes it to court, you'll more than likely have already spent more time locked away than the crime deserves."

"Tell me this, Mr. Know-It-All. What happens if you fail at this and I am declared mentally fit?"

"The charge—"

"Don't bother to answer. I already know what would happen. They'll send me straight to jail," I say.

"I can assure you that will not happen. I will not fail."

"You're also the same person who came in here thinking he had good news."

Think, Brianne. Think fast. You need them to declare you mentally ill and unstable. You already know how to beat those charges and resume your normal life. You'll be practicing and seeing patients in no time.

"Listen, Brianne. I understand you know the process. However, as your attorney, I can assure you this is a good thing. Do you understand? Brianne?"

It's showtime, Brianne.

After repositioning myself, I sit silently, motionless. Mr. Scardingo repeatedly shouts my name. I gaze into the far distance, at an imaginary fixture in front of me. Then I release all the pent-up hysteria and let loose in a fit of choking and sobbing, a fit so powerful in its intensity that it shakes my body violently.

"Would you like me to get someone? Are you all right? Brianne?" He begins to panic. He jumps to his feet and steps over to the door. "Guard? Someone, please come and help her," he calls.

"Tiny robots have been implanted under my skin to control me. I was going the extra mile for my patient. That's what real doctors do."

He looks back at me. "What are you saying, Brianne? You're not making sense." He turns his attention back to the door. A guard is now standing on the other side of it. "I apologize. Never mind," he says, dismissing the guard.

"It was a form of final humiliation. She humiliated me at the funeral. I mean my patient, and I did what any doctor would do."

"Who is *she*, and what are you speaking of, Brianne?"

"I made sure Sienna . . . I mean Sage . . . was asleep. The girls stayed in the other hotel room. It gave me the perfect alibi."

"Alibi?"

"Please just hear me out. Everything that I have done has been for the recovery and healing of my patients. I hadn't planned to hurt Terianne. When I attacked her, she didn't look like the person I met the day before. I saw Chuck. She was no longer a woman. It was Chuck.

"After putting Sienna . . . Sage . . . to bed, I got into the car and drove over to my house. I couldn't find my key, so I knocked on the door, hoping Mason was home. His car wasn't outside, and there was another car out front, which I didn't recognize. In any event, I knocked, and an almost familiar voice that I'd heard before invited me in. When I stepped inside, I didn't see anyone, and I made my way to the kitchen area, where noise was coming from. Then I saw her . . . him, and she said, 'What are you doing here? Aren't you Simone's friend?' And I said, 'How do you know Simone, Chuck?' Well, she stared at me like she had no idea what I was talking about, and then she said, 'Who is Chuck? Get out of here, before I call the police.'

"I yelled, 'You raped me, you bastard,' and I grabbed the knife off the cake dish on the counter. Using all my might, I swung and connected with him until he lost his balance. Once he did, I made sure to stab him in the neck, knowing that'd stop him from existing. Noticing I'd accomplished the task at hand, I ran upstairs and found a dress. I ran back downstairs with it, then removed his garments and dressed him in the black sequin dress. After turning him over, I cut holes in the back of the dress, exposing his buttocks. That was the final and ultimate humiliation for him after what he'd done to me. But as I was admiring my work, I no longer saw Chuck. Terianne was lying lifeless on the floor.

"It dawned on me at that moment, the only way I was able to assist my patient with finding closure was to make the abusers pay for their sins."

CHAPTER THIRTY-FOUR

The Proposal
Alonzo . . .

Despite everything that has transpired this past week, including in the moments right before the opening, it looks to be a huge success. Tracy persuaded me to leave the kids with her and Dale. I am glad I listened to them. I came in right on time. My beautiful bride is about to speak.

When she steps up to the podium and everyone applauds, I call, "The world is yours."

She clears her throat, exhales, and begins to speak so eloquently. "I am going to share with you why you're here and how New Beginnings came about. If you're not already aware, I am Candice Brown. My goal today is to give you my position on helping women, both in this room and outside, so that you better understand the issues of sexual violence against women and teenage pregnancy.

"At the age of fifteen, I became pregnant, and my biological mother threw me away. She sent me to Hope House from the confines of her hospital bed. Hope House was supposed to be my source of solace. I had no idea what motherhood entailed. Ms. Nancy and Ms. Jasmine gave instructions on the fundamentals of motherhood, which helped prepare me and my house sisters for this lifelong journey. However, nothing compared to being and becoming a mother. I cannot imagine going through life without the emotions that come along with motherhood. There are days when I feel as though I can conquer all that life has to offer with my children in tow. And then there are days when I want to run away and question every decision that I have ever made. Feeling it all, the good and the bad, gives my life purpose. I know I would not have been able to overcome the obstacles and setbacks of motherhood and the life I was handed without the sisterhood from my house sisters.

"As a teenage mom, you're left feeling alone, ashamed, and unsure of yourself. But all of that subsides when you realize that you're not alone, that there are other teen moms just like you, and together you can see and help one another through the challenges set before you. Teen pregnancy rates remain high, and no, we cannot save and help every teen mom. However, we will try to help as many as we can here at New Beginnings.

"At the outset, when I decided to reconstruct Hope House and transform it into New Beginnings, there was some backlash. I thought carefully about whether I should speak about this today, and it was the negative comments and outlook that motivated me to do so, because there is still censorship with sharing and talking about these things." She exhales and fiddles with her locket before proceeding.

"My first night at Hope House, I was sexually assaulted. It left me very ashamed. Even more embarrassed than I was before my arrival. I couldn't process what I did to deserve any of it. I questioned God's love for me, along with posing a host of other questions. You'd think that it would have prompted me to seek help. However, after sharing what happened to me with my house sister, she helped me see that this was the new normal. Where were we to go? Even when we tried to leave, everything backfired on us. We were stuck, confused, and afraid.

"After years of abuse, we finally stood up for ourselves. In standing up, we . . . I attended therapy and learned I did nothing to deserve what happened to me or to make any of it happen. This caused me to want and make change, which is where New Beginnings came into focus. Just like I did, my house sisters received a new chance at life. I want to be able to afford other single mothers the opportunity for a new beginning. At New Beginnings, we will ensure safety, stability, and success stories for all our teen moms.

"Lastly, I urge everyone to stand up for each other. We have to be courageous and fearless. No matter what happens in your lives, I encourage you to speak up when things are wrong. Don't live in fear. There is always a way of escape. It doesn't seem like it when you're in it, but I am living proof that there is a way out. We have to unite together! Today I, Candice Brown, can boldly say that I am not scared. I am not a victim. I am a survivor. And we will birth survivors and conquerors here at New Beginnings. Thank you for listening."

The crowd explodes in whistles, cheers, and applause, and Candice leaves the podium without a dry eye in the room.

I have never been prouder of her. She did an amazing job. Hopefully, my surprise will seal the deal, making this day one of the best days of both of our lives.

Following Candice's heart-wrenching speech, Joanne gives the guests a tour of New Beginnings while Candice cries her eyes out in front of me.

"I did it, Alonzo. I did it. I didn't hold back. I spoke up for all of us. For Simone and Nakita. We are not victims. I am not a victim. I shared my story, and I feel good about it."

"You did an amazing job. I recorded you, so you, Ms. J, your dad, and the girls will be able to listen together. They will be so proud of you, just like I am."

"Thank you for being here for me. When I saw you, it made everything easy for me. I could not have done it without you. I love you so much, Alonzo."

She wraps her arms around me.

I kiss her lips and take this as my cue. After breaking our lip-lock, I drop down on one knee.

Looking up to her, I say, "I found the source of my smile the day we reconnected when I found you at Jenna's. Will you let me be the reason for your smile? You are the one. You are the one I want to spend my every waking moment with. With you and our beautiful babies, my life is complete. I want to grow old with you, Candice Brown. Your dad gave his blessing. Now please make my heart skip another beat. Will you do me the honor of being my wife?"

With tears on her face, she replies, "Yes. I would love to marry you."

I was so nervous before I proposed that I was sick to my stomach. Not nervous about whether she would say yes, but nervous because the proposal included asking her in front of our guests. By the time I kneeled down, everyone was making their way back downstairs. It was too late to change my mind, and besides, Candice's eyes were already about to pop out of her head. But I just felt a sense of calm right before popping the question. Being with Candice is fated; it feels like destiny!

When she said yes, I shed a tear!

A Year Later . . .

CHAPTER THIRTY-FIVE

Life Goes On
Simone . . .

This past year has been one for the books. I am still having trouble digesting the fact that Dr. Binet stabbed Terianne to death. I went to visit her six months ago, and it made me sick to my stomach. Just thinking about it now gives me chills all over again.

As soon as the front door opened, my stomach rattled. After entering, I was prompted to sign in and to deposit my coat in a bag to be placed in a locked room. As I followed the herd of visitors shuffling down the hall, my nerves switched into overdrive. What kind of place is this? *I wondered. I nervously eyeballed my surroundings. The place had the look and vibe of one of those haunted insane asylums that you'd see in an old scary movie. Possibly worse. It was depressing in there.*

After I entered the visiting area, I looked around in search of Dr. Binet. A smile played on her face when she spotted me. Unsure of what to do when I reached her, I let an awkward hello slip from my lips. She, in turn, greeted me with a kiss to my forehead. Then we both took a seat. The woman before me did not look like Dr. Binet or the Brianne that I once knew. She appeared to be heavily medicated, with vacant eyes. Her hair was greasy, and she looked as if she'd been wearing the same black dress for days. There were stains everywhere.

"Sienna, you're growing up to be such a beautiful woman. Thank you for visiting Mommy at work," she half mumbled.

"I'm Simone, Dr. Binet."

"I know you're upset with me for leaving you in the car. You don't have to pretend anymore. I will make it up to you." A lone tear rolled down her face. "I'm so sorry. I never meant to hurt you, Sienna. I need you to forgive me."

With matching tears now streaming down my face, I played along, "I forgive you."

"That's my girl. Mommy loves you."

I forced myself to smile.

"I have patients coming soon. We can have lunch, and then you'll have to be on your way, princess. This is going to be another all-nighter. They're shorthanded."

Trying to knit together a conversation from the tangled comments that emerged from my lost and confused doctor friend, I did the best I could to pretend all this was normal.

Next to spending the night in a cell, and having my youth stripped from me, that visit is by far one of the scariest moments of my life. I pray for Dr. Binet every day. I wouldn't wish what she's going through on my worst enemy. No one can pass judgment. None of us can say what we would have done or how we would have handled losing a child. Especially when the child's death is a result of our own negligence. I personally wouldn't be able to live with myself if I harmed Sage.

Today we're helping Judith move back home. That whole situation with her entailed another nerve-racking day. It just so happened to be the morning I was released from the holding cell. After picking up Sage from Candice's, we went to brunch, and while eating and celebrating Candice and Alonzo's engagement, like clockwork Ms. J received a frantic call from Judith. Of course, since we were in a celebratory moment, Ms. J answered on the speakerphone. It wasn't too loud that it disturbed the other patrons. But it was loud enough for us to hear.

"Hold on a second. It's Judith. Hey, Judith. You're missing the celebration. Where are you? Yesterday was another one for the books. Despite it all, it turned out fantastic. I'm still struggling with holding back my tears," Ms. Jasmine said.

"Sorry I couldn't make it to the opening. I was in the emergency room with Chandler."

"Oh no. Is he all right? What happened to him?"

"I—I walked into the bathroom and—"

"Where are you? We're on our way," Mr. Dee said, cutting her off.

"I'm at the house. No one's here, so I phoned," Judith added.

Cutting our brunch short, Dale paid the check as we scurried, the kids in tow, and made our way to the cars.

Upon reaching the house the three of us once shared in record time, everyone took a deep breath. Then we all entered.

"Where's my grandbaby? Is he all right? What happened?" Ms. J called, her voice shaking.

"I'll take the kids to the playroom," Dale volunteered.

"I will give you hand," Alonzo and Jenna volunteered in harmony.

Judith appeared. "He's fine. He's in the playroom. I didn't mean to frighten you. I was giving Chandler a bath, and he began fussing about his water gun, so I left for five minutes tops. When I returned, Elliot was leaving the bathroom, zipping his pants. I freaked out and rushed straight to the ER with my baby."

"Jesus, no!" I covered my mouth to prevent myself from screaming.

"Thank God he didn't touch him. He was just using the restroom. I panicked," Judith went on. "How could I have been so dumb and have moved my son in with a man I don't even know and clearly don't trust? I am so sorry for fighting all of you when you were trying to make me see the truth."

"No need to apologize. We are just relieved nothing happened to you or Chandler," Candice responded and hugged her.

"Is it safe to say the honeymoon is over and you're moving back home?" I jested, observing all her bags on the living-room floor.

"Yes, Mrs. OCD. And guess what? I put some of my bags in your room, for old times' sake."

"I have missed your sloppy butt so much," I told her and we embraced.

So our prodigal sister is returning home, and she has decided to undergo extensive therapy. She and Elliott have agreed to take things slower. He refuses to give up on her. They're attending couple therapy sessions as well. Not only are Judith's love life and emotional state in a better place, but her desire to reconnect with her family has also been fulfilled.

Judith and her siblings were separated from their mom when she was younger. Her mother, Cindy, was a single mom of three who balanced a job and school in an attempt to make a better life for her children. Because of an outstanding car loan payment, her car was repossessed. A year or so later, her paycheck was garnished $383.00 biweekly. As a result, she lost her home. Unable to move or even afford a new place, Cindy was forced to separate her family. The two younger kids were able to stay with her. Judith was sent to live with her grandmother on her father's side. Long story short, Judith's stepbrother Eddie raped her and impregnated her. No one believed her rape story, and in turn, Judith's grandmother shipped her straight to Hope House.

Elliott has a private investigation firm, and as a birthday present, he reunited Judith with her family. Talk about weeping. When her family showed up at the house, we cried so hard that each and every one of us had trouble breathing. Candice, the angel from God that she is, purchased Cindy a house here in Connecticut, and they're moving into it today. It has been converted into a mother-daughter home. Judith's siblings are married and have children, and they are here for a couple weeks.

As for Tracy and me, after everything that transpired with Jenna, Dr. Binet, and me spending a night in prison, we were in desperate need of a vacation. Neither of us had ever been to the Big Apple, and we thought it'd be the perfect place to go. We were anxious to get out of Connecticut. Without question, we fell in love on our first visit. The museums alone were everything. There are a dozen different museums there. The best one for me was the American Museum of Natural History. Tracy and I are natural history fanatics; the dinosaur skeletons on display were everything to us. Let's not forget Central Park, the Statue of Liberty and, oh my God, Times Square. Our hotel was in Times Square. We can now say that we understand why New York City is considered one of the most sought-after vacation destinations. And Times Square has everything from cafés and eateries to theaters and shops within walking distance.

On the third week of our vacation, Mr. Dee and Ms. J came into the city, because we had raved so much about the place. They took part in the daytime activities, and for the first time in our lives, Tracy and I took advantage of the nightlife. That was how we met Ethan and Evan. They're handsome, chocolate single fathers. Sadly, seven years ago their wives had a girls' night out and never made it back home. Both of the women lost their lives in a horrific accident.

Ironically, the four of us were out vacationing in New York to escape our everyday lives and hadn't been out in God knows how long. Well, for me and Tracy, it was a first. The last time Ethan and Evan enjoyed New York City's nightlife was before they lost their wives seven years ago. After meeting them, Tracy and I ended up extending our vacation, which resulted in us now having a live-in nanny. Candice hired one for herself and thought it'd be a great present for us while we were on vacation. Tabitha, our nanny, accompanied us on our long New York vacation. We trusted that she was a perfect match, given the screenings and standards that Candice and her team adhered to.

Who would have thought that a year later, Tracy and I would move to New York? With the help of our new best friends, we purchased houses in Roosevelt, Long Island, a block away from each other. We can talk and see one another from our backyards. We'd been here for only a month before we had to fly back to Connecticut to help Judith move. It had been hard leaving Connecticut and the only family that we've known; however, it was long past time for us to grow up and move on. Not to mention, Ethan and Evan now live in New York as well. They had houses in New Jersey. In hopes of climbing out of the slump they've been since losing their wives, they decided to relocate. The evening we met them, they were celebrating the closings on their new homes.

Although the four of us have been friends for only a year, we've grown very fond of one another. We are taking things slow, and our kids have had several playdates with their girls, Ella and Bethany. Our boys love them. I just hope Ms. J and everyone else takes to them the same way that Tracy and I have. They're all here in

Connecticut now. We invited them for dinner to meet our family. Ms. J has a dinner party planned for everyone to attend tonight. It is going to be a full house. Thank God the weather is nice. I don't think all of us would be able to fit inside the house. Her yard is enormous. Actually, the perfect fit for our family reunion and meet and greet.

Ms. J has been taking cooking classes and has decided to go French for this dinner party. When I walk outside minutes before the guests are supposed to arrive, I peek at the food on the long table. Everything looks great. I just want to know, Where's the chicken or maybe some macaroni and cheese? In any event, it looks so pretty out here.

"Um, Ms. J?" I say when I walk back into the kitchen.

"Yes, baby?"

"I just wanted to know, Is there any American food? Better yet, any soul food? I came home looking forward to a belly-aching home-cooked meal. You have winter salad in the spring and veal, Ms. J. What happened? What did Mr. Dee do? Why do we have to suffer?"

"If you don't carry yourself outside . . ." She cracks up. "There are two themes and menus. It wouldn't hurt you not one bit to try something new."

"I only saw one theme and menu."

"Keep looking. Better yet, go and answer the door. I believe your friends are here."

"Tracy? They're here," I yell. Then I turn to Ms. J. "How do I look?" I ask her.

"Why in God's name are you hollering?" Tracy says from the far corner of the kitchen. "I am right behind you."

"I didn't see you."

"That's because your blind behind was in here complaining, knowing Ms. J would not have a dinner party without her famous fried chicken."

"Thank God for that."

"I believe you two were waiting for these handsome men," Jenna says as she leads Ethan and Evan into the dining area.

"Ye-yes, we were," I stutter as I step from the kitchen into the dining area.

"A year later and I am still taking your breath away," Ethan teases.

"No."

"Yes." He kisses me on the cheek.

Grabbing him by the hand, I introduce him. "Ethan and Evan, this is my Ms. J. Ms. J, this is Ethan and Evan."

"Nice to meet you two. I've heard so much about both of you. But something is missing," Ms. J remarks as she walks up to the two men.

"What's that? I swear I bathed," Evan tells her, clowning.

"I see why these girls are head over heels for you two. But where are your little ones? I was looking forward to finally meeting them."

"They're with our mom. We wanted to have some alone time with the girls, without the kids, on this trip," Ethan explains.

Without question, everyone is quite fond of Evan and Ethan, almost as fond as Tracy and I are. Other than playdates, we haven't been on any actual dates. They wanted to surprise us this weekend and take us out on our first date.

CHAPTER THIRTY-SIX

The Road to Recovery
Jenna . . .

Today, a little over a year later, I now know and believe it wasn't my fault. However, I also know it wasn't a smart move for me to stay at a stranger's home. Although I had looked up to Omarion as a friend, he was no friend. At the time I didn't know Omarion, the rapist, that well, yet I trusted him. The problem was, even though I knew it happened to people—hell, it had happened to my sister and the rest of the girls—I had naively thought I never could be raped. I guess I had removed myself from the reality of what had happened to Candice and the girls. I had never put myself in their shoes. I hadn't been able to imagine going through any of that and must have believed it couldn't happen to me.

Rapist has always seemed like a bad word to me, but I've replaced his name with *the rapist*. He took so many things away from me. I can't say that one is more painful or shocking than the other. He raped my head more than my body. The most challenging part was extinguishing my damaging thoughts. I had relived what he said and did to me so many times.

And to think he started off by instilling so much confidence in me and other women that attended group. He boosted our self-esteem. But Omarion, the rapist, had everyone fooled. He looked and acted like a nice guy. He always smiled and was helpful. It was clearly part of his act, and a successful act at that, because once news got out about his arrest, five other women came forward and admitted to having been sexually assaulted by him. They believed it was their fault, just as I had. Well, he won't be seeing the light of day for a long time. He needs to rot in jail. I wasn't mentally ready to attend the court proceedings right after I was raped, as it was too soon for me. But I will be at every hearing in the future and will protest if the authorities think about releasing him.

No, I have not fully recovered from the assault, but I am in a better head space than I was before. I ended up having to go inpatient for thirty days. Just thinking about the day that led to my therapist, Jahnice Fahey, making that decision frightens me. I thought I was doing well, considering. I did the best that I could by hanging on to Candice's courage and strength. Living in denial was what I was doing. It took years for her to become who she is today. Time was what I needed, but I didn't see it that way at the time.

When I learned of Candice and Alonzo's engagement, that's when everything hit me like a flood. I envied her for moving on. I still felt I deserved what had happened to me. I continually beat myself up over it, to the point where I felt numb. I remember one day in particular that was especially bad.

You cannot relate to Candice. You're not her, *I kept thinking*. You walked right into your rapist's bed. This is all your fault. You deserved it. You teased him, you confused slut. *My numbness went up a notch.*

"Auntie Jen, can you help me with this puzzle?" Amiya asked, pulling me from my thoughts.

Trapped in numbness, I opened my mouth to respond, but I couldn't locate my voice. Instead tears communicated what I was battling on the inside.

"Hey, princess. Let Daddy see that puzzle," Alonzo said, coming to the rescue.

I could feel the breakdown coming, and I wanted to prevent it from showing up now in front of the kids, so I dashed upstairs and climbed into the linen closet, tripping over a hanger. I could not let anyone see me like this. I tried to hide it from them. They could not find out that I was falling apart, I reached down for the wire hanger that I had tripped over. As I closed the closet door behind me, a safety pin caught my eye.

You can't even keep it together in front of the kids, *I told myself. I scraped my arm with the safety pin.* No, that's too easy. You're trying to ruin those kids and confuse them, just as much as you are. That's why Camilla stopped you from watching over the kids. *I beat my arm with the hanger.*

The linen-closet door opened.

"Jen! Please, no, stop. Dad, come quick," Candice sobbed.

Dad and Candice drove me straight to the emergency room. I was admitted and moved to the psychiatric floor and placed on suicide watch. It was most definitely what I needed at the time. I was no good to myself and a danger to be around, especially for my nieces and nephews. While an inpatient, I learned so much about myself and was able to focus on my needs in order to move beyond the rape. Yes, it happened, and no, it was not my fault. I am no longer a victim. I am a survivor. These are my daily affirmations that I tell myself. I no longer allow negative thoughts to lie dormant in my mind. I have pushed them out altogether.

I am still a work in progress and am taking one day at a time. I've recently moved back into my condo, in hopes of making a full recovery. While in the hospital, one of the residents looked familiar to me. I thought it was the medications, as they sometimes made me drowsy. It wasn't the meds. I was right. My mind wasn't playing tricks on me. Right in the room adjacent to mine was Camilla. How she had ended up here, of all places, was beyond me. The last time we heard, she'd moved with the girls to Ohio. That was a very spooky day when I recognized her as a fellow inpatient.

"Camilla? Is that you?" I whispered from the doorway.

Her beautiful skin was now wrinkled, and she'd aged badly. Could it be drugs? She looked awful.

"Don't you stand there staring at me like I am some kind of exhibit. It's the fault of you and that father of yours that I am here. I tried to find you two when they took my girls away from me. They had the nerve to say I, Camilla Brown, well, Marcellino now that I am no longer with your no good father, was unfit to be a parent. So I had a couple of drinks and couple lines of coke. What was I supposed to do? My husband left me, and my boyfriend tried to take my girls. I bet they won't try to touch me again. I almost bit the ear off that lady at the hospital you work at. You two did this to me." *Saliva leaked from the side of her mouth.*

At that moment, I had so many emotions, so much hurt, pain, anger, sadness, and confusion swirling in my head, that it was hard to sort it all out and think straight. To avoid slipping deeper into despair, I notified one of the nurses, and I was immediately moved to another facility.

Upon my release, I shared the news with Dad and Candice. He is working it out in the courts to gain full custody of the girls. Knowing that there's a possibility for him to reunite with my twin sisters, Casey and Cassidy has him beaming from ear to ear. I am excited about it as well. After everything that I've been through, this is so what I need.

As I continue making progress and embracing my life, I must accept and confront the pain no matter how hard it is. One day at a time, but I know I got this. I've been attending church on Sundays and talking to God more. I never grew up in church, but I remember all the things I'd heard people say about God and who He is to them. I've even attended a few of Candice and the kid's living-room televised services. But that hasn't made me want to attend church, or pray daily, for that matter.

See, I still cannot reconcile the fact that God was not there for me when I really needed Him. And this became clear to me on one particular night. Though I still have trouble falling asleep, this night, exhaustion got the best of me and I drifted off to sleep. I remember Candice waking me from a nightmare.

"No! Please stop! Get off me!" I yelled.

"Jenna, it's me, Candice. No one's here. Open your eyes. It's me." She wiped the tears from my eyes.

"I had a vision of him standing over me, with a knife this time. I hate that this fear is controlling my entire life."

"I know exactly how you're feeling right now, and I am so sorry. Would you like me to lie in here with you?"

"No, I will be all right. I have to get through this eventually."

"I'm just down the hall if you need me. Remember, God loves you, and He has not given us the spirit of fear. I know that sounds crazy right now. But He does love you, and He will bring you through. Talk to Him." She left the room and closed the door behind her.

"Talk to God? Is she crazy? Where was He when Omarion sexually assaulted me? What's today? Saturday, right?" I said aloud, though I was alone in the room.

I got up out of bed and looked at the Winnie the Pooh wall calendar.

"Good. Tomorrow is Sunday. I am going to talk to God, all right."

Well, after getting up before everyone else the next morning, I showered, dressed, and headed down to the church house. Of course, everyone was decked out in their Sunday best. I made my way in, then greeted the usher and had her escort me to the second row. I was early, so there were plenty of seats to choose from. Apparently, that was the first a.m. service and there usually isn't a large crowd that early.

I remember the pastor making his way to the podium. And I remember his words, more or less.

He said, "Good morning, people of God. Today I struggled with a message. I have one written, one that I prepared this week. However, while in my study, God dropped a message of healing those hidden wounds in my spirit. The scars that I am talking about aren't cuts and scrapes you might have received from a fall. He wants me to talk about those hidden, deep, unseen wounds. The memories of abandonment, abuse, and insecurity, all of which cause pain, like wounds."

This isn't how this was supposed to go, *I thought to myself as tears flooded my face.*

"These wounds are not seen, because bodies of flesh cover them. Even though they are covered, they fester and produce anger, hopelessness, and doubt. I am going to talk about two things you need to know and do to heal those unseen wounds of your flesh. First, you must forgive. I am not talking about forgiving the person or thing. I am talking about forgiving yourself. Secondly, turn your attention to God. My God will never leave you or forsake you."

God! I don't understand how you can stand there and talk about this God, who sits on His throne in heaven, looking down and watching innocent women and children being hurt, *I thought*. God! He doesn't care about anyone but Himself. Where was He when . . . ? *My knees buckled, and I fell to the floor, sobbing with everything in me.*

While I was on the floor, I remember it felt like every person in the church came to my aid and wept with me. An older, very mature woman, who I now know is the pastor's mother, Gale, knelt down beside me, whispered in my ear, and asked if she could hug me. In my mind I declined, but my arms turned against me and wrapped themselves around her neck, and I clung to her for dear life. The moment she embraced me, it felt as if she was squeezing the pain away. It was something I've never felt before.

Following that service, Mother Gale took my number, and she has become a vital instrument in my life. It did take me some time for me to even get to the point where I talk to God and do not yell at Him. Reading the scriptures Mother Gale gave me helps when I am feeling lonely and helpless. I now have a peace that is hard to explain. All I know is it has been carrying me day in and day out.

CHAPTER THIRTY-SEVEN

Forgiveness
Alonzo . . .

"I am getting married."

"Zoe, man, we know your bachelor road trip is this weekend," Dre reminds me.

"I don't even remember the last time I went away. This has to be epic."

"It could have been that and then some, but you vetoed the strippers," Matt comments.

"There's more to life than strippers, Matt."

"Says the guy who hasn't felt the warmth of a vagina in decades."

"It hasn't been that long, but it has been a little while. But that is going to change soon. It almost went down after the engagement party. Candice is a whole different person these days. I am loving her and everything that she is transitioning into even more."

"I was busting your chops," Matt says. "You mean to tell me you've never been with this woman? Are you shitting me, Zoe?"

"Yes, I've been with her, Matt. We have a daughter together, or have you forgotten?"

Matt shakes his head. "You two were infants at that time. That doesn't count."

"Again, we needed time. She's been through a lot. Real men take their time, even if it means a few occasions of blue balls. I love her, man, and there's nothing you can say to make me feel differently."

"You're most definitely a different kind of man, Zoe," Matt says. "Love produces a weakness for the other person, and that weakness makes women want you and want you bad. I think you might be the only one in love, because that woman still hasn't allowed you to sniff it at least."

"You know what, Matt?" Dre says, cutting in.

"What's that, Dre?"

"You're an ass," he answers and steps away from the bar.

Following behind him, I shout his name. "Dre!"

He turns around to face me. "What's up, Zoe? You good?"

"I am great. Nothing will change that."

"Good! Whatever you do, don't let that clown get under your skin. What you're doing is commendable. It takes a real man to step up to the plate and love a woman through and past her hurt and pain and into recovery. My pops did the same for my moms, and I grew up with a father in my life because of it."

"Really? I didn't know that."

"Yeah, my mom was an orphan. She was physically and verbally abused by her alcoholic foster parents. She turned to men for comfort, and as a result, she ended up with a guy, my biological father, who was twice her age. Mom had me at a young age. She was fifteen years old when she had me. She said my biological father beat on her for breathing. Long story short, she had trust issues that made it hard for her to love herself. She said she poured all her love into me. She didn't want me to experience anything that she'd gone through. When she met Pops, it took a long while before she allowed him into her heart. He said she was worth the wait. After all that waiting, they'll be married sixteen years next month."

"That is definitely encouraging, Dre. Thanks for sharing."

"No doubt, Zoe. Just make sure you court your wife even while you two are married. That's what my parents do. They said it keeps the spice in their marriage. I hope to find a love like that one day."

"You will. You will. I will be sure to court the hell out of my wife. I appreciate the advice, bro."

I am looking forward to our weekend getaway. My last hurrah at singlehood. Since I have heard so much about New Orleans and have never been, the guys have planned a classic getaway. In their words, we will head to Bourbon Street, where we can party and drink out on the street. We will explore the French Quarter, and then it's back to Bourbon Street for more partying and plenty of alcohol. Of course, Matt threw in a visit to a strip club or two, since we'll be right there, but I vetoed that.

That talk with Dre was real. I've known him forever, and he's never opened up to me like that before. I'm glad I chose him as my best man. It was a tough decision, but when I thought long and hard about it, it really wasn't. Out of all four of the fellas—Dre, Matt, Tone, and Giovanni—Dre has been the most supportive and understanding when it comes to Candice. Especially when I moved out of my parents' place. Dre didn't think twice to let me crash at his place until I found my own spot.

Speaking of my parents, I am leaving the bar and am now headed to their place. Last year, when Dad grew ill, I moved them out here with me, so I can help Mom out as needed. Of course, she didn't need any help. She just wanted me around and wanted to sneak the kids over weekly. I still haven't shared my engagement with my dad. Either he's with it or he's not. Either way, Candice Brown will soon become Mrs. Alonzo DeMartini, with or without his blessing.

When I get to my parents' place, I find my mom in the living room, reading a book.

"Hey, Mom. How's Dad feeling?" I say as I walk in the room.

"He's in the den, fussing at the television and smoking on those things that are literally killing him."

After kissing her on the forehead, I head to the den. The smell of cigarette smoke hits my nostrils before I even step foot in the room. I find my dad flipping through the channels, a cigarette poised between two fingers.

"Hey, Dad. How are you feeling? You know you shouldn't be smoking cigarettes."

"I've already been handed my death sentence, so why stop now? The cancer isn't going anywhere. I am," he tells me. Then he gives me a funny look. "You smell like those people. Go sit over there," he says, insulting me.

"You'd think with all that you're going through, you'd humble yourself and not be so cruel and insulting, Dad."

"No matter what is eating away at my body, it will not change the fact that my only son enjoys lying down and playing in the dirt with black women."

"That's it, Dad. I have had enough. I will not allow you to insult my fiancée anymore. If you do not have anything nice to say about her, you will not be invited to our wedding."

"Wedding? Did you really think I'd watch my son marry a mutt? You're a disgrace. Matter of fact, you're no son of mine—" he says, but my mom interrupts him as she walks in the den.

"Tony, don't be so cruel. This is our son. Our only son. I cannot take this anymore. I will walk out that door with him and never return if you do not take that back. We are going to see our son exchange vows, and you will be on your best behavior, or I will leave. I swear I will leave. My bags are still packed and at the door."

"Settle down now, Greta. There's no need to take things that far."

"Apologize and talk to your son. Please!" she insists, then leaves the room.

"When I was your age or a little younger, son, I fell for one myself. She was my world."

"What are you saying, Dad?"

"Listen to me. Back then interracial dating was a bad thing. I didn't want you to go through what I went through, so I fought your love for that young lady."

"What? This is insane. You've thrown one racial slur after the other, and you're sitting here telling me you've been living a lie?"

"I wouldn't call it that, son. It was a lot. I allowed my anger to get the best of me. For that, son, I apologize."

"What did you go through, Dad? Does Mom know? This is all crazy as hell. How? What? I am babbling, so go on."

"When my family learned I was dating Johnel, I was accused of dating a man. The DeMartini family was against gays and blacks. I am not sure what happened, but after dropping her off one evening, I never saw her again. To this day, I have no idea if she's dead or alive. Do I think my family had something to do with it? Without question. I just cannot confirm it. She vanished just like that."

"I am speechless. Dad, your family was a bunch of mobsters. You know what they did to her. This is nuts. I had no clue."

"I was completely in the wrong, son. I took my anger out on you. It had nothing to do with you or that young lady. I ask for your forgiveness. I would be honored to attend your wedding and see my daughter and grandbabies."

"Mom told you about them?"

"No. Her Bible has their pictures in it. I look at their pictures every day."

"Really, Tony?" my mom says from outside the doorway, where she'd been hiding. She enters the den and practically jumps into the recliner with him.

Stuck where I stand, I stare at them, in shock.

"Greta, I apologize for putting you through living hell for all these years. I know my days are numbered, but I promise to make it up to you until I take my last breath, if you allow me to."

I am not a crying man. Don't get me wrong. I have shed a tear or two here and there, and right now this would be one of those times. My dad wants to meet the kids and Candice. I feel like I am in a dream. If I am, I don't want to wake up.

I'll admit, I think I am going to shit my pants before we get to my parents' house. Thoughts of the past, of my dad badgering me about who he expects me to be with are eating away at me right now. I know we had a moment and he opened up after all these years. But I'm afraid he'll close himself back up. Candice is fully aware of everything and said she can handle it.

Well, there's no time like the present. We are here with our four babies.

"Mom, Dad? We're here," I announce as I walk through the front door, right behind Candice and the kids.

We are greeted by the smell of Mom's apple pie.

"Granny," the kids shout as they storm her when she appears in the foyer.

"Take it easy, kids," Candice tells them.

"They're fine. It's good to see you again, Candice." Tears flood Mom's eyes. "I've prayed long and hard for this day."

"Don't cry, Granny. We will come over again," Amiya says and squeezes her leg tighter.

"Thank heavens I didn't wear any makeup today, with all the crying I've done in a matter of seconds," Candice says as she begins to sob too.

"You don't need it anyway. You're beautiful without it," Dad says as he enters the foyer. He uses his walker to move closer to where Candice is standing.

Hell, now I have tears in my damn eyes.

"I know I am probably not your favorite person, and for that, I apologize, Candice. I'll do whatever I can to make it up to you and these beautiful babies," Dad confesses.

"I forgive you, Mr. DeMartini. I am just glad to be here."

"Call me Pop." They embrace.

Thanks to the fact that I am introducing Dad to Candice and the kids, today is one of the happiest moments of my life. It can only get better from here. And it will when my beautiful bride joins me at the altar.

CHAPTER THIRTY-EIGHT

The Good Always Outweighs the Bad Candice . . .

Meeting Mr. DeMartini, I mean Pop, was the best engagement present I could have received. I've prayed long and hard for this meeting to come to pass. God sure knows how to blow your mind and answer prayers definitely in His time, when we're ready. A year ago, I wasn't in any condition to see or deal with that man. I fought Alonzo when he wanted to bring the kids to see his mom. There was no way I wanted my kids anywhere near his father. I just didn't feel comfortable. But that feeling subsided, and no matter how the meeting could have gone, I was prepared.

Honestly, there wasn't anything he could have said that would have made me change my mind or made me feel uncomfortable. Well, I take that back. If he had done something to one of my babies, I probably would have pushed him and his walker down the steps. Lord, forgive me. I know that was wrong for me to say. In any event, I can see clearly where Alonzo gets his charm from. On the other side of all that pain, Pop is a mushy old teddy bear. We ended up staying the night there. He wanted to help put the kids to bed and make breakfast in the morning for them. Mrs. DeMartini, I mean Greta, said he hasn't boiled water in probably over twenty years. That made my heart smile. It's all about forgiveness.

I am just so happy that things are turning around in everyone's lives. We've been through some terrible storms, but we made it through them. Right now, all my prayers consist of me asking God to continue raining goodness down on us. I need it to stay this way. Even with all the positivity that I shoved down everyone's throat, I was at a breaking point. When I found Jenna in Ms. Jasmine's closet, I literally could feel the world crashing down on me instantly. After Nakita, I didn't want to have to see anyone else in such a low place. I know it's unavoidable. I just don't want to see it.

I am beyond excited that things are turning around. Jenna attends church now. Not in the living room with me, but at an actual church, and she loves it. She said that she wouldn't allow herself to become a religious fanatic and that she just needs the relationship with God. Alonzo and I now also attend Mount Gideon Missionary Baptist Church with Jenna. I understand why she feels at home there. For one, the love that you feel walking through the door is contagious. But it's really like a refuge, where all types of people gather.

The kids have been attending Sunday school and children's church. They love it. I want the best for my babies. I know with having God in their lives starting from their youth, they will have the best. Darren's and Dylan's behavior has been better as well. Going to therapy and attending the Sunday services, I believe, has turned out to be the perfect recipe for them.

Mount Gideon has a full-service ministry for any and everything. My favorite one is couples' ministry. Alonzo and I have gone out on several couples' dates, and it has been great. Just seeing other couples our age love on one another is teaching me a little more about how to express my love for Alonzo and love on him. Primarily, I've thought harder about the respect I need to give him as a man. Basically, it mirrors the same love, respect, and honor that I have for God. Without question, I'm not to put anyone or anything before God, but I am motivated to treat my husband like the king that he is.

I cannot believe I am getting married. Candice Brown, me, is days away from becoming Mrs. DeMartini. The girls are here at my place so we can go for our fitting. Simone and Tracy live in New York now. That still sounds crazy to me, just thinking about it. Who would have thought an extended vacation would lead to them picking up and relocating? I sure never would have imagined it. I am proud of them, though. They're in the process of opening up a day-care center. Tracy said there really aren't too many in the town that they live in. They also hate the fact that Ethan and Evan have some girls sitting for them in their homes while they're at work. Given that, Tracy and Simone decided to save their men and make a living out of it. That was a funny conversation I had with them a few weeks ago, if I do say so myself.

"Candice, I need your advice," Tracy said when she came into my office and we saw each other for the first time in quite a while.

"Well, hello to you too, Tracy. You pick up and move away on me, and that's how you greet me?"

"We have invited you to come down numerous times. You have declined each and every time."

"I know. I had too much going on here. I am planning a wedding, you know?"

"Uh, yeah, that's why I am here."

"Fine."

"Speaking of weddings, you know you will eventually have to consummate your marriage, don't you?"

"I do." I blushed.

"You're blushing? You did it? Were you afraid? Oh my God! Tell me everything. Wait, not everything." She side-eyed me.

"Are you done?" I asked her.

"Yes. Go ahead."

"No, I have not. We decided to wait until our wedding night. It has been hard for him, and recently for me as well. I have been attending bodywork and massage therapy. Let me tell you, it has been amazing."

"Getting a massage is helping you? You want people touching you like that?"

"This is why you need to attend. It's not what you think. Bodywork helped me learn how to be touched again. For so long, as you know, the only touch that I got was always abusive, sexually. I never knew that touch could be otherwise. I forgot because of all the abuse. The therapist helped me to trust again and relax. I learned how to regain control of my body. It took time, but I am okay with hugging and kissing Alonzo now. I used to kiss him with my hands at my sides, because I was afraid. I haven't felt desire for him in forever, and lately, I feel it creeping up on me."

"That is huge, Candice. Like, what do they do? We all need to be in something like this. Do you think they have something like this in New York?"

"I am sure they're everywhere. What? You're thinking about your chocolate twin lover boy in a romantic way?"

"Hush up," she said as the color left her face. "I mean, I get butterflies when he's around or I know he's coming, but that's it. Just tell me what they do there, please."

"Different exercises to help you reconnect with your body and not see it or sex as a bad thing."

"Yes, that is something I need to consider. Now back to what I wanted to ask you."

"I'm listening," I told her.

"Since you know about having a business, I wanted, you to help me and Simone look into opening a day-care center in our town. There isn't any there, and Ethan and Evan need the girls in a facility, rather than having some young girls sitting in their house with their daughters all day."

"So, what you're saying is, you're jealous of these women and want to open up a business to save your man from them?" I burst into laughter.

"You're not funny, Candice."

"You're really not," Simone agreed as she made her way into my office.

"I am sorry. It is funny," I tell them.

It was quite comical and still is to this day, when I think about it. Their ribbon cutting is next month, and they found a bodywork facility thirty minutes away from them, which neither of them can stop talking about. I'm proud of all of them. Judith is a whole new person; she too has started massage therapy. Her mom, Cindy, is the sweetest thing in the world. She fits right in with us, and Ms. J cannot contain her emotions when everyone is around. I swear, she is more emotional than I am.

Although she wasn't awarded custody of Samantha's twins, as their father's parents appeared out of nowhere at the last minute, she is still grateful. The twins' grandparents agreed to keep in touch and make sure Micah is in his sisters' lives. Samantha is in rehab. The courts sent her there this time. She was ordered to go inpatient or go to prison. Inpatient looked so much more appealing to her. She obeyed without uttering a word. Hopefully, this is what she needs, and she will be able to get her life back on track.

The most disturbing thing, and a missing link, in all this is Dr. Binet. My heart aches for her. Between losing Sienna and being a therapist, she created a recipe for disaster. I pray every day that she recovers. Still, I am really worried about her, because each time that Ms. J visits her, she says Brianne appears worse than she did at her previous visit. I cannot go and see her like that. Regardless of the downhill slide her life has taken, she will always be the main ingredient in making me the woman that I am today. Her sessions saved my life, and because of her, I am able to contribute to saving the lives of women who have experienced the traumatic events that I've overcome. I am forever indebted to Brianne, Dr. Binet. I won't ever give up on her. God can do exceedingly more than I can ask or contemplate, so there is still hope for her.

The Wedding

CHAPTER THIRTY-NINE

Let's Get Married
Candice . . .

Today is the day that most little girls dream of. I wasn't one of those girls. I didn't get a chance to dream about my world and my own future, because nightmares were handed to me as a reality instead. Right now, I am at a loss for words, just thinking about how far I have come. In fact, how far all of us have come. Tracy and Simone started a whole new life in New York, and they're happier than they have ever been. Judith is living her best life as well. Reconciling with her mom and siblings has given her a whole new outlook on life. They're even dating. None of us ever thought it'd be possible, but it's happening.

God is giving all of us a second look on what life has to offer. Dad is beyond ecstatic. He has full custody of Casey and Cassidy. They're about a year or so older than Amiya. I swear, they've grown into mini mes. That's probably what sent Mommy dearest over the edge. Thank heavens she has no idea where we stay, and hopefully, it stays that way. While at the court hearing, she threatened to fight for her children. That was another day that I prayed for. Well, not having it done in a courtroom, but I received the closure that I needed. That moment in court is seared into my memory.

"The court has heard testimony from both parties," the judge declared, *"and in reviewing the statements as well as the caseworker's notes, the court has determined that it is in the best interest of the children, Casey and Cassidy, to award custody to the father, Dale Mathews. The court is adjourned."*

"You cannot give my babies to that bigamist. He will ruin them, just like he ruined the rest of his bastard children," Camilla yelled.

Ignoring her outburst, I practically jumped into Dad's arms.

Jenna, on the other hand, focused her attention on Camilla. "Dad is the best thing that could have happened for all of us. You are a sick woman. You're in dire need of a mental health evaluation and Jesus!" she declared and then stormed off, in tears.

"Don't you dare come near me," Camilla ordered as I approached her.

"I just want you to know something. Because of what you weren't to and for me, I am the mother that I am to my children. I thank you for not being the mother that I yearned for you to be. It gave me the drive to be everything that you weren't for me. My children know what love is all from you not loving me. Ironic, isn't it? I'm not even mad at you, either. I forgive you. I wish you the best, Mother."

That conversation could have gone so many different ways, but growth, healing, and maturity allowed me to see the situation for what it was. Don't get me wrong. I wish things could be better. I wish they could have turned out different, but the truth of the matter is, they didn't. Therefore, I was left with two choices: I could pick up the pieces and piece together a better life, or I could wallow in self-pity, anger, and disappointment. I'm glad I chose to pick up the pieces to happiness.

Looking in the mirror at myself right now as I sit in the dressing room at the church brings tears to my eyes. I remember when this was one of the hardest things for me to do. Mother's face was all that I wanted to see, so that she'd love me. Today she is the last person I'd like to see in this mirror. I love everything about the person gazing back at me.

"Isn't she radiant?" Ms. J tearfully kisses me on the cheek.

"Please stop it, you two. You're going to mess everyone's makeup up," Jenna says, butting in.

"You're right. Let's try to pull ourselves together," Ms. J agrees.

"How can I? Look at all of you. You all are beautiful. I am so glad I am able to share today with you. I only have one wish that would make this day even better," I say.

"What is it? Do we have time to make it happen?" Jenna panics.

"No, we cannot fix it unless we can turn back the hands of time."

"What are you talking about, C—" Jenna cuts herself short, realizing what's missing.

"I just wish Nakita were here," I say and fall apart.

"She is here with us, baby. She's in your heart. Nakita will always be with you, because she's in your heart," Ms. J tells me in a soothing tone of voice.

"She's right, Candice. You know Nakita would cuss you out if you didn't pull yourself together and prepare to meet your man at that altar. Besides, she *is* with you. Look at Adrianna. She looks and acts just like her mama." She points as the kids make their way into the dressing room.

Boy, is she right. Adrianna is the spitting image of Nakita and is quick tempered just like her. I chuckle, just thinking about how feisty that little one can be.

I peek outside the dressing room, and as I take a look at everyone who has gathered, my tears evaporate and happiness infiltrates my entire being. I could not have asked for a better outcome. Cassidy and Casey are flower girls with Amiya and Adrianna. All the boys are a part of the bridal party as well. My babies are the ring bearers. They look so handsome.

"Oh, look at you, Dad," I whisper when he steps up to me. Tears make another entrance.

Dad looks so handsome. He's usually in sweats, a T-shirt, and sneakers. I don't remember the last time saw him in a suit.

"Hello there, princess. Stop fussing over your old man. Leave that to the ladies."

"Dad, don't even go there," Jenna says right behind me and rolls her eyes.

"I am messing with you, Candice. Seriously, I need you to get your face cleaned up and to put that beautiful gown on, so I can walk the most beautiful bride that I've ever seen down the aisle."

"He's right. Reeky, can you do something about the girl's racoon eyes? Ms. J says as she stands next to me in the dressing-room doorway. "I don't need my babies coming out here, looking a mess. I'll help get these little babies settled until it's time." Ms. J turns, calls the kids over, and escorts them out of the dressing room.

I go back over to the mirror and take a seat. Reeky, the makeup artist, freshens my face, but then tears well up in my eyes as I admire my gown.

The dress is perfect for a princess. It is sleeveless, drapes the floor, and has a sweetheart neckline. What I love most about it is the way it laces up in the back and has beaded crystal sequins with a hint of lavender. Purple was Nakita's favorite color. She loved every shade of purple, so I added the lavender in the dress in her honor.

I'm so in love with this dress. My train is to die for; it is so long, and it's adorned with the same crystal sequins throughout. Perfect dress to wear, because I am marrying the perfect man, a man who will love me the way that I need to be loved. I cannot wait for him to see me in it.

Of course, the flower girls have dresses that are nearly identical to my gown. Not a mirror image, but they are made from the same material and have the same beading. My girls have on lavender floor-length gowns. The gowns are the perfect fit and complement all four of them.

"Well, my darling, it's that time," Dad says as he takes me by the hand. He leads me to the entrance to the church.

"I'm so nervous, Dad," I say when we step outside.

"You will do great. I am so proud of you. My life is complete because of you girls. I love you, baby girl. Now let's go and melt Alonzo's heart some more."

This is the most surreal experience I've ever had in my life. I take a deep breath as the church doors open. Everything around me seems like a blur as I walk through the doorway. Out of my peripheral, I can see our guests beaming at me. It's impossible to look their way. I can't take my eyes off my husband-to-be at the end of the long aisle. Tears threaten to fall, and I give in to them in defeat. I am floating. I don't want this moment to end. I take my time walking down the aisle to join my love.

Once I come to a stop near the altar, Pastor Pennon begins to speak. His words are all a blur to me until he poses a question to my dad.

"Do you wish to give the hand of your daughter Candice in marriage to Alonzo DeMartini?" Pastor Pennon asks.

"I cannot give my baby girl away. I am allowing Alonzo to borrow her for the balance of their lives," Dad says, his voice cracking. Turning to me, he whispers, "It's okay to cry, princess. Hell, it appears to be contagious. I love you, baby girl. That man right there is compassionate. He has made you happier than you've ever been in your life. I give thanks to God that he found you. You both have my blessing and support. I guess I am giving you away, princess." He lets go of my hand.

When I take my position at the altar, Alonzo grabs my hand, and I feel tears do a number on my face.

"You're breathtaking. I am the luckiest man in the world," Alonzo whispers, choking up.

Pulling us from our moment, Pastor Pennon continues. "On behalf of Alonzo and Candice, I would like to thank you all for being here this afternoon. For taking the time to be a part of this day. This day would not be possible without their love for one another, without God's grace, and without the love and support of everyone gathered here today."

Dre, Matt, Giovanni, and Anthony whistle, clap, and cheer.

"Please be seated," Pastor Pennon says, trying to regain control of the ceremony.

"Thank you," he continues once everyone is seated. "On this day we celebrate the marriage of Alonzo and Candice. A physical and emotional joining that has the promise of a lifetime. And at this time, Derek Young will open us in prayer."

Mr. Derek makes his way to the pulpit. "Let us bow our heads in prayer. Heavenly Father, Alonzo and Candice are here today to stand before you and become husband and wife. We ask that you join them in this union and continue to pour your love and favor on their lives. What you have joined together cannot be broken. We thank you for your covering. In Jesus's name, we pray. Amen." He leaves the pulpit and returns to his seat.

"Now we will have the exchanging of the rings and the vows," the pastor says, "The bride and groom have prepared their vows."

Alonzo clears his throat as tears stream down his face. "I, Alonzo, take you, Candice, to be my lawful wedded wife. I promise to be everything you need me to be. When you're sick, I will be there. When you are tired, I will be there. I will be there through all the good times and the bad. I promise to love you without a second thought. I will be your biggest cheerleader and will encourage you to continue achieving all your heart's desires. I want to grow old with you, Candice. I will never lie to you, Candice. I will love you until the very last beat of my heart. I will cherish you and our beautiful children for as long as I live." He pauses. "Can I kiss her now?" he asks Pastor Pennon.

"We're almost there," pastor says, and his voice cracks.

Now it is my turn. "Alonzo, today I give you my whole heart and every single part of me. You are my only true love. I love you, Alonzo. I have loved you since I was fourteen years old. I thank you for never giving up on me. For being a man of your word and for showing me that there are real men who love, respect, and cherish women. I thank you for loving me through the heartache and pain, even when I didn't know how to love you or myself. You are mine—the missing piece to my puzzle. You are the only man that I'll ever want and need. Even through sickness and health. Come what may, I will always be right by your side. I cannot wait to begin making everlasting memories with you, now that we're officially starting the rest of our lives together."

"Now you may kiss—" Pastor begins, but Alonzo is a pace ahead of him.

Alonzo pulls me in, lifts my veil, and allows our lips to become one for the first time as husband and wife.

Trying to hold back his tears, Pastor Pennon announces, "Ladies and gentlemen, it is my honor and privilege to be the first to introduce you to Mr. and Mrs. Alonzo and Candice DeMartini."

The weeping attendees erupt in cheers!

The End